Hannah

Jerry Eicher

Book List of Published Novel Titles

A Time To Live
Sarah
Sarah's Son
Hannah's Dream
Hannah

The Adams County Trilogy:
Rebecca's Promise
Rebecca's Return

Hannah

Fiction/Contemporary

Published by Horizon Books
768 Hardtimes Rd.
Farmville VA 23901

www.readingwithhorizon.com

Editors – Jon Marken, Kyra Marken

Cover design by www.KareenRoss.com

ISBN   978-0-9787987-4-1

DEDICATION

Dedicated to the hope of a better tomorrow.

CHAPTER ONE

HANNAH BYLER AWOKE with a start. She sat upright in bed listening, steadying herself against the wall, feeling the rough bark of the logs under her fingers. The wind outside the small cabin stirred in the pine trees. The moon, already high in the sky when she went to bed, shone brightly in the log cabin window.

Her eyes searched for the lighted hands of the small alarm clock her mother had given her as a wedding present. Beside her was the deep, even breathing of Jake. She had grown accustomed to the sound in the few short months of their marriage.

What had awakened her? She was about to decide it was her imagination when fear rose in her chest and her heart beat faster. Yet she heard no sound, just the sense of presence outside the cabin walls.

"Jake," she whispered, her hand finding his shoulder in the darkness. "Jake, *vagh uff.*"

"What is it?" he asked, sleep in his voice, speaking louder than she wished he would at the moment.

"I don't know," she whispered again, hoping he would get the hint. "There's something outside."

Jake listened, sitting up with his arms bracing themselves on the mattress.

"I don't hear anything," he said, a little quieter this time. "There are all kinds of noises in the mountains at night."

"I feel something outside," she insisted, certain she was right.

Hannah waited, unsure what Jake would do, still not totally used to his ways. She watched his form in the darkness, half expecting him to lower his head back down on his pillow, tell her the fears were imagined, and go back to sleep. Instead he pushed down the covers, his feet on the way to the floor.

A loud snuff outside the log wall stopped him. They both froze. Hannah didn't recognize the sound; no animal she knew ever made such a noise.

"It sounds like a pig," Jake said, his voice low. "What are pigs doing out here at nighttime?"

"It's not a pig," Hannah whispered back, gauging by her fear. No stray pig, even in the nighttime, could create such tension. "It's something else."

"But what?" Jake asked, the sound coming again, seemingly right against the log wall.

Hannah lay rigid, filled with an overpowering sense that something large and fierce stood outside.

"I'm going to see," Jake decided, and Hannah made no objection, not certain at the moment if words of protest would even come out of her mouth.

By the light of the moon through the bedroom window, Hannah saw Jake bend over and feel under the bed for his flashlight. Someone had given it as a wedding present, jokingly calling it a Wild West staple, something he must have. He moved towards the door of the bedroom.

From somewhere Hannah found the courage to follow, staying close behind Jake. Their feet made little groaning sounds on the wooden floor. Jake slowly pulled open the wooden front door, his flashlight piercing the darkness. He swung the beam left and right.

"Nothing here at least," he said quietly, stepping outside.

Not sure what to expect, Hannah looked toward the edge of the porch. "It was around the corner," she whispered, her own voice loud in her ears, her fears and the stillness amplifying the sound.

Jake walked towards the corner of the house, giving Hannah the courage to step out on the porch. Alone she would have cowered in the house, but with Jake's form ahead of her, his shoulders outlined from the reflected light, she followed at least that far.

Jake stopped momentarily, then stepped around the house, taking the light with him. Only a low glow remained in Hannah's line of vision. She now saw the full moon playing with the shadows. In the distance, the misty line of the Cabinet Mountains accented the utter ruggedness of this country, so alluring to her in the daytime, now threatening and very dangerous.

For the first time since moving here with Jake — just after their marriage — she wondered whether this place was a little too much for the two of them. Was a cabin lying a mile off the main road, up this dirt road into the foothills of the Cabinet Mountains, really what she wanted?

"It's a bear," Jake's voice came from around the corner. "Come take a look — quick — before he's gone."

"Gone," she half-whispered.

"Come see," Jake's urgent voice came again.

Again finding courage from somewhere, she went, stepping around the corner of the house, following the beam of Jake's flashlight. Its broad light pierced the night over to the edge of their clearing. At the end of the beam, a furry long-haired animal, as large a bear as she had ever seen in the zoo, stood looking back at them, its raised head sniffing the air.

"It's a grizzly," Jake said, tension in his voice. "See its hump."

"Then why are we out here?" she asked, nearly overcome with the urge to run, desperate for solid walls between her and this huge creature.

"The men at the lumber yard said there aren't any around. Mostly black bears down in this area," Jake said in her ear.

"Shouldn't we be inside?" she asked the question another way, pulling on his arm. "It's not going away."

"It will sooner than if we go inside," he told her, his light playing on the creature, its head still in the air, turned in their direction.

"I'm going inside," she said, her courage wholly depleted.

"It's going," Jake announced, so she paused. They watched, fascinated, as the great creature, bobbing its head, disappeared into the woods.

"It's gone," Jake said, his voice still tense. "That was a grizzly."

His light on low now, they started back. Hannah followed Jake's lead, although she felt like running ahead, fear seeming to grow in her the closer she got to the front door. Suddenly the looming slat door looked thin and unprotecting against the hulk she had just seen disappearing into the dark tree line.

"What if it comes back?" she asked, at his side now, her steps matching his.

"It won't. It's just passing through," he assured her. "They don't like humans. They're wanderers anyway. It'll probably not come this way again. Ever."

Not exactly reassured, Hannah shut the door tightly behind them, pushing the latch firmly in place.

"Bears hang around," she told him. "This one could be coming back."

"Then we'll deal with it. Maybe the game warden can help. I doubt it will return, though." Jake was fast losing interest, she could tell.

Climbing in bed, Jake snuggled under the covers, pulling them tight up to his chin. "Cold these nights," he commented. "Winter's just around the corner. I have to get some sleep."

Hannah knew this to be true. Jake's job on the logging crew involved hard manual labor that required a good night's sleep.

"I hope it's not coming back," she told him, following him into bed.

"I doubt if it will," he said, but she could tell he was already nearly asleep.

To the sounds of Jake's breathing she lay awake, unable to stop the thoughts. Home, where she had grown up in Indiana, now seemed far away, a hazy blur against the fast moving past few months.

What is Mom doing? she wondered. *No doubt comfortably asleep in their white two-story home. Secure, another night just like the night before, facing another day just like the day before.*

Thoughts of her earlier summer in Montana — tending to Aunt Betty's riding stable — pushed into her mind. This country had seemed so glorious then and she had dreamed of returning. Back home in Indiana, with Jake back at his home in Iowa, she had almost lost the dream and then regained it.

First had come the wedding — she smiled in the darkness — after a flurry of letter writing and visits by Jake to Indiana as often as he could. Betty hadn't gotten her wish for a wedding in Montana, for her mom had put her foot down. The wedding was even better — she smiled again — than the one in which she had refused to marry Sam.

Their hearts had been drawn back to Montana, though — to the land and to the small Amish community just off the shadow of the Cabinet Mountains. They had made no secret of those plans, and a month after the wedding they had moved.

What in the world are we doing here? she now asked herself, almost sitting up in bed with the suddenness of the thought. *Out here in the middle of nowhere? Is this where my dreams have led me?*

She lay in the darkness, wishing for close neighbors, wishing she could get up, walk to the front door, and know that someone else lived within calling distance — or at least within running distance, if it came to that. Now, with a bear around, a night wanderer with mischief on his mind, there was nowhere to go. She shuddered.

She wondered whether she could outrun a bear, even if a neighbor's house stood close by. She pictured herself lifting her skirt for greater speed. How fast could bears run? Could they see well at night to scout out their prey?

Shivering in the darkness, she listened to Jake's even breathing, wondering how he could go on sleeping after what they had just seen. A grizzly — Jake had been sure of it. A grizzly sniffing around their cabin, outside their bedroom wall. Why was he not more alarmed?

She had always thought she was the courageous one, wanting adventure, coming out to Montana on her own that first summer. The mountains had fascinated her, drawn her in, given her strength. Now tonight those same mountains had turned on her and given her a bear for a gift, a grizzly. Even the stately pine trees, with their whisper that soothed her before, now seemed to be talking of dark things she knew nothing about, things too awful to say out loud. That was why they whispered.

She turned in the bed, hoping Jake wouldn't be disturbed by her restlessness. She thought of his job on the logging crew, really a job of last resort. Yes, it was a blessing when offered, as they needed the income, but now it was becoming more and more of a burden. Jake didn't complain, but the burden became apparent in the stoop of his shoulders when he came home at night. It revealed itself in his descriptions about operating the cutter, navigating the steep slopes and dealing with logs rolling down the sides of the mountains. She also heard it in his descriptions of Mr. Wesley, his boss. She had met Mr. Wesley once when he stopped by the house to hire Jake. He operated the largest timber company in Libby, and his huge, burly form matched his position, nearly filling their cabin door that day. She had been too glad Jake was getting a job to worry much about Mr. Wesley, but after he left she was glad she wouldn't be seeing him every day.

Hannah shivered again, feeling the same chill seeping into the house that Jake had felt earlier. Winter was coming to this strange land, and neither she nor Jake had ever been through a winter here.

Willing herself to stop thinking, she suddenly knew. There had been something she wanted to tell Jake but was waiting until she was certain. On this night, the night the bear came, she was certain. The strangeness of how she knew puzzled her. Could a bear's night visit and this wonderful news have anything to do with each other?

CHAPTER TWO

H ANNAH WOKE WELL before dawn. The alarm showed ten minutes till the official rising time. Expecting to be groggy after the night's events, she was surprised at her clearheaded state of mind.

Sliding quietly out of bed, she avoided waking Jake. He could have his last few minutes of sleep uninterrupted. Shutting off the alarm, Hannah walked out to the large front window of the cabin, its metal frame outlined by the setting moon. She stood looking towards the east where the sun would soon be coming up.

Jake said windows were a problem in log cabins. He was surprised one this size had not broken with the movement of the logs over the years. A blessing of the Lord, a sign, she had thought — one of the things that persuaded her to accept Jake's decision to buy the place.

The loneliness of the area had been exciting at the time. This morning it felt empty, a void that needed filling. She looked for signs of the first sun rays above the Cabinet Mountains, finding only stars, their brightness still undimmed.

Waves of homesickness swept over her. Home. There her mother would be up about this time, perhaps even before this, making soft noises in the kitchen as she prepared breakfast. There, Hannah would be awakened, not do the waking, as she soon would do for Jake.

The responsibilities of the day came pressing in on her, disrupting her thoughts. Jake's breakfast needed making and the last of the garden things needed bringing in. Was this how it was, or would be, she wondered — life, simply with its demands, driving away the dark thoughts?

One bright thought hung on the horizon, not unlike that vigorous twinkling star above the highest peak of the Cabinet Mountains. Her mother and father were coming to visit before Communion Sunday. They would see Aunt Betty, her mother's sister, but Hannah knew the real reason they were crossing all those miles. They were coming to see her. Was this then what was provoking her homesickness?

It was possible, she decided. The grizzly visiting last night was still on her mind, but she decided to give it little weight. No doubt it was what Jake said, just a passing experience that wouldn't be repeated.

Walking into the bedroom she shook Jake's shoulder. "Time to get up," she said softly.

"Where's the alarm clock?" he wanted to know, his voice tired.

"I already shut it off."

"You're up. Little early."

"I just woke. Maybe the bear last night," she suggested as explanation.

"Yeah…maybe," he agreed, sitting up now. "There was a bear last night — wasn't there?"

"Yes."

"He was just passing through. They don't have bears that hang around — in this area," he said, repeating his arguments from last night.

"I'm getting breakfast ready," she said, not disagreeing enough to protest.

"I'll be out," he muttered. "Is it looking like rain?"

"Not that I could tell."

"Boss thought it might. Hopefully not. I really can't lose the wages."

"Are we short on money?" she asked, thinking the amount in the bank account had looked okay the last she looked.

"Now it's okay. Winter's coming though. Won't be as

much work then. We have the mortgage payment to make, too."

"I'll get breakfast," she said again, stepping out to the kitchen. Glancing around, Hannah saw she needed to make a quick trip outside to the little shack Jake had built over the spring. The spring came out of the ground some fifty feet from the cabin, and the spring house served as their refrigerator.

Reaching it, she took a dozen eggs from the wooden pine shelves. On her return, she felt chilled in the morning air and wondered why she hadn't noticed the cold earlier. Last night, when she was out with Jake spotting the grizzly, the air had not seemed so cold.

Back in the house, she thought about Jake's fear over the growing scarcity of work. Hannah's dad had always taken care of money problems — at least she assumed he had, never having heard her parents talk about them. Now, she figured, part of being married was dealing with money, but she never imagined exactly how that would work out.

Jake was talking to her, and she was uncertain what to do. Wouldn't God take care of them? Jake would find work somehow, and if there wasn't work, they could skimp on the money they had. Then there were the things from the garden she had canned this summer. Some potatoes were still out there, and corn. That would help, she comforted herself. *They could always save more, couldn't they?*

Bending over her oven, she lifted the lid to start the fire. At home, they had gas in the kitchen that lit the oven and burners at the turn of a knob, not exactly like the electric ones the English used, but certainly better than what she had here. Yet she was happy. Jake had purchased the old wood oven in Libby, secondhand, at a price they could afford.

Jake also kept a box of kindling wood in the kitchen, sitting in the corner. This morning she did the usual piling of wood, having figured out the best procedure by trial and error. She was now able to get a flame going rather quickly.

Hannah had the pan warmed by the time Jake arrived in the kitchen.

"I'll take three eggs this morning," he said, letting her know his departure from the usual two.

Sometimes she made him oatmeal, but Jake preferred his store bought cornflakes. Hannah had never told him of the times she winced at the price when making the purchase at the IGA in Libby. Her mother usually did the grocery shopping when Hannah was growing up. The few times she did make the Saturday trip into Nappanee, paying the bill had not been on her mind. Now things had changed.

Placing the rest of the breakfast items on the table, she finished the eggs, then joined Jake, pulling her chair up across from him. Together they paused in silence with bowed head. Jake didn't pray out loud yet, which was fine with her. Hannah figured he would get around to it when the time was right.

"Mom and Dad are coming the week before Communion Sunday," she reminded him.

He nodded his head, his mind apparently elsewhere. Turning to look outside, she saw the sun sending its first streaks of light over the Cabinet Mountains. The glory of the sight, as the first colors broke, prompted her to abandon her plate and walk to the window for the best view possible.

"I'm not tired of it yet," she half-whispered, more to herself than anyone else, gathering courage for the day ahead.

"It is beautiful," Jake agreed from the breakfast table. "It's even nicer from the side of the mountain looking east."

"Could you see — well?" she asked him, knowing he was referring to his time as a fire spotter working for the forest ranger, before they were married.

"They were nice. I enjoyed them." Jake reached for the cornflake box.

She knew the moment had come to tell him, as joy circled her heart. The night's event with her morning doldrums were forgotten.

"I'm expecting," she told him, freezing in place from the rush of emotions that rose in her.

His cornflake box stopped in mid-air, a few flakes falling out, softly landing in his plate. "You...are?" He paused, looking intently at her.

"Yes," she said, knowing her smile was lighting up her face. "I'm sure."

"A baby," he said, giving her a trace of a smile in return. Then a soberness filled him.

"Aren't you glad?" she asked, concern in her voice.

He nodded, "Of course. It is just...I will be a father."

"But you want to be?" she asked, sitting down across from him again, the concern now on her face.

"Oh, yes," he said, nodding again. "But am I fit to be a father? That's the question."

"You are," she said, puzzled that he should feel that way. "I think you'll make a good father. Is it the money?" she asked, wondering if that was troubling him.

He didn't seem to flinch, which reassured her. Rather he seemed to be pondering before answering.

"Maybe partly. I know we don't have much, but many young parents are like that. I don't think a baby makes it worse. No," he shook his head, apparently coming to a firm conclusion, "I worry about myself, I guess. It will be a heavy responsibility. I didn't think it would happen this soon, I guess."

"Well you're married," she stated, half teasing. "What did you expect?"

He grinned, "I guess I was just thinking of you."

"The rest comes with it," she assured him, smiling.

"Is there a midwife around close?"

"I'll have to ask Elizabeth. She'll know what the other women do."

"The other women," he said musingly, pouring milk into his cornflakes. "Makes us sound old."

"You ever thought of moving back east?" she asked him, remembering her homesickness from earlier. "You ever think about work there...with the way it is here? Dad could probably get you a trailer factory job pretty easy."

"I don't think so," he said, shaking his head. "I like it here."

"I do, too," she agreed. "The bear was a little scary last night. You think we can make it — on the logging income — with the baby coming?"

"You're not thinking of moving? Leave the community here?" He looked at her strangely. "And this country.... Who wants to go back and live where it's flat?"

"We could go back now...long before the baby comes, and get settled in."

He shook his head again, firmer this time, she thought.

"We've never lived through a winter either. You could be out of work for a long time."

The shake was still there, but not quite as firm.

"The bear last night. Maybe that was a sign to us."

This brought a chuckle, Jake's spoon stopping midway to his mouth. "Surely you've learned your lesson about believing in signs, haven't you?"

"I suppose," she said, and couldn't help smiling.

"It almost got you married to that...Sam boy."

"That's a little mean," she informed him. "I was just trying to find the will of God. Sure...I wasn't too good at it, but we made it. Didn't we?"

"Yes." He found her eyes across the table, letting tenderness show. "Plus I had my own troubles. With or without signs."

"So you don't think it's a good idea? Moving back east?"

"The bear will go away," he assured her. "I'm not going back east."

His last spoonful of cereal was going towards his mouth when they heard the sound of a vehicle coming to a stop outside, followed by a sharp rap on the slab door.

"Who could be here this time of day?" Jake asked.

Chapter Three

"Good morning, Mr. Brunson," Jake said, after opening the front door.

Hannah heard the sounds of a reply but couldn't understand the words. What Mr. Brunson was doing out this early in the morning she couldn't imagine. He lived further in on their dirt road, a small two-story home built by Mr. Brunson himself before she and Jake had moved into the cabin.

"No log cabin for me," he had told her once with a chuckle when she remarked on the uniqueness of their own home purchase. "I like eastern living too well." Why Mr. Brunson liked that kind of living while staying in Montana, she had wondered, but figured it was none of her business to ask.

She was used to seeing him drive by in his beat-up Ford pickup, waving to her if she was outside, and stopping in for vegetables from her garden all summer. He paid well, much better than she could have gotten selling anywhere else, even if she was raising vegetables to sell, which she wasn't.

"Please come in," she heard Jake saying, holding the door open. "We were just finishing breakfast."

"Wouldn't want to disturb that," Mr. Brunson said, stepping inside, removing the John Deere cap Hannah was used to seeing and running his hand through his thinning white hair. "Just thought I'd come down. See how you folks were doing this morning."

"Okay, I guess," Jake told him. "There was a bear here last night. We figured it was just passing through. Didn't think we were in any danger."

"It was a grizzly, wasn't it?" Mr. Brunson's face looked grim.

"I think so," Jake agreed. "We went outside after we heard noises. It looked like it had a hump on its back."

"That's what I thought. I didn't get that good a look — but it was big. One of my hogs I was fattening is gone. I was hoping it hadn't done any damage down here."

"You think the bear got it?" Jake asked, his interest clearly stirred.

"Can't prove it for sure — I guess."

Hannah could see the man's tense jaw from where she sat. Getting up she went out to join the two men.

"Good morning," Mr. Brunson smiled his greeting.

"It sniffed around our bedroom wall," Hannah told him, the memory returning. "You think it's coming back?"

"If my hog tasted good, which I'm sure it did. Wouldn't surprise me. I'm going down to talk with the game warden first thing."

"Will they do something?" Jake wondered. "Grizzlies usually don't come this far down. At least that's what the locals said."

"I haven't been local long enough to know." Mr. Brunson's face was grim again. "I just don't like bears walking around my back yard, picking up my pig."

"Did he eat it somewhere?" Hannah wanted to know, wondering if Mr. Brunson had found the feeding site of the ill-fated hog.

"That would prove it," Jake said. "If you found the kill, the game official would have to do something about it. Which would solve our problem too — with the bear coming back."

"Don't count on it," Mr. Brunson grinned. "It's the big bad west out here. Both man and bear go free."

"I like this country though," Jake was quick to defend.

"Hannah was talking just this morning about wanting to move back east."

"Bear or no bear, I'm staying," Mr. Brunson said, not too cheerfully, Hannah thought, for one so committed to the land.

"Same here," Jake joined in, apparently glad for what support he could get.

"You haven't had breakfast, have you?" Hannah asked Mr. Brunson.

"No — haven't had time. Too many bear troubles," Mr. Benson chuckled.

"Come on in. The stove is still warm. I'll fix you some eggs and toast," Hannah told him. "Jake still has a few minutes before he leaves for work."

"Oh, I couldn't be a bother. Really," Mr. Brunson was quick to say, moving towards the front door.

"We insist," Jake joined in. "Hannah is good at frying up eggs."

"I would guess so." Mr. Brunson didn't need much persuading, following Jake out to the kitchen and taking the chair offered him.

Stirring up the fire again, she moved the still warm pan back on, thinking fast whether she could add something else to the breakfast menu. There was sausage in the spring house. Should she get a piece for Mr. Brunson to eat with his eggs?

Deciding that she should, and that Jake wouldn't mind, she said, "I'll be right back" and left Jake and Mr. Brunson talking about the best way to get action from the game officials on the grizzly.

Taking a knife and a plate with her to the spring house, she found the sausage and cut a piece off, adding it to her plate. Reaching for the boneless ham, she cut enough off for Jake's lunch sandwich.

Back in the house, Jake was up and standing at the counter, working on his lunch pail preparation, which she usually did.

"I'll help you in just a bit," she told him, as he was looking for something in the cupboards.

"Chips," he said.

"Third drawer down," she told him. "On the left."

The crunching of the bag told her he had found it as she broke the eggs into the now hot pan, adding the sausage beside them.

"I'm sorry about this," Mr. Brunson commented. "You really didn't have to fix breakfast."

"I'm glad to. It's no problem," Hannah assured him, keeping an eye on the crackling pan while she gave Jake a hand with his ham sandwich.

"I really have to go," Jake told them, Hannah's attention having returned to the breakfast making. "My ride's due soon."

"You do get out early," Mr. Brunson commented. "You like logging, Jake?"

"It's work," Jake half grunted, not that enthused. "I liked the forestry job the other summer much better."

"Why aren't you doing it then?" Mr. Brunson wanted to know.

"Too far to drive every day, plus you have to live up in the cabin. I don't think they take married couples."

"No, I don't think they do," Mr. Brunson agreed.

"Breakfast," Hannah announced, setting the plate of eggs and sausage in front of Mr. Brunson. Moments before, she had toasted a piece of bread freehand over the fire.

Mr. Brunson didn't miss the maneuver or fail to notice the results. "Right nice bread toasting there. I'll have to learn that myself."

"Doesn't work on electric stoves," Hannah told him, not sure what appliances Mr. Brunson had.

"I have gas," he grinned. "Think it would taste the same?"

"That's how we toasted at home. Mom always did. Tastes the same — I think," Hannah told him, glad Mr. Brunson liked the results of her attempt.

"I really have to go." Jake stood in the kitchen opening with his lunch pail. "See you tonight."

"Be careful," Hannah told him, remembering the night's events and hoping they didn't portend any future problems.

"Thanks for asking me to breakfast," Mr. Brunson said, his grin broad, his fork poised above the plate.

"You're welcome," Jake said, already opening the front door. The latch fell into place behind him as he stepped outside.

Hannah took a chair at the kitchen table as Mr. Brunson began eating without prayer. Her astonishment must have shown, because he stopped, took a look at her face, and said sheepishly, "I'm sorry. I guess I've been uncivilized too long."

"I didn't mean to say anything," she told him quickly, hoping she hadn't caused too much embarrassment.

"I used to pray," Mr. Brunson said. "Just needed a reminder." Pausing, he bowed his head.

"How long have you lived here?" Hannah asked him, never having asked before but feeling free now.

"About ten years," he said somewhat soberly, and Hannah wondered at his tone.

"From the east?" she asked, assuming that from what she knew of him.

"Yep — Boston. Big city. Needed some country I guess."

"My mom and dad are coming to visit soon," she volunteered, leading up to a question that bothered her. "I never see any visitors at your place."

"I guess you don't," he said, running his hand over his head. As he ate his last egg, Hannah noticed the piece of sausage was already gone and wished she had cooked him two pieces. Jake seldom ate sausage.

"I'm an old man," Mr. Brunson offered, interrupting her thoughts.

"Surely you have family," she said confidently. "They never come to visit?"

"One brother," he said. "Lives back east too. He's about as old as I am. Doubt if he wants to travel much."

"No wife?" she asked him, watching his face. "Surely you married."

"Well…" he told her, but kept his eyes on the plate of now finished breakfast. "My brother is. He married — younger — has two children, but they are in business. Don't have much interest in me, or Montana." Mr. Brunson gave her a wry smile, but she knew his eyes weren't expressing the same emotion. They looked far away and pained.

"Boy? Girl?" she asked, meaning the brother's children.

"Two…I mean, one each," he said, correcting his confusion, but she wondered whether the mistake had really been accidental.

"Your parents gone?" she asked as she got up and took his plate, stacking it beside Jake's on the countertop.

"I'm pretty old." He gave a genuine chuckle now, followed by genuine sorrow. "They died a long time ago. I was young — still in my twenties. Mom followed a year after Dad. They were great people."

"I'm sure they were," Hannah said, touched by Mr. Brunson's emotion. "I wouldn't know what to do with both my parents gone."

"I suppose so," Mr. Brunson agreed. "Just be thankful for what you have."

"God has been good to us. That's what Dad would say."

"He is a wise man," Mr. Brunson agreed again. "Now thanks for the breakfast. I must be going. Tell Jake his wife cooks a great breakfast."

"You're welcome," Hannah said, feeling warm circles run around her heart at the praise. A further thought occurred to her. "Maybe you could come for supper some night when Mom and Dad are here?"

"Oh," he seemed genuinely surprised. "I wouldn't want to be a bother."

"You wouldn't be," she assured him. "Dad would enjoy meeting you."

"Well," he seemed to hesitate, and then smiled, "maybe I will."

"I'll send Jake up then — when I know the night. If you can't come that night, maybe some other."

He found his John Deere cap on the floor by the front door. Hannah noticed his hands fumbled slightly as he put it on. She also saw there was moisture in his eyes as he left.

I wonder if he really has family, she asked herself, as Mr. Brunson's truck started up outside, but then decided it really was none of her business. Walking back to the kitchen she began washing the breakfast plates. Outside the first rays of the rising sun lit up the east side of the Cabinet Mountains.

Chapter Four

Hannah began her work for the day by carrying the ears of corn from the garden to the front yard. Her arms loaded high, she guessed at the quantity she could can that day. Her mother, Kathy, had always made such decisions for these projects at home, but there was obviously no mother around now. Wishing she could at least consult Aunt Betty, she gave up that thought too. It was simply not practical with the distance involved and the time such a trip would take. She was on her own.

Adding wood to the kitchen stove before husking the corn in the yard, she was reminded of how difficult a wood stove could be. Compared to the gas range she was used to at home, this was, well, a thing of the wilderness. The land of dreams, she thought with a grim smile — Montana.

But I loved him and this place, she reminded herself, letting the memory of her courtship with Jake warm her heart. *At least I got myself away from Sam — poor boy,* she thought. Then she sobered when she remembered that it was now Annie who was comfortably settled and married in Indiana. Annie might be hard at work on Sam's farm his father had given him, but she was safe from bears. Hannah made a face at the wood stove.

She had been invited to Sam's wedding — she and Jake — so Sam must have carried no bad feelings. Annie had looked radiant that day, and Sam all shiny in his new black suit, his hair slicked down over his forehead. Hannah had noticed Sam blushing as the bishop married them.

So…but she wasn't going to think about that anymore. This was where she wanted to be and belonged, with Jake and now him. Hannah smiled, remembering the life inside of her, already thinking of the coming baby as male. It seemed as natural as breathing to her. Jake needed a boy. Not that he had ever mentioned it exactly, but she wanted to give him a boy. She wanted his firstborn to be the delight of his eye, the pleasure of his heart. This child would be that — she was certain — and a joy for both of them.

Making sure the fire was burning steadily, she added another piece of wood before taking a chair outside in the yard. Sitting near the corn she pulled off the husks, throwing them in a pile nearby. Jake would carry them into the garden for mulch later when he came home. Jake was like that, usually willing to help her with such things — even when he came in from work exhausted.

She must be careful, though, she told herself, not to impose on Jake too much. This was especially true with the baby coming and the extra work that would make. Her mother had once mentioned something to that effect about her father, but Hannah couldn't remember the exact reasons her mother had given. She just knew she didn't want Jake to be overburdened. He already had enough to do.

With the corn husked, she left the ears lying on the ground and returned to the kitchen. Getting her pressure cooker off the bottom shelf of the cabinets, she added water carefully to the right level. She then tapped the pressure gauge to check it, not certain if this was a true test, but it was all she knew how to do. The little black needle bounced in response to her taps.

She had purchased the cooker at a local garage sale soon after they moved here. The item had not been among the gifts at the wedding. She remembered with regret that it had been among the items given at her aborted wedding to Sam, but Kathy had insisted all those items be returned.

I married for love now, she told herself grimly, tapping the round gauge again, getting another little bounce out of it, *not for cooker or farm. This thing had better still be working,* she thought, not certain why she was questioning the cooker this morning, since it had been functioning okay all summer. Perhaps it was the fright from last night. Whatever, a malfunctioning gauge on a pressure cooker was not a trifle.

"You'll be a good boy," she told the cooker, laughing at herself. "I do need a baby — I'm talking to the kitchen pots."

Leaving the control knob off, Hannah pushed the cooker to the side of the oven and returned to the yard to cut the corn from the cobs. When she came back inside, she carried enough corn for one batch. Filling the jars, she was pleased to find there was still corn left.

She dropped the filled jars into the cooker and moved it back on the oven. Hoping she could get through cutting enough corn for a second batch before the cooker whistled, she went back to the pile in the yard and sliced away, glad this job would soon be done.

When she stepped back inside, her delight was dampened by the discovery the fire wasn't cooperating and the cooker wasn't boiling as it should be. Searching for the cause, she found the ash pan full and had to remove the sliding tray, carry the contents to the edge of the woods, and dump them.

Jake, because of his fire spotting days, had frequently warned her of the danger of fire from ashes. Back home in Indiana, there was no oven to make fires in and few woods to burn up. Here, though, there was great danger, so Jake had cleared a little area by the side of the garden to dispose of them safely.

Usually Hannah would have dumped the ashes without much thought, but this morning everything seemed to need extra care. Taking the tip of the pan, she spread the pile thin, knowing that spread ashes would cool faster. Not that there was any danger, she told herself — Jake had built this fire pit to take care of that.

Walking back inside, she found the oven fire already burning much better. She added extra wood to keep it moving along. The whistle of the cooker came none too soon, sounding only moments after she had packed the second batch of corn into the jars. Checking the strength of the fire, Hannah placed the control knob on the cooker. The pressure was steady, so she left the kitchen to check the garden and plan the rest of her day.

She knew of a few tomatoes still left on the vines, but she walked the row to be sure of the number and counted enough to easily make another batch of tomato juice. That would come in handy this winter, since both she and Jake enjoyed tomato soup.

Visions of the two of them — soon to be three, she reminded herself — sitting in the cabin with snow flying around outside, eating popcorn and tomato soup some evening, were delightful. When, then, should she tackle the job? Today yet? Deciding the task to be a little too much, she glanced up and found the clearness of the sky reassuring. With no rain in sight, the tomatoes could be done tomorrow.

She returned to the kitchen knowing the cooker needed to be watched closely. A look at the gauge assured her all was well — five more degrees and she could slide it off the hot part of the stove. She added another piece of wood.

Not wanting to go far or wait in the kitchen, Hannah stepped into the living room where two of Jake's shirts needed mending. She had draped them yesterday over the couch. Not a good practice, she knew from her mother's instruction to keep such things in the sewing room. Here there was no sewing room and little space to keep mending projects.

With her mother coming to visit, perhaps she should think of someplace else to put the mending. But her mother was sensitive, she reminded herself, and would understand how little space they had. For that Hannah was thankful.

It was about then the cooker blew. The noise hit her like a dull blow to the head, resounding throughout her body; her mind refused to believe the message. Hannah Byler, the just lately Hannah Byler, had blown up her pressure cooker.

Her first thought, as she turned towards the kitchen, was this was not something one could hide under the proverbial rug and prevent anyone from finding out. The emotion of what had just happened swept over her. Few Amish women blew up their cookers, and those who did were not forgotten quickly.

Others would be thankful she was not in the kitchen at the time, but at the moment she wished she had been. The thought flashed through her mind that a few burns would help stir up sympathy. Instead, she was coming out unscathed.

Her first look into the kitchen quickly dissuaded her from her wish. The lid lay mangled on the floor, having left a deep gash in the wood ceiling. Corn and glass pieces were splattered on every wall except the one by the living room, furthest from the stove. Great clouds of steam rose from the oven top, where much of the spilt water had landed. If she had been here, she was certain the result would have been more than a few burns.

Hannah's next thought was of Jake and how he had to come home to a wife who blew her kitchen to pieces. It wasn't as if he didn't have enough to do already. She felt an urge to rush into the cleanup — to sweep up the pieces of glass, to pull the corn off the log sides with her fingers, to wipe up the water, to make things as if this had never happened. Instead, she felt a great weariness come over her. Returning to the living room she ignored the mended shirts, sat down on the couch, lay her head against the back, and broke into tears.

CHAPTER FIVE

HANNAH SPENT THE rest of the forenoon cleaning the kitchen. The immensity of the task was soon evident, not just in removing the corn and glass pieces stuck to the walls, but in repairing the damage where the metal fragments had hit.

One of the upper cabinet doors was broken, which she knew Jake would have to fix. The rest were water stained but looked to be okay after she wiped them down. The tear in the ceiling she figured no one could fix, and that it would remain there forever. A symbol, she thought despairingly, a reminder for all the world to see of the young woman who blew up her cooker.

When the corn came off the walls, it left little yellow stains behind, until she thought of letting it dry out first and then sweeping it off with the broom. Most of the glass fragments she got up while waiting for the corn to dry. Looking angrily at the old stove, the handiest thing to blame other than herself, she could find no damage whatever to its hardy exterior.

"You'd live forever — you mean thing," she told it. "No matter what happened."

There was then the problem of what to do with the remaining batch of corn. Hannah no longer had a pressure cooker to work with. Throwing the corn away was simply out of the question, so that left only one course of action.

Too anxious to feel hunger, even though lunch time had

arrived, she hitched their young driving horse, Mossy, to the buggy, and left without eating. Mossy was the name of the horse when Jake made the purchase. How such a name came about, Jake said he had no idea, since the horse seemed to have plenty of speed. Getting him to use it was another matter.

The drive to Betty's place seemed to take forever. Hannah urged Mossy to move faster, but he protested by swishing his tail back and forth. She slapped the lines again. Mossy increased his speed momentarily, then lapsed back into a steady gait.

Finally she arrived, seeing the *Horse Back Riding* sign from her days running the riding stable still hanging in its old place. She knew Betty's oldest daughter, Kendra, now helped her mother with the horses. As Hannah was tying Mossy to the hitching rail, Betty came rushing out of the kitchen door, her working apron around her waist.

"What's brought you around, this time of day? My, it's sure nice weather for this time of the year."

The sound of her aunt's voice pushed Hannah where she didn't want to go, the tears threatening again. "I wondered if I could borrow your pressure cooker."

"Why, dear?" Betty was not put off that easily, her eyes searching Hannah's face. "You have one yourself. Don't tell me you are doing two at the same time with that old stove of yours. You're liable to blow the old thing up working it that hard. Didn't your mom ever tell you that?"

The blowing up remark brought the flood of tears. "I already blew up the cooker," she got out, choking on the words.

"You blew up the cooker — oh, my word." Betty was all sympathy. "Just blew it up? Why? Was the gauge stuck — surely that's what it was. Did you check? You weren't in the kitchen at the time, surely?"

"I don't know," Hannah told her miserably. "I tapped the gauge like usual. It's an old cooker, of course, but the needle bounced."

"Then no one can blame you. Not for a thing." Betty got right down to the encouraging part. "You're not hurt are you? Were you close by? Surely not? You look okay."

"In the living room — really I'm okay," Hannah assured her, then almost wailed: "Now I'll be known as the girl who blew up her cooker. Mom will think me completely careless. And she's coming in a few weeks."

"Now...now," Betty used her best comfort tone, but there was a chuckle in her voice.

"It's not funny," Hannah said, indignantly.

"I guess not. But really," Betty still chuckled, "you ought to be thankful. For a girl who can blow up her cooker, yet not have a scratch or burn on herself.... This is good. Look on the bright side of things. You survived walking out on your own wedding. Now that — I told myself, even though I understood and all — that would take years to live down. Now look at you. Married already and well settled in. You have nothing to worry about. Maybe your kitchen does. Not you. You need help cleaning up?"

"No. I'm already done." Hannah didn't look too convinced from Betty's speech.

"So you need a cooker, and I'm canning myself," Betty got back to business. "That's just the way things.... Well, don't worry about it."

"Oh," Hannah was quick to say. "That's different. I'll go ask Elizabeth. Maybe I can borrow hers."

"That's further the other direction," Betty said. "I couldn't let you do that. Now, wait a minute. My old one is still in the basement."

"Your old one." The horror crept into Hannah's voice.

Betty chuckled again, "Don't worry, this one won't blow. It's been faithful for years. The only reason I got a new one was so I'd have two at the same time. Today though — don't worry — I'm only using the one."

"You sure?" Hannah wasn't entirely convinced.

"You can't blow two in one day," Betty assured her.

To which Hannah said sarcastically, "Me...not blow two.

Anything could happen right now. At least it feels that way. There was a grizzly past our place last night. Mr. Brunson came down this morning. It got his pig, he thinks."

"My...my...you are having your troubles. Bears aren't such a big thing around here though. Especially on the main roads. They don't bother much. And people have them back off the roads — like where you live. Happens all the time."

"That's really comforting."

"It's Montana. The mountains. You'll get used to it. If it bothers you too much, the game warden will probably have the bear moved."

"That's what Jake and Mr. Brunson want to look into."

"See there, it'll be okay. Now the cooker. Just give me a minute and I'll dig it out of the basement."

Hannah waited by the buggy, and Betty was soon back as promised, putting the cooker behind the seat.

"I'll get the cooker back as soon as I can," Hannah told Betty as she climbed in. Mossy wearily lifted his head to look back at her, as if checking to see if he needed to move again.

"Don't worry. Keep it till you're done. I'll only need one for the rest of the season."

"Maybe Jake can buy me a new one."

"That might be a good idea," Betty said with a chuckle, stepping back as Hannah got Mossy moving.

Jake found Hannah in tears that evening when he came into the house swinging his lunch pail. She was still working in the kitchen, lifting the last of the canned corn from Betty's used cooker. That she had also managed to prepare a small casserole for their supper didn't enter her calculations as a reason for the tears and exhaustion, as she told Jake the story, pointing dismally at the mark in the ceiling and the damaged cabinet door.

"You shouldn't have made supper then. With all that going on," he told her.

"Then what would we have eaten? You have to eat. I can't let you starve. What kind of wife would that be?"

"Still a very good one," he assured her. "Now what needs to be done around here? It looks like you've cleaned up already. Let me take out the water in the cooker."

"It can go down the drain. The corn husks still need to be picked up. They're in the yard, and now it's almost dark already."

"I can still do it," he told her, lifting the warm cooker from the oven and carefully pouring the hot water down the drain for her.

"Do you think I'm an awful cook?" she asked him, hesitantly. "I just blew up my kitchen."

"Of course not," he said, without even pausing to think. "Grandma Byler blew hers up years ago. Except she got some nasty burns. We can be real thankful nothing happened liked that. What if you had been in the kitchen?" She was certain his eyes were full of genuine concern. "It does happen. Grandma has been a family story for years."

"That's just what I was afraid of," she wailed.

"One way to get famous, I guess." His grin brightened his face. "Maybe I'd better get those husks in the garden before dark."

"It's not funny," she retorted, to which he said nothing, chuckling on his way out.

When Jake came back, Hannah had the supper plates laid out and the casserole in the middle of the table with its simple complements of bread, jam, butter, and corn.

"I'm sorry there's no cake or something," she told him, pulling a chair out and motioning for him to be seated.

"This is plenty," he said, his face long, she noticed. "Let's pray," he added, and started before she could ask why.

When they were done he answered the question without being asked. "Boss said winter jobs might be hard to come by."

"What does that mean?" she asked, pushing the casserole in his direction and turning the spoon towards him.

"He said" — Jake had a catch in his throat — "if anyone could, we should best be looking for other jobs. Winter's coming up, I guess. Our work might be cut back. I think, though, he was talking about me."

"Surely not," Hannah replied, as Jake passed the casserole back. The smell stirred her hunger, forgotten for so long in the hurry of the day. Jake's words didn't take immediate effect, as if she heard them from a great distance.

"I'm afraid so," Jake replied, and now the full import of his words dawned on her.

"So what about paying the mortgage?" she asked, fear in her voice.

"I guess we must trust God," Jake said, without much confidence in his voice.

Just like her father would say it, Hannah thought, yet it sounded strange coming from such a young man. *Yet her young man,* and she was young too, Hannah reminded herself. Maybe this was how it went? How you learned things? Just by doing them, even though you felt scared.

"I guess we must," she told him, not really feeling very trusting about it — but there, she had said it.

"Maybe I can find something else," Jake was saying without much confidence either. "It's kind of late in the year."

"Do you think it's a bad sign?" Hannah asked him, the fear coming back.

"What?" he wanted to know.

"Me…blowing up the kitchen today. And the grizzly? Are things going to be hard for us? What about the baby?"

She saw Jake's face darken momentarily, but then he collected himself. "There is always a way out. Somewhere. Hasn't God been good to us so far?" Jake gave her a thin smile. "You didn't marry Sam. We have each other. Now a new life coming. Ours."

"I didn't know it would be like this, though." Her voice was hushed. "Is it like this for everyone?"

"I don't know." He found her eyes. "I've not been here before. But God will take care of us."

She saw his tenderness and let her own face soften. "I guess you're right. I'm just afraid sometimes."

"I think everyone is," he assured her.

That night they awakened to the sounds of grizzly outside.

"Just let him be," Jake whispered in the darkness. "Maybe the game warden will do something about this now."

Hannah said nothing, finding Jake's hand until it was quiet outside.

CHAPTER SIX

HANNAH SAW JAKE off as usual before the sun was up, watching him walk to the blacktop road for his ride. She had raised the question again at the breakfast table about moving east, to which he had said no.

She could tell he thought the bear was the root of the problem, the reason she suddenly wanted to move east. Gently but firmly he took charge of her fears, reassuring her that things would get better soon. He thought Mr. Brunson might stop by and could go to the game warden with the bear problem. If not, maybe he would run across an opportunity to report the matter.

Hannah thought their problem was more complicated than that. Wasn't Jake close to losing his job with winter coming up? The bear's appearance might have marked the start of troubled times, or so it seemed to her, yet matters now looked bigger than just the bear.

True to Jake's hope, Mr. Brunson's pickup truck stopped in front of the house just as the sun was rising. To save him having to walk in, Hannah went out to meet Mr. Brunson in the yard. He stayed in his truck and waited.

"Nice of you to come out," he told her when she was within earshot. "Old bones hurt in the morning."

"Jake was hoping you would stop by," she said, standing beside his truck.

"Bear back?" he guessed.

Hannah nodded. "We heard him again. Don't know

what he wants though. Nothing missing this morning."

"Wish I could say the same." Mr. Brunson's face darkened. "Found my hog this morning between our two places. Not much left of him, I must say. Think the bear came back last night to finish the feed."

Hannah made a face at the image. "Jake was hoping you could tell the game warden. Maybe today? Don't think I like a bear wandering around."

"That's where I'm going now," Mr. Brunson said emphatically. "I got a picture of the eaten hog to prove the matter. Going right into town and see what can be done. Maybe we can get some action tonight. If not...." Mr. Brunson's face darkened again, then he smiled when he saw Hannah watching him intently. "No... I suppose not. Better not shoot the thing myself. Law's kind of hard on such things."

"Don't be giving Jake any ideas," Hannah told him. She could just see Jake out with his hunting rifle, the darkness throwing off his aim, enraged bear arms reaching for him.

"We wouldn't want to do that," Mr. Brunson assured her. "Nice fine associated with the penalty too."

"That we couldn't afford," she said with certainty. "This bear could be quite a problem it seems."

"That's what the law is for in this country — one would hope," Mr. Brunson said, his face grim. "Let me see what I can get done today. See you after Jake gets home — maybe. I might be able to give you and him both some good news."

When Mr. Brunson left, Hannah wasn't sure whether to be relieved or not. From what he was saying, the game warden would soon do something about the bear, and that would convince Jake there was no reason to move back east. She was surprised at the extent of her disappointment. Her thoughts about moving back to Indiana had taken firm root, seeming to sprout trunk and twigs all of their own.

Then again, she certainly didn't want the bear around, so it was best for Mr. Brunson to head to the warden's, even if it meant staying in Montana. Jake sure had his heart set on staying. He seemed to think he could find work somewhere to survive the coming winter, even if the logging business got a little slow.

If that was what Jake wanted then she had better support him, she decided, whatever her own inclinations. Hannah really had not the heart to do otherwise, unless, she told herself, she was absolutely certain the circumstances warranted such action. As of yet, that was not the case.

"So...*Sees Montana, sie mie blumm,*" she said out loud to the heavens, glancing upwards at the lingering redness of the sunrise before walking back in the house. Hannah laughed at her own words, humming them with a tune of her own making, thankful no one else was there to see or hear. "Sweet Montana, be my flower."

Back in the kitchen, Betty's pressure cooker still sat on the back corner of the counter where she had left it after yesterday's corn canning. Hannah eyed the cooker warily, her nerves still raw, the memories still vivid. Should she, or shouldn't she, take on the tomatoes today?

Jake hadn't said anything about the weather, which he usually did if a major rain was moving in. He liked to pass on the reports given to him by his boss. Perhaps he had been distracted, Hannah thought, making a face — she had given him plenty of distraction. *Not everyone's wife blows up the kitchen,* she winced at the thought.

Stepping outside again to confirm her earlier observation, she saw streaks of red still hanging above the rising sun and decided the tomatoes had to be done today, whatever her feelings about the cooker. Her mom had often moved up their scheduled wash day in response to a red sunrise.

Hannah got her bowls from the pantry and headed for the garden. She soon abandoned her effort to calculate how much she needed for two batches of tomato juice, simply picking what was there. The ripe tomatoes were going to waste anyway.

Halfway down the row, the tomatoes suddenly ceased. She kept looking, finding a tomato here and there, but not nearly as many as there should be. Her suspicions roused, she found evidence in a flattened tomato, the moistened ground showing bear prints. The distinct claw marks were in front, with wider indentations on the sides and back.

A shiver ran up Hannah's back. The bear had been right here, where she stood now, its huge furry body lumbering down this row of tomatoes. Did bears eat tomatoes? This one, at any rate, seemed to have been sampling them.

She gathered courage to check further down the row, wondering if the bear was still around. The protection of the log cabin seemed far away. She held panic at bay, though, figuring grizzlies had enough sense not to come out in the daylight.

The tomatoes did reappear a few plants down, and Hannah finished filling the bowl, deciding there were still enough for canning. She returned to the front yard, set up the strainer, and began work.

It was a messy job, tomato juice splashing on her apron no matter how carefully she worked. She had never appreciated this part of the process but thought that doing it for her own home would make it more tolerable. Of this she was mistaken! Still she continued, mashing the tomatoes through the strainer, adding salt to the mixture from memory. What must be done must be done, she told herself.

When the cans were filled, she carefully set them in the cooker. Tightening the lid, she slid the cooker onto the hot part of the stove. With skepticism she eyed the gauge, which seemed to be working; still she worked outside the kitchen while the cooker was heating up. Glancing back in every few minutes to check the pressure, she moved quickly at 11 pounds and slid the cooker off the hot area.

For the next 15 minutes she made quick trips back and forth between the kitchen door and the stove, maintaining the pressure at 11 pounds. Finally, with a deep sigh of relief, she moved the cooker completely off the heat. The point of danger over, Hannah stayed in the kitchen. When the pressure had gone down completely, she undid the top with a gentle pop and a small cloud of steam rose.

While the cans cooled on the kitchen table, she repeated the entire process and still had tomatoes left. Wondering whether it was time to quit, she decided instead to press on, figuring Jake would understand if she had only leftover casserole for supper.

When he got home, Jake found her happy in her accomplishment, rows of red tomato juice jars lined up behind her on the kitchen counter. Some of the cans were still popping softly, finishing sealing.

"Our winter stash," she told Jake, letting her joy wash away her weariness.

"You were canning all day," he said, obviously impressed. "Why didn't you take a break from yesterday?"

"It might rain tomorrow, that's why. I didn't want to be searching for wet tomatoes in the mud."

"It will rain," Jake said, surprised. "The boss said so. How did you know?"

"The sunrise was red."

"I guess it was," he said. "I didn't notice. We're not even going to work tomorrow. I guess the percentage is pretty high."

"So what are you doing tomorrow, then?"

"Maybe I can talk to the game warden — about the bear."

"Mr. Brunson stopped by this morning. He was going in today. Said he found the place where the bear ate his pig." Hannah made a face, pulling the wrapper off the leftover casserole and opening the oven door. "Hope you're happy with leftovers."

"That's fine. Mr. Brunson say if he'd let us know?"

"Said he'd stop by when you were home if he had news."

"Hopefully it's good then. Guess I'll wash up," Jake said, disappearing in the direction of their small bathroom, its water flow, like that of the kitchen, fed by the pressure from the spring.

Moments later Hannah heard Jake pumping air into the

gas lantern they used for evening light. To keep expenses down, they used gas only in the evening, and then only in the living room, using kerosene lamps otherwise. That was Hannah's idea, but she doubted whether it actually saved that much.

Jake never complained, though, seeming to like the routine. He hung the lantern on the center ceiling nail and sat down to read. Hannah figured he was into the *Readerîs Digest*, the latest edition having just arrived in the mail. In the kitchen, she continued setting the table by the light of the kerosene lamp.

"It's ready," she told Jake, sticking her head into the living room, giving him a tired but warm and happy smile.

After supper, Mr. Brunson did stop in as promised. He took the chair Hannah offered him.

"Game warden said he'd stop by tomorrow. Don't know what he'll do, but I had my pictures."

"Hannah said you found the place," Jake told him.

"Mighty nerve, that's what I say. Coming right up to our places like this." Mr. Brunson didn't sound happy at all.

"Hopefully something will be done then," Jake responded. "I'll be home tomorrow. So maybe that will help — if the game warden comes."

"He'd better. Supposed to rain tomorrow. Who knows. Goodnight then," Mr. Brunson said, getting up to leave.

Jake shut the door behind him as Mr. Brunson stepped outside. His form passed the front window, highlighted by the light from the gas lantern.

That night the noises from the bear outside were even more pronounced. Perhaps he was emboldened by the pouring rain that lashed the logs of the cabin, Hannah thought. She lay in bed unable to ignore the sounds until Jake finally got up and yelled fiercely out the front door.

"Should do it," Jake said wearily, climbing back into bed.

Apparently it did, because there was silence the rest of the night.

Chapter Seven

THE RAIN WAS still coming down in sheets when Hannah and Jake woke. Since Jake planned on staying home, no alarm had been set, but from long habit they didn't miss the time by much.

"I can't sleep," Jake announced after a few tosses and turns. He propped himself up in bed on his elbows, looking around the dark room.

"Me neither," Hannah agreed, but stayed in bed while Jake dressed and left. Before she could decide whether to get up too, she heard the noise of Jake preparing to light the gas lantern and then the hiss of its light filling the living room. Stray rays came into the bedroom. Groaning, she halfheartedly got out of bed. Jake was home today, and she figured it was time to get up.

Walking into the living room from the dark bedroom, Hannah wished she could turn on some inner light this easily and get rid of the gloom she was feeling. Perhaps, she thought, the cause was the rainy day and that bear last night making itself at home in their backyard.

"You going to have breakfast soon?" Jake asked with hope in his voice as she walked past.

"I can," she told him. "Little hungry myself. You want anything different since you're home?"

"No," he shook his head, busy reading the Farmer's Almanac.

Hannah didn't know if all men were as unimaginative

49

as Jake when it came to food, but she decided a rainy morning called for something special. If nothing else, it would serve as a little cheer for herself.

"I'll make some bacon," she told him, thinking of their breakfasts at home with her mom preparing it. Jake glanced up, but went on reading.

"Can you get me some from the spring house?" she asked him.

"Sure," he said, then seemed to hesitate, apparently remembering the rain. "You want the bacon that bad?"

"Yes," Hannah told him, suddenly stopping by the kitchen opening, the horror of the thought occurring to her for the first time. "What if the bear got into the spring house? Maybe that's what he's after?"

"Could be," Jake allowed, producing his raincoat from the small closet by the front door. "He can't get in though. I built it strong enough."

"How do you know?" Hannah wasn't convinced.

"I just know."

"You've never been in bear country before?"

"No." Jake still didn't look concerned. "I'll check, but he didn't get in."

True to his word, Jake was back in the house quickly, a grin on his face. "Told you," he said. "That's what he's after, though. Partly at least. Big claw marks on the logs."

"Did he get in?"

"Of course not," Jake chuckled. "It's built strong enough for any bear."

"You think we should tell the game warden about this?"

"I suppose — if he comes out." Jake sounded skeptical. "It probably won't help our case though."

"That's what I was thinking." Hannah took the bacon from him, disappearing into the kitchen. With the fire soon burning in the wood stove, breakfast was on its way to the table.

Afterwards, Jake did look pleased, Hannah thought, with the extra she had put into breakfast.

"You like it?" she asked him.

"Good as Mom's," he grinned, meaning it as a compliment, but Hannah felt uneasy. She had always assumed she measured up to Jake's mom.

"I make it as good as I can," she told him, not meaning to leave any trace of what she felt in her voice, but Jake looked up anyway.

"It's better," he said.

"I'm glad then," Hannah allowed. She didn't want to fuss with him, especially on his morning home. "What are you planning for the day?"

"Book work?" He made a face.

"The checkbook is balanced," she said, thinking of adding *what little there is in it*, but refraining. Jake tried hard enough without her making things worse for him.

"I know," he nodded his head. "Just looking at my" — then changed the word with a smile — "*our* financial situation."

"We're making do," Hannah assured him. "But just barely. The bank payment on the house takes a large chunk each month."

"How else could we have done it?"

"Rented — I guess," she told him, making a face. "This is such a nice little cabin though. Dear and all."

"Reasonable, too," Jake reminded Hannah, "for this area. It was quite a deal. Both Steve and Betty thought so."

"I know," Hannah said, knowing Jake knew of other people who said the same thing — like Bishop Nisley himself — but apparently thought mentioning her relatives was in his best interest. "It was a good idea," she assured him.

"We'll make it somehow," he sighed, getting up from the kitchen table. "Though I don't quite know how."

Hannah cleaned the kitchen, the rain still beating on the window pane, while Jake busied himself in front of their little desk cubicle in the living room. Jake had insisted on making the entire piece by himself. Hannah wasn't really surprised that he was good at it, and told Jake so.

The top was a plank of large log, sawn in half and smoothed with a varnished finish. For legs, Jake used hickory, with the cut knots showing their full glory. On the right side, two slabs of log formed the vertical frame for the drawers, which slid on wooden slides, softened by stick-on cloth gliders Jake purchased at the hardware in Libby.

"We're still making it," Jake announced from the desk, his voice glad, filled with relief.

Hannah said nothing, wanting Jake to enjoy the moment without her input. He deserved to succeed, she thought, feeling a sorrow gather around her heart. Would the effort, though, not be better spent back in Indiana where Jake would get paid for the real value of his work? Here, it seemed to her, there was a lot of heavy hard work, with less money coming in than what she was used to seeing her father make.

Pushing her thoughts aside, Hannah concentrated on the kitchen. By midmorning, the rain slacked off, and Jake was on the verge of venturing outdoors when Mr. Brunson's truck pulled up in front of their cabin. Along with him was a dark green, clearly marked state vehicle.

"Mr. Rogers," he introduced the officer, when Jake and Hannah stepped outside. "Mr. and Mrs. Byler."

"So you've been having bear trouble?" the young officer smiled, looking like a game warden, Hannah thought. His uniform was a little torn down by his ankle, but his step forward strong when he shook hands with Jake and offered a nod in her direction.

"Noises around the cabin," Jake told him. "A few nights already. Last night was pretty bad again."

"Rain doesn't stop them much," the young officer chuckled. "Forging for the winter, I'd say. Won't be long before the snows start. Let's take a look around then. Ought to be some tracks out yet."

"It just rained hard," Mr. Brunson injected, not sounding too happy. "Don't be telling me there was nothing. He was here at these young people's place. I've got my pictures of the eaten hog. That ought to prove something is going on."

"Don't worry," the officer grinned. "I believe you folks. Let's see what we have."

Jake led the two men, with Hannah following behind, showing them the spot along the bedroom wall where the noises had come from. The officer bent close to the ground for a better look, grunting as his finger drew the outline of a faint print.

"Bear all right."

"So you're not going to say we made it up," Mr. Brunson snapped.

"I said I believe you. Even without evidence." The officer seemed unruffled. "Bears are always possible around here."

"Grizzly?" Jake asked him.

"You know it was a grizzly?" the officer asked. He looked sharply at Jake.

"Yes," Jake told him.

"How could you tell?"

"Hump on its back. Big one, too."

"You saw it?"

"The first night," Jake assured him.

"A good look?'

"Sure. With my light."

"Let me see your light," the officer said.

"See, I told you you wouldn't believe us," Mr. Brunson got in. "These are nice young people. There's no reason for a grizzly to be haunting them at night. Let alone eating my pig."

"Let's see the light," the officer repeated, then continued studying the ground as Jake went to get it.

"Anything else bothered around here that you know of?" he asked, directing his question in Hannah's direction with a turn of his head.

"The bear was in my garden," Hannah told him. "I found paw prints. Then Jake found scratches on the spring house this morning. I haven't seen those yet."

"Missing anything?" the office asked, looking up at her.

"Maybe some tomatoes. Don't know if bears eat tomatoes," she grimaced. "Nothing missing in the spring house. Jake built it strong."

"You can say that. I stopped by while he was building," Mr. Brunson jumped in.

"You keep meat in the spring house?" the officer wanted to know of Hannah, ignoring Mr. Brunson.

She nodded. "We don't have refrigeration." Adding with a smile, "Cheaper that way."

"I suppose so," the office allowed, standing up again as Jake came back with his light. "Also attracts bears."

"Now don't you go blaming us," Mr. Brunson said, sounding irate. "These young folks are doing real well here. They don't need a bear messing things up. Folks ought to be able to live the way they want without the law coming and saying otherwise."

"I wasn't saying that," the officer answered Mr. Brunson this time. "Just mentioning it. If the bear didn't get in, or thinks he can't next time, he probably won't be back."

"Now don't be saying that either," Mr. Brunson said, still sounding angry. "Ignoring the problem won't solve it either."

The officer ignored Mr. Brunson, reaching for Jake's light. He flicked the switch, sending the beam first against the wall of the cabin, then out across the garden. Even in the day, with the sun trying to break through the clouds, the light reached underneath Hannah's tomato plants.

"Good enough," the officer grunted. "So it might be a grizzly."

"That's what the man said," Mr. Brunson snapped.

"A black bear isn't much of a problem," the officer directed his remark toward Jake, ignoring Mr. Brunson again. "Problem bears can be disposed of easily — if we have to. Grizzlies, as you might know, are another matter. Where this one came from, I don't know. There are some in the south Cabinet area — usually stay there — or maybe from the Bitterroot or Bob Marshall. Either way, we could have him trapped and taken back, but it might not do much good. Bears are like that."

"So why not just take him out," Mr. Brunson wanted to know. "If you can't do it, I can."

The officer looked at Mr. Brunson skeptically. "Let me tell you. I hope you're just joking. Grizzlies are protected around here, Feds and all. Unless you want to tangle with them, let alone us, better leave this bear alone."

"That's what I thought," Mr. Brunson fairly growled, his voice low in a tone Hannah had never heard him use before. "Little use you people are. Home and property could be eaten up with no help coming from the authorities."

"Let's take a look at this spring house of the Byler's." The officer gave another sharp glance at Mr. Brunson. "Then I'll file my report. We'll see that the problem is taken care of one way or the other."

"What about my property?" Mr. Brunson wanted to know, not sounding mollified at all.

"We'll take a look at that too," the officer said, his voice constrained, Hannah thought. She felt her body tremble at this exchange between the men. *I'm not much of a pioneer woman. Here I thought I was tough and all, dreamy-eyed with my cabin and Jake — now I'm just water on the inside when the first big problem comes up.*

Walking over with Jake, the officer looked carefully at the spring house, lifting the heavy door and then letting it swing shut.

"It's built well," he concluded. "Should be okay, if you keep it shut tight. Never let him get in though. Once he does, you'll have to tear this down. Bears would never forget such a haul. This would give them a big one."

"Sounds like you plan on this being a long-term problem," Mr. Brunson growled again.

"We'll do something," the officer said, assurance in his voice. "I'll see what can be done."

"You'd better," Mr. Brunson told him.

The officer asked a few more questions of Jake and Hannah and then left. He followed Mr. Brunson further up the dirt road, going up to look at the site where Mr. Brunson's pig had been eaten.

Around three the rain started again, chasing Jake from the yard inside the barn where he began cutting wood for a project. He had been working for some time now on a log dresser for the master bedroom. *For their baby*, Hannah thought, feeling the warmth circle her heart. Yet she knew Jake had started the project before she told him, so it couldn't be just for that. The thought of the baby still gave her comfort, diverting her attention from the troubling bear.

The rain also brought Jake's boss just before supper, his truck rattling to a stop in front of the cabin. Jake opened the door for him with a smile. "It's good to see you," he told him, stepping aside to let the burly man come inside.

"I can't stay, son," he said, his eyes downcast. "Sorry. I have bad news."

"Yes," Jake said, a catch in his throat that Hannah heard all the way out in the kitchen.

"I just lost my next contract. The big one behind the Cabinet Mountains. I'm afraid I have to lay off half the crew until work picks up again, with winter coming and all."

Jake said nothing.

"I'm sorry, son," the man's voice reached Hannah clearly, carrying genuine compassion in it. "I know it's hard for all of us. That's why I came to tell you myself."

CHAPTER EIGHT

THE REST OF the evening seemed to drag on forever. Jake sat in the living room with its beaming light, but he was in his own world. Hannah shed her tears in the kitchen, taking care to hide them from Jake. He was going through enough, she figured, without seeing her cry on top of everything else.

"You want some supper?" she asked when she could trust her voice not to break down on her.

He shook his head, his eyes staring blankly out the front window. "We have to have money to live on," he said softly.

She felt like saying the old cliche *we can live on love* but restrained herself, the silliness of it almost bringing back the tears.

"I'll make you supper anyway," she told him. "You need it."

"I need a job," he said, his voice flat. "I need to take care of you — the baby." His voice was so broken she felt the tears sting again, emotions welling up, pushing themselves out with strength beyond her ability to contain. She wrapped her arms around his shoulders, letting the tears come, not caring they dampened the top of his head.

"We need to go back to Nappanee," she told him, wishing she wasn't saying it but unable to help herself. She saw their condition in its starkest terms, the falling darkness outside driving her thoughts.

"We can't," he said, his voice still flat but determination surrounding its edge. "We can't leave this place."

"But why not?" she protested. "The baby's coming. Winter will soon be here. You heard what the officer said — they're not going to do much about that bear. It's a grizzly, and they're protected by law."

"We can't," he said quietly, his elbows now on his knees, his face in his hands. "We belong here. Both of us. To this place. This country. This church. I just feel it. Felt it since the first time we came here. It was to be you and me, together. Here."

"But what if things change? We all dream," she told him, knowing her own tendency. "Sometimes it's not right, not what we think it is."

She felt his shoulders stiffen under her hands as he said, "We're supposed to stay here."

"And starve? Lose the cabin? At least if you sold now you could get plenty of money for it. In the winter, who knows? There might be no buyers then."

He turned to face her, his young features drawn in pain. The tears stung her eyes again as he took both her hands in his.

"It might be easier," he nodded his head as if the thought was still forming itself. "But to do what is right is always best."

"What is right about this?" Hannah took one hand out of his, motioning with a broad sweep meant to include the land, the cabin, the people who lived here, and the bear.

"I don't know," he said, his face puzzled, still in thought. "We just need to stay. I'll go look for work tomorrow. Something will come about."

"There are plenty of jobs at home. I know Dad could get you in where he works. They pay gobs of money."

"Let's try here first," he sighed, weariness filling his face, his youth making it look so out of place, Hannah thought. She took his hand again, compassion stirring in her heart.

"You are the brave one," she told him. "I always thought I was, but you are so much braver."

"No," he shook his head. "You really are. You married me." A slight grin played on his face. "Any regrets yet?"

"Don't say that," she chided him, meaning it. "Of course not."

"Sam wouldn't be out of work," he said, searching her eyes cautiously.

This made her laugh. "Me, a farmer's wife. No, I don't think so."

"Is that the only reason?" he asked with concern.

She laughed again, thinking of Sam. "You, silly. Of course you."

"Just checking." He let go of her hands. "Still have supper plans? I feel a little better."

"What about that girl?" Hannah asked him, now that the subject had been brought up. "Wish she hadn't jilted you? She was much better looking than me."

"No she wasn't."

"But she left you."

Jake shrugged his shoulders, keeping his eyes on her face. "That's just because she was wiser. Wiser than I was at the moment. I just became wiser later."

"Oh? You just saying so?"

"Of course not. Why are you asking these questions? Really."

Hannah let a smile play on her face. "Maybe it's the bear."

"That's right," he agreed. "It's the bear. We'll blame him."

"Supper now?"

"Supper," Jake agreed. "A good one."

Hannah sent Jake out to the spring house for ham, potatoes, and a head of lettuce, the rest of the supplies she needed already in the kitchen. When he brought the items in, he stayed and helped do what he could. Hannah got him to peel the potatoes, finally telling him to wash the bowls she was done with when he got too much in the way. This kept Jake occupied until the gravy was done.

They sat down to the meal an hour later, mashed potatoes and gravy, corn from her garden, salad with cut tomatoes, and cake left over from earlier in the week. Jake bowed his head for prayer, surprising her by praying out loud. The words sounded out of the prayer book at church, but they soothed her spirit.

The tears stung again as she pondered what was happening to them; Jake's praying seeming to catch the spirit of her feelings. They were being pushed out of their youth, their innocence, their ideals, into a world neither had ever been in. She could see it in Jake's face as his lips moved, mouthing the German words. She could feel it in her own body now holding their child. She wept from the sheer overwhelming vastness and strangeness of this world that lay before them.

"It'll be okay," Jake's voice reached her, his fingers finding their way to her hand again. "We'll make it."

Hannah wished she had Jake's confidence in the matter, but nodded her head anyway. She didn't want any disruption between them at the moment. Removing her handkerchief from her apron pocket, Hannah used it until her emotions were under control.

"It's hard — I know," Jake told her. "But God will help us."

Hannah found herself taking comfort in the words, but most of all she took comfort that Jake was saying the words. Never before had he said anything like this, in this tone of voice, with this amount of confidence behind it. She clung to the anchor offered, not certain whether it came from Jake, his words, or the God they referred to.

They finished their supper in silence by the light of the kerosene lamp. Jake helped dry the dishes afterward, leaving for the living room after the last plate was done and Hannah told him she would put away the rest of the things.

She lingered in the kitchen, hearing the soft rustling

of Jake turning the pages of whatever he was reading in the living room, watching the moon rise above the Cabinet Mountains. It was full, a circle of shimmering glory suspended above the tops of the last pine trees that formed the boundary between land and sky.

Here the moon stirred her in ways it never had in Indiana. She had never figured out why, wondering if it was the lack of factory lights or towns on the horizon. Perhaps the mountains themselves gave off this feeling of wildness, this untamed shiver that ran down her back.

This land had always seemed to be her friend, especially on nights like this when the moon ruled the sky. Yet now she had a deep unsettling feeling that nature had a mind of its own, a mind unfriendly to the presence of humans, regarding them as interlopers much as she did insects in her garden. She shook her head but was unable to shake the sense of uneasiness.

Finding some comfort when she sat next to Jake in the living room, she felt like pulling blinds, though there were no blinds to pull on her front window.

"It quit raining," Jake said, more to say something than anything else, she thought.

"It has," she agreed.

"I'm going into town tomorrow, to Libby."

"Oh," she looked up in surprise, wondering what Jake would want in town. They had little money, or need to spend it, with or without his status of joblessness.

"Bishop Nisley mentioned the hardware store might have a job. The manager had asked him about Amish labor the other week. I just thought of that."

"What do they pay?" Hannah wondered.

"I don't know, but anything is better than what I have."

"I would hate to see you just give away your time. They can't pay much."

Jake looked at her. "We will make it. God will help us. It starts, though, with doing what you can do, even if it doesn't pay that much."

She thought the thought, and then couldn't keep from saying it. Outside the full light of the moon shimmered through the living room window.

"The trailer factories pay pretty well. Maybe God wants to help us that way?"

"We are staying," Jake said quietly. "This is where we belong."

The room settled into silence again, comfortable enough, Hannah thought, but still quiet. Why it bothered her tonight she wasn't certain.

"Has the *Family Life* come this month?" Jake wanted to know, getting up with the obvious intention of looking for it.

"Yesterday. It's in the bedroom."

Jake came back with it, looked at the table of contents, then flipped quickly to his selection. Hannah watched him read, apparently a full-length article, which she found a little unusual. Normally he read the letters to the editor first and then worked his way further in.

Tonight he did not flip pages, reading intently. Curious, Hannah leaned over to read the title of the article. *Learning To Make Home Businesses Profitable.*

"Interesting," Jake mumbled, his eyes not leaving the paper.

"What's interesting?"

For an answer he read out loud, his eyes retreating up the page a few inches: "The larger Amish communities have long prospered in the area of small business, many of them having ready and willing buyers available in the pool of tourists who visit their areas. This has produced cottage industries of furniture makers, vegetable growers, goat farmers, and a number of others specific to the area.

"Now, though, the need for small businesses is growing, especially in our smaller communities without readily available factory jobs. They also provide options for younger families in communities where farm land now sells at exorbitant prices."

Jake stopped reading, adding on his own, "It goes on with many good ideas on how to start and what one might do."

"You're going to start your own business?" Hannah asked, the question on her face as well as in her voice.

Jake shrugged his shoulders, his eyes going back to the article. "I don't know. It's interesting reading."

"What would you do?"

"I don't know."

Certain Jake did have an idea, Hannah felt like probing deeper but decided against it. Enough was enough for one day. When Jake got up to go to bed she couldn't help asking, though, "You think the bear will be back tonight?"

Jake glanced out the window, seeming to ponder the bright night sky. "I don't think so. He didn't get much here last night. Maybe he's done."

"I hope so," Hannah said, getting up to follow Jake into the bedroom.

Falling asleep easily, she woke only once, late in the night, with the moonlight still full on their bedroom window. She listened for strange sounds and, hearing none, slipped back into sleep.

CHAPTER NINE

JAKE PREPARED TO leave for town and job hunting right after breakfast.

"The hardware will be open by the time I get into town," he told Hannah, heading to the barn to harness their driving horse.

Watching him drive out towards the main road, Hannah felt forsaken, even though she was used to him being gone each day. Perhaps it was the uncertainty of what he would find once he got to where he was going, she figured, stepping outside to look at the Cabinet Mountains.

Morning was usually a time she enjoyed being outside; the ever-sharp freshness of this country invigorated her. Today, though, the mountains looked forbidding, the clouds still hanging heavy on the peaks.

Well, she told herself, *it's just the weather. Jake will know what to do.* But the uneasiness wouldn't leave.

Starting on the breakfast dishes, she heard a pickup truck, its sound coming from further in towards the mountains. Knowing it had to be Mr. Brunson, she went out to the driveway.

"Good morning," she hollered to him as he rolled down his window, hoping he had good news on the grizzly.

Mr. Brunson shook his head, seeming to know what she wanted. "Sorry. The state isn't going to be much help."

Hannah's face fell as she envisioned many more nights with the bear outside the cabin walls.

65

"Said winter will be here soon. Has to hibernate then — all bears do. He thinks the pattern might change in the spring."

"I guess we'll have to live with him then," Hannah said, despair in her voice.

"Like I said. Sorry. I'd shoot the thing, but you know how that would go."

Hannah nodded, not wanting to encourage law breaking. Then she blurted out the news, the desire to share with someone too great. "Jake lost his job last night. Boss stopped in after you left."

"I'm sorry to hear that. And winter coming." Mr. Brunson looked concerned. "Any prospects?"

"He's in town looking right now. Hopes the hardware may have an opening."

"Something to get through the winter?"

"I think so," Hannah said, figuring Jake didn't want too many of their troubles spread around.

"Hope he finds something." Mr. Brunson put his gear shift in reverse. "Hope the bear agrees with the warden."

"Don't forget about supper," Hannah told him. "Mom and Dad come in a few Sundays. Staying all week."

"To a good supper then," Mr. Brunson said with a smile. "Will be nice to meet your folks." Then he left, backing out of the driveway and giving her a final wave as he drove towards the main road.

Hannah felt the aloneness creep in again, wishing it were Sunday already. She would see Betty or Bishop John's wife then. There were others too, but Betty and Elizabeth's handshake and perhaps Betty's hug when she told her about Jake losing his job would be of great comfort.

When Hannah was growing up, Betty had always seemed much older, almost ancient from a little girl's perspective. Even a few summers ago, when Hannah had spent time taking care of the riding stable for Betty, it had felt that way. Of late, though, the distance between them had become much smaller. How that could be, Hannah wasn't certain.

Being ancient herself was not an attractive answer, but maybe that was what was happening, Hannah thought. She did feel kind of ancient all of a sudden, with the bear, the baby, and now Jake losing his job.

The baby. For the first time that morning joy filled her. *A child, her and Jake's child, and she had not told her mother yet. Should she? This life inside of her. This new beginning. This great unknown. Was this what all parents felt?* She supposed so, but it felt very much like her own feelings and hers only.

How strange, she thought. She didn't even know whether the child was a boy or a girl, yet it didn't seem to matter. Was that how her mother had felt — not knowing, yet feeling the capacity to love regardless?

How would this child turn out? Would it look like Jake or her? When it lay in the crib, so small and newborn, would Betty say she could tell exactly where this child came from? *Likely so,* Hannah thought, chuckling at the vision of Betty bent over the side rail, certain in her discernment of the distant lineage of this newcomer.

Her mother, Hannah remembered, needed to be told. Writing seemed to be the thing to do. Already she could feel the words forming in her mind, finding their expression in letters on the page. Yet she paused. Her mom was coming soon, why not wait?

Yes, she decided quickly, she would wait. It would be more fun, closer. She felt the tears burn in her eyes. How wonderful it would be to tell her mother while she was sitting in the living room. This would make it so much more real, surrounded by the walls of her cabin — her and Jake's cabin.

Still communion Sunday seemed a long way off. Her parents would have the spare bedroom for their visit, and that needed preparing, or at least a good cleaning. Hannah knew she would in her nervousness see dust and dirt everywhere. At present, there was no use starting the cleaning. The room would just get dirty again.

No, it would require a last-minute rush to prepare, making everything as spotless as it could be — for a log cabin, Hannah thought grimly. One negative of a log cabin, but she supposed her mother would see the plus side too. Romantic was not a word her mother would use, but Hannah liked it, and with the child coming, she and Jake were well on the way to making the place home.

Suddenly she remembered where Jake had gone this morning. So quickly she had forgotten, and forgotten also why she wanted to move back east. Did she really? Thinking of her mother coming brought back the earlier feelings of why she loved this place. Surely it was not all being taken from them?

Probably this was what Jake was feeling, being less shaken by the present than she was. This was good, then, this remembering the reason they were here. Her mother's coming was already serving a good purpose.

Finding comfort in the thought, she returned to the kitchen and then went to the spare bedroom. It was as she knew it would be — not clean, but clean enough. Specks of dust stayed on her fingers when she ran them under the dresser lip.

"Log cabins," she muttered. "Sweet things indeed."

Well, the dust would simply have to be handled the day before her mother arrived — amidst the rush of everything else — but it couldn't be helped. Once here, her mother would pitch in and help with cooking, so even the planned supper with Mr. Brunson was not a major concern. Perhaps they could have Betty and Steve over that night too.

But her vision of the cabin bursting with her cousins and Mr. Brunson, plus the table full of adults, was a little too much. *No*, Betty and Mr. Brunson would have to be split up into separate nights. With a week to work with, this should be no problem, she decided.

The clatter of Jake's buggy on the gravel took her out to the porch again. The look on his face was all the information she needed.

"I'm sorry," she told him, even before he stepped up on the porch.

He shook his head, looking as if his shoulders carried a great burden. She was struck again by how out of place it looked on someone so young.

"Nothing," he said simply. "Mr. Howard said in a few weeks maybe, when the snow season starts, but not now."

Hannah searched his face, hoping to find in it the strength she saw earlier, but Jake looked scared.

"What are we going to do?" she asked.

"I don't know. I think I might have to start some business on my own."

"Like you were reading about in the Family Life?"

Jake nodded.

Hannah wasn't sure what to think. "You'll need money for that."

"I know," Jake agreed.

"But from where?"

He shook his head.

"My parents are coming soon. Maybe you could ask them," she offered.

Jake shook his head again. "Not your parents. We're not asking them for money. I'm not taking the chance of losing it."

Not sure whether Jake was being stubborn or strong, she studied his face.

"I'm not asking," he repeated, seemingly reading her thoughts.

"But the baby," she said.

"I know. Something will have to be done," he replied, lapsing into silence.

"I'll have lunch ready soon," Hannah said after a few moments, hoping that would provide some comfort to his obviously bruised feelings. She wished she could do more, but nothing presented itself. Moving back east crossed her mind again, but her own thoughts from earlier kept her from voicing the idea. It might be best to take things slowly.

"I'll put the horse away," Jake said, returning to the hitching post where Mossy stood patiently waiting to be let out of the buggy traces.

Hannah had sandwiches ready thirty minutes later, and Jake sat down at the kitchen table. Outside the early clouds still hung around, now having grown darker.

"You think it's going to rain?" she asked, wanting to make conversation more than anything else.

"It could." Jake didn't offer anything more.

"You think the logging job might be back in spring?" she asked, wanting to know the answer this time.

"I doubt it," he said quietly, but didn't elaborate.

"Why?" she asked.

"Something about the business," Jake offered. "Don't exactly know why. Don't think it's prospering very well. Logging's not the thing to be in right now."

"Did your boss say so?"

"Not in so many words. Picked up the idea though."

Trusting Jake's instincts in the matter, she decided now was the time to bring up the subject again.

"Think we should move back east?"

"You want to?"

Hannah wanted to say *yes* to try to sway him, but in a way that wasn't true.

"I didn't," she said, settling on those words.

"I don't either," Jake said. "I think we should stick it out a little longer."

"But how long?"

"If God wants us here, we should stay," Jake said.

Not sure how to take that, as if God came down and told people where to live, Hannah puzzled over how to answer.

"We have to do what's best," she ventured.

"I know," Jake said. "I'm trying."

They finished their sandwiches in silence — not uncomfortable silence, Hannah thought, just troubled. She wished it wasn't so, but having Jake around for the rest of the day turned out to be more disturbing than she had expected.

He sat around and read for a while and then went out to the barn.

She had supper ready at the regular time, the thought of his usual coming-home time bringing a fresh stab of pain. Jake looked pained, too, as he sat at the kitchen table. Hannah could tell he wasn't eating as much as usual.

Later, they read by the light of the lantern, its hiss drawing them into sleepiness and away from their troubles. Hannah was the first to suggest they go to bed. In the morning, Jake got up and announced that a light dusting of snow had fallen. He stayed by the bedroom window till Hannah joined him, curious. Together looked out at the clear marks of the grizzly's night visit.

"I didn't hear anything. Did you?" Jake asked.

Hannah shook her head.

"That might be the last of him," Jake said, sounding as if he knew something about the habits of bears. Hannah had forgotten to tell him the news Mr. Brunson brought. At this moment she hoped both the game warden and Jake were right about the matter.

CHAPTER TEN

THE SNOW SOON disappeared once the sun came out. Hannah was glad, not yet ready for winter, even if this was Montana. The thought of a howling whiteout surrounded by mountains intimidated her.

Driving to church the next morning, she ventured to ask Jake, "You think winter's coming early?"

He shrugged. "Don't know the country well enough."

She didn't press the subject, since Jake was not in his best mood. With the odd jobs around the house soon gone through, he sat around much of yesterday, time obviously weighing on him. Thankfully today they had someplace to go.

Jake brought Mossy to a stop in front of the barn. Church was being held in the house, but Jake couldn't get close enough to the walks with the other buggies already gathered in the yard, so Hannah would have to walk from here.

"As close as I can get," he said, apologizing with his tone.

"No problem," she told him. Walking wasn't something she found disagreeable.

Betty was already in the kitchen when Hannah got inside. Making her way around the circle, Hannah greeted each woman in turn. Stopping in front of Betty, she felt the urge to whisper news of their troubles, but decided not too. It might be considered disrespectful to be talking too long, even with a relative, since other women were in line behind her.

Betty seemed to sense her thoughts, squeezing her hand before letting go. There would be time after church over Sunday lunch to discuss the matter. Not knowing they had been running late, Hannah was surprised when the line of women began moving almost immediately towards the living room.

She caught sight of the clock on the wall — it did say five till nine, so somewhere she and Jake must have misjudged the time. Marking the thought down as something to watch for in the future, she joined the line of women, taking her appropriate place near the end, almost the last one before the young unmarried girls started.

Only Sylvia Stoll was behind her, having married Ben Stoll a month after she married Jake. She knew Ben from her stay with Betty, when she thought of him as the scared logger, she remembered with amusement. His obvious interest in her hadn't gone anywhere, for more reasons than one. Ben had found Sylvia in Iowa a few months later, and from how it looked they were well matched, each the rugged type well suited for this country. Not like she and Jake, she thought with a shiver — maybe they were out of place in this wild country. It must be the winter and the threat of severe snow, she decided, causing these thoughts. She stilled them, shifting on the hard bench.

Beside her Sylvia sat without moving. Hannah wondered if Sylvia too had a secret of a coming birth, but that was not something one went around asking about. That she had one was joy enough.

The song leader announced his selection in a loud baritone, his voice reaching throughout the house. It was strange how the babies upstairs didn't wake up from the pronouncement, or perhaps they just get used to it, Hannah thought skeptically.

Half expecting it, Hannah was not surprised when Jake led out in the next song. Jake was such a good singer he got his turn on a regular basis.

She listened to his voice, full and with such depth of

emotion. He held the notes to their proper length, swinging them up and down as expertly as she had ever heard anyone do. This was her man, and the half source of the life growing in her. Thrilling at the thought, she hoped Sylvia didn't read anything on her face. As much joy as she had, this was still intensely private, even though Sylvia might be experiencing the same thing. Here in church, surrounded by these people, she had forgotten the storm clouds gathering at home. Even now as she remembered, the thoughts still did not sting quite as much. Jake, if he could sing like that, would find some way to keep things going. If not, then maybe he would listen to her soon and consider moving back east.

Yet the thought of moving brought a pang of regret, more so than it had at home, she noticed. But she must face reality. Even Betty would agree with that, she was sure.

The two ministers, led by Bishop Nisley, came down soon after Jake finished, finding their places on the bench up front. There was nothing unusual about the sermons and nothing to indicate what was to come.

After testimonies, Bishop Nisley got to his feet, his eyes intense, and said, "Will the members please stay. The rest are dismissed." There was nothing unusual in that either, since this was pre-communion church. The surprise was yet to come.

All the non-members filed out, mostly children and some young people, followed by several woman who would prepare lunch for them. For the next hour Bishop proceeded to go through the written and unwritten rules of the *ordnungs briefs*. Some of the session was just lecture, some of it a reminder of broken rules, and some of it a question of whether new rules should be added.

Bishop said there was a question raised over how long newly purchased homes could keep their electric power. A reasonable amount of time was allowed now, like two years, Bishop thought, receiving nodding agreement from several of the men. This allowance was intended to reduce the financial hardship caused by the transfer, especially for young couples.

But some believed allowing two years was too lax. Should this rule be amended to one year? The extra time might simply promote complacency and unwanted accommodation to English ways. Several of the men, Hannah noticed, nodded their heads, but several weren't looking too happy either.

In the questions and vote that followed, the proposed change raised enough objections that Bishop cancelled the move, stating that the time allowed would remain two years. Hannah felt relief. Though she and Jake had no electricity left at their place, she didn't know what the future held, and their own financial hardships made her sensitive to others, such as young Sylvia sitting beside her. Hannah knew Sylvia and Ben's place still had full electric power, including lights, and might well be the reason the rule change was brought up. The ministers could be getting nervous, she thought, when time went on and young couples made no attempt to start the changeover. Yet she didn't want to prejudge. There might be good reasons Sylvia and Ben hadn't switched.

Bishop continued with his closing remarks, noting that communion service would be held in two weeks and Bishop Amos Yoder from one of the Nappanee, Indiana, districts would be traveling here to participate. Afterwards a new minister would be ordained. That was, of course, if there was no objection from the congregation, which there wasn't, as a quick vote proved.

Bishop dropped the news just like that — no warning, no preparation, just the cold hard facts. Several of the men shifted on their seats, Hannah noticed, and a few women in her line of vision suddenly became very interested in their children. The new minister could be anyone, provided he was male, preferably married, and in good standing as a member.

Hannah felt the chill reach her, too, because Jake did qualify, but surely he was a long shot. He was simply too young for such a thing. Perhaps he could sing, but that didn't translate into minister material. As for exactly what did translate into minister material, she didn't know, nor did anyone else for that matter. There was no set pattern, no guidelines to go by except those read from the scriptures, and those, of course, fit most of the men in church, since speaking ability, elegance in bearing, or commanding presence were not listed as qualifications.

The tension subsided as church dismissed. If any of the men felt like the executioner's ax was poised over their necks, the feelings got lost in creamy peanut butter sandwiches, hard cheese, and the crunch of sweet dill pickles.

Betty found Hannah after the first table setting was through. "You like the snow?" she teased.

"Hope it scares away the bear," Hannah whispered, not wanting the news to spread too far.

"It should," Betty smiled reassuringly. "It's probably just a fluke."

"Hopefully," Hannah said, not convinced at the moment.

"You get the pressure cooker to work?" Betty whispered now, obviously trying to keep the accident secret between them. "I did write your mother about it."

"Yes," Hannah grimaced. "Finally got enough nerve to go back into the kitchen."

"I can guess," Betty smiled again. "It could happen to anyone."

"I suppose so," Hannah allowed, then got to the news she really wanted to share. "Jake lost his job."

"You don't say!" Betty was all sympathy. "Has he found anything else?"

"Not yet. Went to the hardware on Friday. They're not hiring until the snows start good."

"Brings in the skiers," Betty nodded in understanding. "Makes sense. What are you doing till then?"

"Jake will think of something," Hannah told her, more confidence in her voice than in her thoughts.

"I hope so. Let us know if it gets too bad."

"I will," Hannah said, meaning it, but wondering if she would actually have the courage to ask for help. Begging was embarrassing regardless how you sliced the thing.

"Is your mom staying with you?" Betty asked, eyeing Hannah.

Knowing the look meant Betty wanted to share, Hannah didn't give an inch. "At my place. All the nights."

"Supper at least?" Betty glared at her. "I'll have to steal them a little. You'll come over for supper one of those nights, won't you?"

"Of course," Hannah agreed quickly, delighted at the invitation.

"What do you think of the minister thing?" Betty was whispering again.

"Surprising," Hannah told her, because it was, and because the answer seemed safe to say. Discussing the subject was not considered good form, and she hoped Betty wouldn't go any further.

"There's Steve now," Betty said, changing the subject as Hannah had hoped. "I'd better get ready to go."

"Will you be at the singing?" Hannah asked her, thinking she and Jake might go. If nothing else it would get them out of the house. With Betty and Steve going, Jake might be easier to persuade.

"Don't think so," Betty said, already walking towards the kitchen and her wraps.

Ten minutes later Hannah saw Jake hitching the horse and joined him at the buggy by the time he was done.

They drove home in silence, Jake making no mention of the day's events, seeming to be lost in his own thoughts.

"You want to go to the singing?" she asked him.

Jake shook his head as Hannah expected him to.

CHAPTER ELEVEN

THE FIRST TWO days of the week Jake found some repairs to do on the spring house. He said he was strengthening it from the bear. On Wednesday, he headed back into town looking for work. How Jake expected an Amish man to find any, Hannah wasn't certain. It seemed to her an impulse-driven move, born of desperation.

It was Betty, stopping by in the middle of the afternoon, who brought the first good news. She said Bishop Nisley could use some help with barn repairs. Nothing was said about pay, nor did Hannah raise the issue. She knew it was charity, even though Bishop probably needed the repairs. With the whole winter still ahead, he just as easily could have waited.

Mr. Brunson stopped in just as Jake was coming in from the main road. Hannah saw the two standing by the barn, talking at length. Wondering what they were saying, she was ready to walk out when Mr. Brunson left, heading back towards his place.

"Just checking on the bear," Jake said as explanation when he came inside.

"Find any work?" Hannah asked, because it was the question of most interest to her.

"Mr. Brunson asked that too," Jake said dejectedly. "He must have seen me hanging around the house."

"I told him about it the other day," Hannah volunteered, hoping that would ease Jake's feelings.

"That's what he said. I still think he saw me." Jake slowly sat on the couch, his whole body language one of discouragement.

"Betty stopped by," she said. "John has some barn work for a few days."

"So it's come to that?" Jake asked, staring out the window.

"Better than sitting around home," she told him.

"I suppose so," Jake allowed. "Mr. Brunson said he's seen nothing of the bear since last week."

"Neither have we, now that I think of it," Hannah agreed.

"Snow must have scared him into the mountains."

"So much for that then. Maybe we'll see him next spring."

"I suppose so," Jake agreed half-heartedly, his mind somewhere other than bears, Hannah could tell.

"You going to bishop's tomorrow?"

Jake nodded.

"Maybe we should think about east," she ventured. "Winter is coming fast."

"Not while people are helping us," Jake told her. "It just wouldn't be right."

"They would help us in Indiana too," Hannah felt compelled to say. She wasn't making much of an impact on Jake, though, she could tell from the look on his face. It made her half wish the church people wouldn't help, especially if Jake was going to take it the wrong way. Then, ashamed of her attitude, she told herself she ought to be glad for any work Jake could get.

Hannah made a point of preparing a good supper, thinking to cheer Jake. Since he was going to work tomorrow — work that no doubt would be difficult — she figured he needed it. When she called Jake to the table, the way he looked at the mashed potatoes, gravy, and ham made her glad she had. His eyes were hungry enough, but the doubt on his face still troubled her. He was seeing the days ahead, and the dismal view was obviously spoiling his usual enjoyment of a good dinner. Hannah resolved to do all she could for him. What that was, she wasn't certain.

After supper Jake got out his Bible, reading it at length in the living room. Hannah hoped he would find some comfort. Perhaps she should try it herself, she thought, but wasn't certain where to start.

Jake solved the dilemma by asking her to sit beside him. "I want to read this," he informed her.

He then proceeded to read out loud, "I will lift up my eyes unto the hills from whence cometh my help. My help cometh from the Lord which made heaven and earth."

Jake paused as Hannah thought of the Cabinet Mountains. Normally she would have readily agreed with the words about looking to the hills, but lately she wasn't sure anymore. The mountains had become dangerous to her.

Jake continued, "He will not suffer thy foot to be moved. He that keepeth thee will not slumber."

"You think that's true?" she asked him.

"I don't know," Jake said. "It's in the Bible."

"That's always true, isn't it?"

"Yes." Jake's voice sounded hesitant.

"No moving of the foot, and God never sleeps," she said thoughtfully, thinking on the words.

"Sounds comforting."

"Until you're out of work," she finished for him.

"Yes," Jake agreed. "Well, tomorrow I go to Bishop Nisley's. Let's be thankful for that."

"Yes," Hannah agreed, but inside she was wondering whether going east wasn't the best thing to do. Yet raising the point would just trouble Jake, and he did need his sleep for tomorrow's work, not some argument with her.

Getting up, she went back to finish in the kitchen while Jake continued reading. She heard him leave for the bedroom soon after and followed when she was done.

Dropping off to sleep easily, Hannah woke only once during the night, hearing nothing unusual. She got up to fix

Jake's breakfast once the alarm went off. Jake was already in the barn, harnessing Mossy for the ride over to Bishop Nisley's. Fixing his lunch while Jake ate, Hannah packed extra, just in case, then stood by the front window to watch him leave.

Surprised when snowflakes started falling, she assumed this explained the grizzly's continued absence. At least this was one blessing to be grateful for, though snow wasn't exactly what she wanted. In Hannah's mind it was much too early to snow, but this wasn't Indiana, she reminded herself.

Jake got back before dark, his face happy though tired, which was good to see, even if the job didn't pay much.

"Supper's ready," she told him. "Going back tomorrow?"

"Yes," Jake said. "The rest of the week. We might get done early on Friday."

Hannah didn't ask about next week, figuring she would find out soon enough. It was a joy for her to see Jake peacefully reading in the living room. He hadn't looked so since losing his job with Mr. Wesley.

When Sunday came around, Hannah hoped someone from the community would have heard about their situation and would offer Jake at least temporary work. It was not to be, though, as church dismissed without even Betty asking about Jake's job status.

Kathy and Roy were coming on Thursday, which gave Hannah plenty to do, but not Jake. Finally she gave him a broom and wipe cloth, showing him how to spray the soapy water lightly, setting him to cleaning the spare bedroom. He did a good job, she had to admit, but he didn't look happy afterward. Not in the way Bishop John's work made him look, she thought with distress, but that was to be expected.

Somehow they made it to Thursday, with Hannah biting her lip more than once, wanting to bring up the subject. It was obvious to her that moving back east was the only option left to them. They simply could not continue like this. With her parents coming, it would be an excellent time to raise the question, make plans, and get the support they would need for the move.

Even with winter moving in, they would fare much better in Indiana than here. Renting would be an option, one they should probably choose, but Jake would have to make that decision. Perhaps if he was able to get a high-paying factory job, with her father's help of course, they might be able to afford the payment on a small place.

They had formed attachments to the cabin, the mountains, and the people, but she supposed time would heal the separation. Betty would be the hardest to leave. Hannah could imagine the tears when Betty was told the news, but facts were facts, and the biggest fact was the mortgage payment on the cabin.

Hannah knew Jake was thinking about the mortgage too as he studied his checkbook at night. The cost of groceries must be on his mind as well, and now her mom and dad were coming to visit.

Feeling a little guilty about it, she still gave Jake the list of groceries she needed, sending him into town Thursday morning. Jake studied the list long and hard, she thought, but left with Mossy without saying anything. He came back with everything, even down to the maple syrup she wanted for at least one breakfast of pancakes and eggs.

It would all work out, she told her conscience. Mom and Dad were part of the ticket to get them back on their feet financially, so they were worth the investment. Plus they were her parents, and she would do the same for Jake's, if and when they would visit. Maybe that would happen in Indiana? If it did they would be served the best pancakes with maple syrup she could make, Hannah promised herself.

Jake was sent up the hill to Mr. Brunson's, bearing a reminder of Friday night's supper invitation. Betty had already spoken for Tuesday night, making the decision after church on Sunday. The van bound for Indiana was leaving on Wednesday, so Tuesday was the last night her parents would be in Montana. Hannah's heart thrilled at the thought of almost a week of family, with Communion stuck right in the middle.

Jake returned with the news that Mr. Brunson was down with the flu. Still, he hoped to make the Friday night date. If not, he would bring word himself, even if he wasn't feeling well, so Hannah would know. Jake said he thought Mr. Brunson would come — something about looking like he needed company.

That evening the van pulled in while Hannah was fixing supper, the pies still in the oven and the casserole cooling on the tabletop. Jake came out of the barn to meet the arriving vehicle. Hannah rushed out to find her parents already pulling suitcases from the van, having shaken hands with Jake. Her mom was telling Jake what a nice place they had.

"It's wonderful," her mother gushed, as Hannah came close enough to hear. "I remembered the area, but it's even better in the fall. And your little cabin — what a place to live."

Kathy looked up to see her daughter. "Oh my," she said, gathering Hannah in her arms for a long embrace, then letting go with a question on her face. "You're not? I mean... really?"

"Yes," Hannah said simply, not surprised that her mother should guess.

Jake's face was the color of beets, she noticed, but he'd get over it. Maybe when the baby was actually born it wouldn't seem such an embarrassing subject to him.

"Well come in. Looks like you're the last ones dropped off?" Hannah asked.

"Yes," Roy agreed, "we are. The others had to get to their places first. We're just the little peas in the pod."

"Roy," Kathy said in mock horror, laughing. "He's tired from the trip."

"Hard van seats," Roy agreed, going around the front of the van to speak with the driver.

"The driver's staying in Libby for the week," Kathy said as explanation. "I guess we're all on our own till then."

It was then that transportation crossed Hannah's mind. "Oh," she gasped. "I hadn't thought of that. We only have a single buggy."

Kathy followed the train of thought, instantly waving her hand at Roy to hold the van driver. "So when will we need to get around?" she asked Hannah.

Hannah thought frantically. "Sunday. I think only on Sunday. Betty can come get you on Tuesday."

"Roy," Kathy rushed up to him, "we need transportation on Sunday. They only have a single buggy."

Hannah's father nodded, stepping back up to the van window. What followed must have been arrangements for the driver to meet them here on Sunday morning. Hannah knew such things cost extra money, since drivers for the Amish charge by the mile. The striking difference between their two worlds struck her hard. Her father had not hesitated, as she knew Jake would, to spend the extra money. But perhaps she was soon going back to their world? The thought comforted her.

CHAPTER TWELVE

J AKE AND ROY quite quickly got settled in the living room,
since Jake had always been comfortable around Hannah's
parents. For this Hannah was thankful. Sam, she thought,
would have worked too, but she couldn't imagine him carrying on the type of conversation Jake and her father did — one
of the signs, among others, she had chosen correctly.

"A log cabin," Kathy said, looking around the kitchen
and, Hannah was sure, seeing all the dust and pieces of
food from the cooker explosion she had missed. Now that
her mother was here, things she had never noticed before,
or missed in cleaning, seemed to be waving their hands for
attention. "The explosion didn't do too much damage," her
mother added.

"It's a log cabin. They get dirty quick," Hannah muttered, figuring the obvious might as well be stated. No use
pretending she had a spotless Indiana Amish house.

"I didn't notice," Kathy assured her. "I was just looking
at the logs. They seem tight enough."

"There's dirt," Hannah said, not backing down. Her
mother would notice soon enough. "We like it though."

"I suppose you do. It fits the country and the mountains, almost right outside your doorstep."

"That and bears," Hannah said, startling Kathy.

"Bears? Really?"

"Yes. Grizzly too." Hannah made it sound as bad as she
could.

"Did you hear that Roy?" Kathy stuck her head excitedly back into the living room. "They have a pet grizzly."

Roy chuckled, "Jake was telling me. Trying to get in the spring house."

"What are you going to do about it?" Kathy's eyes were wide. "At least you don't have little children yet."

"The game warden thinks it might change its ways. Next spring that is. I guess he's holed up for the winter now, with the first snow here. At least headed for the mountain. It got Mr. Brunson's pig, too."

"Mr. Brunson?" Kathy suddenly sounded more interested in Mr. Brunson than the bear.

"He lives up the road. I invited him for Friday night supper. I think he could use the company, as I never see anyone visiting him."

"This Mr. Brunson." Her mother's eyes were following her, Hannah could tell. She felt like chuckling, but waited instead for the question. "How old is he?"

"He's a grandpa," Hannah chuckled now. "Like real old."

"You sure?"

"Mom, you'll see," Hannah assured her.

Her mother didn't look convinced. "Sometimes you can't tell."

"Really, Mom," Hannah said, making a face. "Jake likes him."

This seemed to satisfy Kathy, and she changed the subject.

"When are you coming to visit Indiana?"

"You know we can't. We're too poor," Hannah said quickly, then took the opening. "We might move back though."

Kathy raised her eyebrows.

"Jake just lost his job. Bishop Nisley gave him some work last week, working on his barn, but this week he's had nothing."

"Just like that. Moving? I thought Jake's job was long term?"

"We're in trouble." Hannah felt like she was justifying herself, which she supposed she was. "We have the mortgage to pay."

"Most people do," Kathy told her, glancing around the kitchen. "Are you cutting your expenses close? I see all kinds of food around."

"Mom," Hannah said as explanation, "you don't come every day."

"We know how to live without money," Kathy said. "We had our hard times too."

"I never noticed." Hannah knew she was still trying to justify herself.

"It was while you children were young," Kathy said. "But you should be talking about this to Jake, not me. Is he agreeing to this move?"

"No," Hannah admitted. "But he's thinking about it. Dad might even be able to find him a job."

"We'll let Jake look to that," Kathy said, disapproval in her voice. It stung a little, but Hannah felt desperate, having had Jake around the house all week. Something simply would have to be done.

With her mother's help, supper was a breeze to prepare. Jake, all smiles tonight, asked Roy to say the prayer. It was good to hear her father's voice again saying the simple German words of petition to God. Not that Jake couldn't pray, she told herself, but he just didn't have the gravity of tone, the years of experience behind his voice.

"So," Kathy said when Roy was done. "You will make us grandparents. The first experience for us. You feel old yet, Roy?"

"Real old." Roy made a face, pretending a deep regret for his future status.

"Your parents already have grandchildren?" Kathy directed her question in Jake's direction.

"A couple." Jake's face wasn't quite as red, Hannah noticed. Maybe he was getting used to the subject. "Eight, actually. Another one on the way, perhaps. My oldest sister."

"Lost track already?" Roy chuckled.

Jake made a face. "You know. Older brothers and sisters."

"Just like a man," Kathy said. "Don't even try."

"Babies are important," Roy said in a saintly voice, teasing, Hannah knew. Jake must have understood too, because he smiled.

"They are wonderful," Kathy proclaimed. "I can't wait."

From the look on her father's face, he seemed to be agreeing.

"I lost my job," Jake announced, apparently not having told Roy earlier.

"That's what Hannah said," Kathy spoke up.

"She's already told you?" Jake shrugged his shoulders.

Kathy said quickly, "I guess women get concerned sooner."

That seemed to satisfy Jake. "I think the hardware may have some work soon, now that snow is falling. At least that's what the man said."

"You ever think of starting your own business?" Roy asked, as Hannah's heart sank. Having her father give Jake encouragement might be exactly the wrong thing. Moving back to Indiana seemed a much better idea to her than a risky venture into self-employment.

Jake's smile broadened, though. Apparently he didn't notice Hannah's downcast face. Under the table, Kathy gave her a squeeze on the arm and a comforting smile. She said without words that things would work best with the man leading the way. It was a lesson Hannah had grown up with, but this was different, wasn't it? Her mother's eyes said no.

"I was thinking of making furniture," Jake said. "Log cabin things, that sort of line. Might be a big seller out here. Or even shipping across the country."

"You have talked to someone?" Her father agreed with Jake, Hannah could tell.

"The hardware man," Jake said, supplying information

new to Hannah. So also did his next words. "He could even give the business a place to work from. A web presence too. Maybe its own website, he said. I would make the furniture, maybe on the side to start with, then full-time if things took off."

"How much money would you need to start up?" Roy wanted to know.

"None, I think." Jake seemed to be running the thought through his head. "Mr. Howard at the hardware would supply the working space. Supplies shouldn't be that expensive. We'd just start out slow, selling as we made it."

Hannah's shock must have shown plain enough for even Jake to notice.

Her father saw, because he said, "News to you?" with what sounded like sympathy in his voice, but he still was on Jake's side, Hannah could tell.

"I'm sorry," Jake managed, finally looking at her. "I guess I never told you."

"I guess you didn't," Kathy said, for which Hannah was deeply grateful. At least someone felt a little irritated besides herself.

"It was just thoughts, conversations," Jake said as explanation. "Nothing solid. I was waiting until I know for sure."

"Understandable," Roy helped Jake out.

"I do suppose it's a surprise to Hannah. You think it's serious?" Kathy asked, on whose side at the moment Hannah didn't know.

"I hope so," Jake nodded. "Mr. Howard has high hopes. But he's still thinking about it."

This too was news to Hannah, but she kept her composure. There would be time later to speak with Jake. Apparently there were things going on she knew nothing about.

"The factories are hiring," Roy said, even though Hannah was sure her father knew nothing about her desire to move east. "The economy being good and all."

Jake showed no interest, his attention on the casserole in front of him.

"You think Jake might be able to get a job?" Hannah went ahead and asked, since Jake obviously wasn't going to.

"Hannah," Kathy said mildly enough.

"I know she wants to move east," Jake volunteered, not seeming too upset. "I don't know sometimes what to do."

"Oh, really," Roy commented, "so you're thinking of moving. I know it's a toss-up sometimes. When you're young, that is. Move here or move there. This job or that job. When you're old like us, grandparents almost, it gets a little harder."

"We probably have to do something," Hannah spoke up again. "I'd go for moving back east. You might even help us find a place. You probably know of a house for rent right now."

Her father nodded, confirming her guess.

"Simple choices can have long consequences," he added. "You'll have to think about it."

"Mary and Laverne are getting married this fall yet," Kathy announced.

Hannah supposed her mother wanted to change the subject, which was fine with her. The move was obviously something for her and Jake to discuss again later.

"Well it's about time," Hannah followed her mother's lead. "They've been sweet on each other since school."

"Sometimes those take longer," Kathy grinned. "Don't know why."

"They all take time," Roy agreed, "some just longer than others." As if that made any sense at all, but Hannah figured her father wanted to stay in the conversation.

"I'm sure Mary would have had you as one of her bridesmaids. You're married, of course, now," Kathy said. "Probably use her cousins."

"You think so?" Hannah felt honored even at the thought of being included. "I guess Mary and I were close."

"Who is this Mary and Laverne?" Jake wanted to know.

"School," Hannah told him, knowing he would understand.

Jake nodded his head, then turned towards the front window as a buggy came in the driveway.

"It's Betty," Hannah said excitedly, thrilled that her aunt and uncle would come over unannounced.

"My, my," Kathy said, rising from the table. "I wonder if they've had supper?"

"Now, Mom. Don't you worry," Hannah said quickly. "We'll just see. This is supposed to be my worry."

"I guess so," Kathy said, sitting back down, plainly still worried.

Jake went to open the front door as Steve and Betty came in, exchanging warm greetings all around. Kathy and Betty got a little emotional as they gave each other a hug. Hannah could tell that her dad and Steve pretended not to notice, finding seats in the living room and launching into a conversation with Jake about the weather.

"Have you had supper?" Hannah asked Betty as soon she could get a word in edgewise.

"Of course," Betty assured her, wiping a stray tear off her cheek. "I guess it gets lonely out here. It's sure good to see family."

"It's good to see you too," Kathy said quickly, meaning it with all her heart, Hannah could tell.

"Well…I'm here," Hannah said, placing an injured tone in her voice.

"That's why you're staying too," Betty told her, making Hannah wonder if Betty knew anything about moving — but that wasn't possible, she figured.

The evening went by much too quickly for Hannah. With Betty to help, the kitchen was cleaned up in no time, and the women joined the men in the living room. There were moments when she forgot the log walls of the cabin or the mountains outside with its menacing grizzly. They were all just family again, Indiana family, safe and secure, laughing and reveling in each other's company.

This was the way it was meant to be, she told herself, glancing over at Jake more than once. He seemed to be joining in with no reservations, thrilling her heart and firing her dreams. Jake was such a nice fit for her, and he would easily fit in once they moved back to Indiana. Of this she was certain.

Later, after Steve insisted Betty and he must leave so he could get some sleep for work tomorrow, she lay beside Jake in bed wanting to bring up the subject of moving. Yet the evening seemed to have said enough already. Surely Jake could see for himself how things were going. She decided she had better not say anything more.

Besides, Hannah wasn't certain if pushing worked with Jake, and she didn't feel like risking it. The matter was simply too important. When she had second thoughts a few minutes later, it was already too late to bring up the subject. By the sound of Jake's deep breathing she could tell he was asleep. The day was enough, she decided again. There was no way she would wake Jake.

Checking once more to make sure the alarm was set, she fell asleep quickly.

Chapter Thirteen

H ANNAH COULD TELL Jake was irritated when the alarm went off, but she ignored him. It might be a little early to get up, but she wanted to get into the kitchen before her mother had any chance of getting up.

Kathy could easily be awake already, with the strange country and all. Coming into her own kitchen to find her mother already making coffee, or some such thing, would be just too much to bear. *A little foolish,* she allowed, but it seemed a matter of importance at the moment.

The kitchen was dark, though, as she stumbled around lighting the kerosene lamp. The flame flickered, casting its shadows on the rough log walls. Everything seemed less lonesome this morning with her mother and father in the house. Hannah sighed deeply, letting the feeling soak in.

Childish, she told herself, as the tears threatened to come. *Why was she crying over such a thing? You are no longer a little girl. A woman,* she told herself, thinking of Jake sleeping back in the bedroom. The feeling of his arms around her when he held her close was something she never wanted to do without. *Then why was she crying, thinking of her childhood?*

Probably because she wants both, she mused.

"Good morning," her mother said behind her, having made no sound coming into the kitchen.

When Hannah jumped, Kathy chuckled. "Sorry. Just couldn't sleep. Must be the higher altitude or something."

"You'd be up anyway," Hannah informed her mother.

"Want some coffee? Was just thinking of heating the water."

"That would be great," Kathy yawned, wrapping her housecoat tighter around herself. "Chilly up here too."

"Winter comes early," Hannah said with wariness in her voice. The season had lost much of its friendliness. Indiana winters might seem threatening too, but with a factory job for Jake and its steady income, snow would be more like a friend again.

"Life getting to you?" Kathy asked. "Talk to Jake about moving last night?"

"No," Hannah said without going into details.

"It's just as good. Perhaps God wants you out here?"

"Maybe," Hannah allowed, not really wanting to discuss the subject. "I guess we'll have to see. What do you want to do today?"

"I don't know," Kathy yawned. "Maybe see your mountains up close. Go for a walk. I see your dirt road goes further back in."

"That's where Mr. Brunson lives," Hannah said, to which Kathy raised her eyebrows.

Hannah decided right then and there that her mother needed to meet Mr. Brunson. Since he was coming for supper, an earlier meeting would be just the thing. Kathy could get to see him and relax her fears. A walk and a meeting of Mr. Brunson could be managed at the same time.

"That's what we'll do," Hannah decided.

"What is that?"

"Go for a walk up the road, see the mountains, and then you can meet Mr. Brunson before he comes for supper."

"That's what you said." Kathy seemed to thinking of something else.

Hannah waited, starting the fire in the stove, figuring her mother would say what was on her mind soon enough.

"Sam's wife Annie is expecting too," Kathy finally said, although Hannah thought the news hardly warranted the serious tone.

"They also found a growth when she went to the doctor the first time."

"Oh!" Hannah exclaimed, knowing this news qualified the mentioning.

"It wasn't breast cancer. Benign, they said. Still" — Kathy's face turned towards Hannah in the flickering light — "quite a scare for a young couple."

"Is she okay?" Hannah asked, thinking of young Annie. *How would it be to face something like that while carrying your first baby?*

"Doctors performed the surgery a few days later. The family's trying to keep it secret, now that it's not cancerous. I think those things get out anyway."

"I see," Hannah said, easily imagining Sam having such sentiments. "I'm just glad it wasn't more serious."

"And so young. It wouldn't seem fair. But then God knows best."

"Poor Sam," Hannah said, saying what instinctively came to her mind.

"Not really," Kathy chuckled. "They are a well-matched couple."

"Better than me," Hannah said.

"I suppose so," Kathy allowed. "You should have thought of that before you made your father pay for the wedding."

"I'm sorry," Hannah said, knowing her mother was only half serious. "At least I found out in time."

"Just barely." Kathy made a face, getting up to open a cabinet drawer, looking for the coffee can, Hannah figured. Her mother found the can on the second try. Such efficiency, Hannah thought, even in a strange kitchen. Must come from experience, or perhaps just from being her mother.

"So where is this Mr. Brunson from?" Kathy asked, changing the subject.

"I don't know," Hannah confessed. "He was living back there when we bought the place."

"Never has family visiting?"

"Not that I've seen."

"Isn't that strange?"

"I don't know. He's English," Hannah gave her most logical explanation. "That's one reason I invited him for supper."

"No harm I suppose," Kathy allowed. "You going to get the men up soon?"

"You'd better let them sleep in. Jake hasn't got a job, remember."

Kathy nodded. "Once that water's hot. I'd like to see the outside with the sun coming up."

"Those mountains block the view sometimes," Hannah told her. "Depends how cloudy it is."

"Is it cloudy this morning?"

Hannah glanced out the kitchen window, looking carefully. "I don't think so. We can step out and look."

"That teapot will take a while anyway," Kathy agreed. "Let's see what the sunrise is like."

Stepping outside after getting their coats, Hannah and Kathy stood looking towards the Cabinet Mountains. The air was brisk, but not cold enough to spoil their enjoyment of the early morning. Over the tops of the mountain the first rays of sunlight reached for the sky. They noticed a line of clouds not visible from the kitchen window, but it hung low on the horizon and wouldn't obscure the coming light, Hannah figured. It might even enhance the colors.

"Let's get our coffee and watch this," Kathy said with excitement. "I've never seen a sunrise over mountains before."

Agreeing, Hannah followed Kathy back inside, placing another stick of wood on the fire to hurry things along. With the extra urging, the tea kettle soon whistled merrily.

"Sounds of home," Kathy commented, expecting no answer, Hannah figured.

They measured coffee into the filter, letting the steaming water run through and into their cups. Hannah gave her mother the sugar and spoon first, waiting until she was done to stir her own.

Back outside, they stood watching the sunrise as the colors slowly grew. Hannah had watched sunrises in Montana before, but this one seemed to be working hard at putting on its best display. With the low clouds as the backdrop, the red, yellow, and orange streaks reached upwards. Greens and blues soon appeared, each vying for dominance, producing new shades of brilliance every few seconds.

Kathy reached out her arm for Hannah, pulling her close as they stood shoulder to shoulder. Never in her growing up years had Hannah felt this close to her mother. *Was it because she was becoming more like her, now that she was with child? Had they found new territory they could share?*

"I'm so glad you're my mother," Hannah whispered, as the colors of the sunrise deepened even further above them.

Kathy just pulled her tighter, saying nothing.

"For putting up with me," Hannah's voice caught.

"You were always a joy," Kathy's voice came softly. "Regardless. You are a good daughter. And you have a good husband."

Hannah didn't trust her voice at the moment. There was no sense in bawling like a little girl, even though she felt like it.

They stood there for long moments until the colors began to fade above them, the sunlight growing stronger.

"We'd better go inside before you catch a cold," Kathy finally said. Ever the mother, Hannah figured.

Hannah felt like telling her she wanted to stay out here forever, to never move from this spot, but that was silly. One always had to move on, it seemed.

In the kitchen again, they got the breakfast pancakes ready, placing them in the oven for keeping until the men got up. When eight o'clock came around with no signs from the bedroom of men waking, they made enough eggs for themselves and ate, figuring the men could eat when they got around to it.

When her dad got up around nine, he found a seat in

the living room and began playfully reprimanding his wife and daughter for neglecting him. Hannah chuckled as her mom played along.

"You have to fix your own breakfast. We already ate ours," Kathy said.

"That's what I thought," Roy said in his mock bitterness. "Women become useless in Montana, it seems."

"That's awful," Kathy said in mock horror. "You're talking to your daughter."

"I was talking about you," Roy informed them.

"That's even worse," Kathy told him.

Jake, apparently hearing their voices, emerged from the bedroom, rubbing sleep from his eyes.

"No food services this morning," Roy announced in his direction. "Men are on their own. It's make do or starve."

Hannah watched Jake's face, hoping he would catch on. When he did, she felt delighted that he understood her parents so well.

"When we hunger, they too hunger sooner or later," Jake said, joining in.

"That's a man," Roy chuckled. "Tell 'em."

"Okay," Kathy said in mock resignation. "The pancakes are made. We'll make the eggs. The rest you have to do yourself. Hannah and I have eaten already."

"They don't like us. Just like that, cast aside," Roy said with a straight face. "After all these years. Then gone."

Jake had to grin as he followed Roy into the kitchen. With the eggs made in minutes, Kathy and Hannah left the rest of the breakfast items on the table and the men alone to put things together for themselves. The two women found seats in the living room.

"They don't love us no more," Roy said mournfully, piling pancakes on his plate. "At least the syrup is still sweet."

Jake had to grin at that remark, and the grin became even broader when Roy added, "Maybe that too gets bitter in Montana."

"Watch yourself," Kathy hollered at him from the living room. "I heard that."

"It must be the baby. The nerves," Hannah said in explanation when a tear rolled down her cheek. A great longing to move back to Indiana filled her. That her mother understood the real reason was evident from her smile. Babies could be blamed for a lot of things, but not everything.

"We must cherish the time God gives us," Kathy said simply. "It goes by soon enough."

After they were done eating, the men were informed of the plans to walk up the road to Mr. Brunson's.

"To look at the mountains," Kathy added as further explanation.

Hannah noticed her mother said nothing about the time just spent watching the sunrise. That made it all the more special, a moment shared only by the two of them.

"Well, Jake," Roy said in mock disgust. "They not only make us eat by ourselves. Now we have to walk up the mountain."

"It's nice," Jake informed him.

"Don't you know men are supposed to stick together?" Roy looked hard at him. Jake only grinned, getting his coat from the closet, ready to get out of the house.

Chapter Fourteen

IN THE WALK towards the mountain, Hannah and Kathy led the way. Jake and Roy seemed deep into some discussion. Hannah wasn't sure, but from snatches of it she thought it sounded like Mr. Howard's furniture-making offer. Her father seemed enthused, which she wasn't sure she liked.

Kathy couldn't stop expressing her pleasure over the sight of the mountains, her enthusiasm mounting as they came ever into better view.

"I know I've seen them before," her mother said. "Maybe it's the view from here."

"It gets even better further up," Hannah told her, having been there once before with Jake after they purchased the log cabin. "I imagine you can see them even better behind Mr. Brunson's cabin. I've never been beyond that, though."

Thirty minutes of climbing up the slight grade brought them in sight of the cabin, two stories high, consisting of little more than boards nailed upright with mismatched tin on the roof. Some of the edges even stood higher than the others.

Behind the cabin further up the slight slope was the barn, its structure in even worse shape.

"The house is well insulated," Jake said, since obviously something needed to be said in Mr. Brunson's favor.

"And clean," Hannah added, remembering that point from her brief look inside the abode.

"He's a real nice gentleman," Jake said, and from the

look on Kathy's face, Hannah knew it meant more to her mother than if she had said it.

Without hesitation Jake led the party up to the front door and knocked. Mr. Brunson opened almost at once, clean shaven as usual and with a smile on his face.

"Well, what have we here?" he asked, obviously pleased to see them.

"Hannah's parents," Jake told him. "Roy and Kathy. This is Mr. Brunson."

"Glad to meet you." Mr. Brunson extended his hand.

Roy shook it with a smile, nodding, while Kathy stepped forward, a little more cautiously Hannah thought, but she was smiling, which was good.

"Women got us out walking," Roy said with a chuckle. "Don't let an old man stay in bed long."

"Now that's not true," Kathy retorted. "You slept real late."

"Wouldn't feed us either. Turned us right out on our own." Roy kept a straight face this time.

"Sounds like you have some tough women there." Mr. Brunson was grinning.

Jake chuckled, "He likes stretching things a little."

"Well, you want to come inside?" Mr. Brunson held the door open, and from where Hannah stood everything looked as spotless as she remembered. Barren, but clean. Hannah wondered if Mr. Brunson had more to sit on than the single chair by the leggy platform that passed for a kitchen table.

"Oh, we were just out walking," Kathy told him quickly. "Thanks anyway. Hannah says you're coming tonight for supper?"

"She was kind enough to invite me," Mr. Brunson said. "I hope I'm not a bother."

"Certainly not," Kathy said quickly again. "We're just guests, too."

"I'll look forward to it then. Sure you don't want to come in? Don't have much, but it works for me."

"I'm sure it does," Kathy said. "We have supper to make yet."

"If your cooking tastes as good as your daughter's, supper will really be something," Mr. Brunson told her.

Hannah was sure her mother turned a little red as she brushed off the compliment with a shake of her head.

"We train them that way," Roy said with a chuckle. "That is...until they quit like this morning."

"Don't pay attention to him," Kathy told Mr. Brunson. "Does he look underfed to you?"

"Not in the least," Mr. Brunson assured her with a straight face, as if he took the matter totally seriously.

"We'd like to walk up higher," Jake said, surprising Hannah. "I think you have a good view of the mountains a little way up. If that's okay?"

"Most certainly," Mr. Brunson said. "It's not that far. Of course there are better places, but those would be quite a climb."

"Thanks," Roy and Kathy said almost together.

Hannah gave Mr. Brunson a smile as they left with Jake leading the way. Mr. Brunson waited, Hannah noticed, until they were well into the yard before shutting his door. Apparently he was in no hurry to be rid of their company, which bode well for dinner that evening.

Finding the spot he wanted, Jake stopped, motioning towards the Cabinet Mountains. From here they could see the full range of mountains and even further to the north and south.

"I can see why someone would want to live here," Kathy said softly.

Roy nodded momentarily, then muttered, "There's always the thing of a job."

"Oh, you can hunt and fish and ski in the winter," Hannah said, not sure where the words were coming from.

Jake looked strangely at her until she felt guilty. "I'm sorry," Hannah finally said. "This is beautiful country."

"Well...I've seen enough of it," Roy pronounced. "Let

get ourselves back to the house. It's time for an old man's nap."

"And eating," Kathy added.

"Of course," Roy laughed. "That skimpy breakfast we had to make for ourselves was a long time ago."

"See," Kathy said.

"We had better get them back before they die of hunger," Hannah matched her mother's tone. "It's been such a long journey — the heat, the famine, and the thirst."

Jake only chuckled as he led the way back past Mr. Brunson's and down the slope towards the log cabin. Once they arrived, Roy did eat plenty for lunch, Hannah noticed, so he must have been hungry. He also took a nap. Jake, she thought, looked tempted, but resisted the urge, reading the *Family Life* instead.

With her mother helping again, Hannah made the full dinner she had planned — meat, potatoes, gravy, salad with the last of the fresh vegetables, and two cherry pies, cheating by using store-bought fillings. At least it felt like cheating to Hannah. She had always seen her mother make the pie filling from scratch with cherries from the grocery store. Kathy didn't mention the difference, though, and Hannah pushed the guilty feeling aside. It was a time to enjoy family, she decided, not think about unimportant things like how pie fillings were made.

Mr. Brunson showed up well before the appointed supper time and was welcomed in. He took the seat offered him in the living room with Roy and Jake. From the glimpses she got of him while setting the kitchen table, Hannah thought he seemed comfortable enough, joining in the men's conversation.

When everything was ready, Hannah let Jake know and he led the two men out to the kitchen. Standing in the opening, Hannah told each where to sit as they went past — Jake at the head, with Mr. Brunson and Roy on either side of him. Kathy sat beside Roy, and Hannah took the table's end, across from Jake.

Settling into her seat, Hannah smiled at Jake to let him know he could proceed. She figured he would know anyway, but she liked catching his eye, seated there at the head of the table, entertaining real people in their own house.

"Would you please ask the blessing?" he asked Roy, sounding grownup and sober, Hannah thought. Here they were, acting like adults, having a baby, and yet she felt every bit of a child on the inside.

Roy bowed his head immediately, the others following, and began praying. Hannah did steal a glance at Mr. Brunson, who still looked quite comfortable, as if the praying didn't bother him at all.

"You have family around here?" Kathy asked Mr. Brunson as the food began making its rounds.

"No," he said. "No one."

"How long have you lived here?" Kathy asked smiling. "Hannah said you were here when they moved in."

Mr. Brunson wrinkled his brow. "Most of nine years now."

Hannah thought he wasn't quite certain and wondered why. Maybe it was just the fact he was older and his memory was failing him.

"You like living in the mountains by yourself?" Roy joined in the conversation. "Nice country I must say."

"I have a son out east," Mr. Brunson said, a shadow crossing his face. Hannah wondered why Mr. Brunson had never mentioned this son before. Maybe she and Jake just didn't ask the right questions.

"Ever visit?" Kathy asked, passing the bread.

"No," Mr. Brunson said, rather quickly Hannah thought. "Never has."

"You go back east any? Christmas and holidays?" Roy asked.

"No," Mr. Brunson chuckled, a sad chuckle, Hannah thought, but it sounded so nearly like a cheerful chuckle she wasn't sure. She figured it easily could have been misunderstood by someone who didn't know him well. But how well did she know him?

Her parents fell silent. Hannah could tell they were wondering whether the questions had been a bit much. Mr. Brunson must have noticed too, because he chuckled again.

"I guess we're not as big on family as you folks are. It's nice you invited me, though."

That relaxed everyone and the conversation flowed again.

Roy thumped his stomach and pronounced himself satisfied with his last bite of cherry pie. He must not have noticed the store-bought filling, Hannah comforted herself. At the price of groceries, store fillings ought to be as good as homemade, she thought ruefully.

With the men back in the living room, Hannah and Kathy did the dishes, then joined them afterward. Mr. Brunson soon excused himself, thanking both Hannah and Jake for the invitation. He left in his truck, the headlights bouncing up the lane towards the mountain.

"He's nice enough," Kathy said to no one in particular.

"Yes," Roy managed, having found a piece of *The Budget* to read now that Mr. Brunson was gone.

"You have to feel sorry for people without families," Kathy said vaguely in Hannah's direction. "Whether it's by choice or not."

"Think Mr. Brunson had a falling-out with his son?" Hannah asked, remembering the sound of Mr. Brunson's chuckle at the table.

"You never know nowadays," Kathy mused. "The world is what it is."

"What about his wife? He must have had one. And other children?" Hannah wondered.

"Maybe he only had one child. It's possible the way people have children nowadays," Kathy said. "I'm glad you invited him though. That was right thoughtful of you."

Hannah sighed with relief, thankful for her mother's approval. "I thought it was," she said.

Roy yawned soon after that and announced it was bedtime for him.

"You had a nap," Kathy told him.

"I'm getting old," he retorted.

"Then you'll have to head on," she told him. "I don't come to Montana everyday."

Hannah could see her father was fighting sleep and soon gave up, walking towards the spare bedroom with a grumble about no one taking care of him anymore. Jake left an hour later, having completed his *Family Life* articles. Hannah and Kathy stayed up till past midnight.

Something about the lateness of the hour, the chores completed, and the missing men loosened their tongues and hearts. They spoke nonstop about all the things women talk about — what Aunt Martha said, who was going to start courting whose son or daughter, and who knew what about everyone — all the little subtleties and nuances of people's lives.

The torrent finally came to an end as mother and daughter settled into a comfortable silence. They knew their time together would never be as it once was, abundant and available, and each in her own way was trying to come to peace with the fact. The separation had proven more painful than they expected, yet they found in their coming together again a new facet of their relationship quite beyond their imaginations. They had never been so separate and yet so one.

"You really think you might move to Indiana?" Kathy asked, wistfully.

"I don't know. Jake seems so set against it. I wish we would."

"Don't push it," Kathy said, still the mother, and Hannah, now sleepy, suggested they go to bed.

CHAPTER FIFTEEN

IN THE MORNING, Jake took a sudden notion for a trip into Libby with Roy. He wanted to show Roy the hardware store, talk with Mr. Howard again, and maybe pick up something from the grocery store. This last offer he said with a grin, which Hannah knew was meant to mollify any objections she might have.

Hannah had no objections anyway, nor did she need anything from the grocery store. But she didn't think her father's presence would make any difference in Jake's conversation with Mr. Howard. What she didn't know was that Jake did, thinking it would give him greater credibility to have quality relatives along.

Hannah was glad Jake thought well of her family. But she still hadn't warmed up to the idea of a hardware job. They really needed to move back to Indiana, and since Jake wasn't ready yet to face the facts, she would simply wait until he was.

When the men returned just before lunch, Roy expressed himself satisfied with Mr. Howard and the job offer given to Jake. Hannah glanced at Jake, puzzled since her father seemed to be talking present tense. Jake grinned even more.

"He wants me to start Monday. I said I couldn't till Wednesday when my in-laws leave," Jake said, almost gleefully.

"I told him to go right ahead, not to wait." Roy threw his

hands in the air. "He wouldn't listen. Don't blame me if you starve out of house and home."

"For work?" Hannah asked, to clear things up.

"Steady work," Jake assured her. "All winter. We even spoke some more about building log furniture. He showed us the storage room out back."

"It might work," Roy said. "A little small, but it's got heat."

Hannah hoped her disappointment didn't show too much. "That's good," she managed, seeing some of her hope for the Indiana move fading away. *But perhaps the job would only last the winter. Maybe she could make it through the winter. At least they wouldn't go hungry.* "Does the job pay okay?"

Jake made a face. "Not that much. But it's work."

"It's fair," Roy said. "The real money looks to be in the furniture, if you could find a distributor. Market it."

Leaving the men to talk about how to sell specialty merchandise and to whom, Kathy and Hannah went to prepare sandwiches for lunch.

"Cheer up," Kathy told Hannah when they were in the kitchen. "It's not the end of the world."

"I don't look that disappointed, do I?" Hannah asked, hoping it was just her mother's instincts picking up her distress.

Kathy smiled. "You can get your heart set on something. Then that may not be God's will."

"But I wanted to move back to Indiana," Hannah whispered, pretending to wail, distorting her face.

"Just go with the flow of things. It's better that way."

"Maybe we can move back next spring, after the hardware job gives out."

Kathy shook her head. "It's best not to plan things like that. Spring is a long, long way off."

"And a cold hard winter ahead." Hannah gave a shudder.

"But you knew about the winters before you moved here," Kathy reminded her.

"That's different from seeing one staring you in the eyes. And the grizzly."

Kathy laughed, giving Hannah a quick look that softened the moment. "You'll make it. We always do."

Hannah wasn't sure about that but it was good to hear her mother felt so.

With the sandwiches served, no one had any other ideas what to do, so they decided to spend the rest of the day and evening around the house. Roy took a long nap again, while Jake went to clean out the horse stall. It took him several wheelbarrow loads as he dumped the mixture of straw and horse manure on the garden.

Mr. Brunson interrupted him on his last load, rattling into the driveway. Leaving the wheelbarrow in the yard, Jake walked up to the truck. Hannah could tell the news must be interesting from the expressions on their faces. Jake headed for the house immediately after Mr. Brunson left.

"He wants to show us his elk, Roy and me," Jake announced when he opened the door. "Sounds like a big one."

"What?" Roy asked from the recliner, having woken suddenly.

"Mr. Brunson wants to show us his elk," Jake repeated with a grin.

"How'd he get it?" Roy wanted to know, rubbing his face.

"Bow and arrow," Jake said. "He's good at it."

"They're big, aren't they?" Roy got to his feet glancing at the women. "You want to come along?"

They both shook their heads. Roy shrugged his shoulders and followed Jake outside.

"Keeps them entertained," Kathy said when they were gone, to which Hannah added her agreement. It was the women who got the last entertainment, though, when Jake and Roy returned in an hour with a plastic bag full of fresh elk meat.

"What are you doing with that stuff?" Kathy asked in genuine horror, eyeing the bag of redness.

"You're making it," Roy announced. "For supper."

"I'm not. It's elk meat," Kathy said, her tone still unchanged, her eyes big.

"It's the same as deer meat at home," Roy assured her.

"How do you know? It might have an awful flavor." Kathy didn't seem mollified in the least.

Certain she had already eaten elk meat at Betty's place last summer, Hannah jumped into the conversation. "It's okay, Mom. Betty makes it, I think."

"Betty does?" Kathy's horror seemed to be only increasing.

"You probably ate some when you visited last," Hannah said as calmly as she could, feeling like laughing at her mother's distress.

"See," Roy said, his voice triumphant. "That settles it. We are having elk meat for supper."

"I suppose so." Kathy still eyed the plastic bag of meat.

"And Mr. Brunson is coming for supper, since it's his meat," Jake announced. "I invited him."

"But we don't have supper ready," Hannah protested, a thousand thoughts of cherry pies and salad and other fixings running through her head.

Kathy rallied first. "It won't be much. I promise you that."

"Just the meat and some gravy," Roy said, a gleam in his eye. "Has to be tender though."

Kathy glared at him. "That may be all it will be. If it's tough, don't say you weren't warned."

It turned out the meat wasn't tough when Hannah and Kathy got done boiling, then frying, it on the stove. Jake brought in extra wood, having split more behind the barn.

Mr. Brunson had nothing but good things to say about the hurriedly thrown-together supper, pronouncing it among the best he had ever eaten.

"You're just saying so," Kathy told him, nonetheless

enjoying the praise, Hannah could tell.

"Certainly not," he assured her, then started to say something else — but he stopped abruptly, a sad look crossing his face again. Hannah couldn't tell if anyone else noticed, and the conversation soon continued.

After supper the men took turns playing checkers in the living room. Mr. Brunson proved to be quite a challenge for Roy, who considered himself an expert. Jake played once in a while "to calm them down," he said as explanation for Kathy and Hannah's benefit. The real matches were between Mr. Brunson and Roy. The two battled it out, with one man going ahead and then the other, as the women watched with amusement.

Mr. Brunson finally proclaimed it a draw and Roy a worthy adversary. He rose from his chair, extending his hand. "I've got to go, old man. You do know how to play checkers."

"Old man yourself," Roy said with a great laugh. "You are good. You sure you've got to go?" he asked with genuine regret in his voice.

"Yes, got to go. Thanks for the meal again," he said in Kathy and Hannah's direction as he left.

"Nice old man," Roy said, "and can he play checkers."

"You can be thankful to have such a good neighbor," Kathy commented. "Anyone want coffee?"

Roy did and announced his choice with a loud, "Of course."

"Well I knew you did," Kathy told him. "I meant the others."

"Get it brewing. They'll join in," Roy said, great assurance in his voice. "Why would anyone not want coffee?"

"Maybe because they want to sleep sometime before morning," Kathy told him. "You're immune already."

"Make the poor things decaf then," Roy said.

"She doesn't have any," Kathy informed him.

"I just keep regular around for visitors," Hannah told her father. "We don't drink coffee yet."

"What a shame."

Roy was served his coffee in due course and actually got Jake to try some — just a splash or so on the bottom, as Jake put it. After that Hannah had to try some too, at her father's insistence. Just in case, he said, if Jake couldn't sleep they would be in the thing together.

"You're going to ruin both their lives," Kathy told him, laughing.

"Make it better," Roy insisted. "Helps them in their rough times."

Hannah didn't know about that but thought the coffee might help ease her stomach from the elk meat. It turned out not to be half bad.

Apparently not affected by the caffeine, both she and Jake got sleepy before her parents did. Kathy shooed them to bed, saying they needn't wait up as she and Roy were quite capable of putting themselves to bed.

After blowing out the kerosene lamp, Hannah snuggled up to Jake and decided, sleepy or not, it was time to talk about the subject. She asked him if it was out of the question to move this fall, and he said yes. She asked about spring, and he said maybe. The job at the hardware would give them some direction. If it didn't go well, it might be an indication to move. If the log furniture sales took off, it would be an indication to stay. It would all depend.

When she told him she really wanted to go, he said he understood in a tone of voice that sounded like he really did.

"It's just hard to make such a choice," he said. "I would want to do what you want. I have to know it's right though."

"That's nice to know," she told him. "Wouldn't it be nice to be in Indiana? To have a nice steady job? To have Mom and Dad close?"

"I know," he said, "but we have to be sure. Maybe God wants us here."

"Why would He want that?" she asked him.

"I don't know," Jake said, sounding genuinely puzzled. "It's just a small community here. They can always use more people. I don't know."

"You wouldn't stay just because of that?"

"No," he said, rolling over. "I just don't know. We will have to see."

Jake's breathing soon evened out, and Hannah let her worries go, drifting off to sleep.

CHAPTER SIXTEEN

WITH THE PRIOR arrangement to take Roy and Kathy to church, the driver of the van showed up early, for which Hannah was thankful. To arrive late would be an embarrassment, and blaming a van driver wouldn't pass as an excuse.

She and Jake had decided they might as well go along instead of driving their own horse. Kathy and Roy both agreed. Hannah went out to ask the driver if he wanted breakfast and was told he already had eaten in Libby.

They left at a quarter after eight, taking along a prepared lunch. When they arrived at Mullet Troyer's, where church was being held, the driver stopped short of the barnyard, uncertain where to park. The older son came out of his place in the line of men and motioned to a grassy spot behind the barn, away from the buggies.

The practice of placing buggies and automobiles in separate parking was common, Hannah knew. Not that the Amish considered cars evil — it just felt better when they were apart, a neat compartment that kept things in order.

The group split up at the driveway, Jake and Roy joining the men in front of the barn and Kathy and Hannah walking to the house. Betty met them at the front door, apparently having noticed their approach.

"Good morning," Betty greeted Hannah and Kathy warmly, her arm lingering briefly on each of their shoulders. Betty was a touching person, Hannah knew. If this was not church, she probably would be giving them each a hug.

"It's sure a nice morning," Kathy observed.

"Yes it is. Just perfect when we have to sit inside all day," Betty stated matter-of-fact like.

That was another thing about Betty—she just said things, and usually people weren't offended. Though everyone knew the all-day church service, with communion at the end would be arduous, they didn't mention the subject. They didn't even if there was a nice sunny fall day outside and they were inside, trapped, with their backsides flattened out from sitting six hours or more on a hard, uncushioned, backless board bench. Communion Sunday was supposed to be a holy time, a time of reflection on the scriptures, one's sins, and one's place in life.

For a moment, Hannah remembered a minister was supposed to be ordained today. The thought was quickly lost, though, as Betty led the way around the circle of women, each being greeted in turn.

After the ministers' time upstairs, the singing stopped and the preaching started. Bishop Nisley had the first part, starting at Genesis and telling the story up to Noah's escape from the flood with his ark. No notes, no Bible, just a quotation of facts and general plot line by memory.

A minister Hannah didn't know had the next part. Apparently he had come along with the van load, although neither of her parents had mentioned him. He went from Noah's entry into the new world washed clean by the flood until the time of Christ's birth. With the hands of the living room clock now just past twelve, Bishop Nisley dismissed for lunch.

Since the day was so nice, everyone poured out into the yard for lunch, taking short benches with them, if they could be found. Others were given chairs by Mullet until there were no more. He and his family then ate inside at the kitchen table. Kathy found a spot in the yard, with Jake and Roy each bringing a short bench along. They had been quick to grab one while they were still to be had.

Hannah found Jake's boldness amusing today. She assumed it came from the fact Roy was along and gave Jake sort of visitor's rights. Normally, Jake would have been the last to get a bench. He would have settled as some were having to, with one of the long, awkward benches.

They ate their lunch to the chatter of voices all around them, families keeping intact. Only when everyone was done eating did some visiting occur. Several people stopped by to speak with Roy and Kathy. Bishop Nisley soon made an announcement from the front door that services were to resume.

The long afternoon began. Bishop Amos Yoder made his slow way through the gospel accounts, working up to the crucifixion of Christ. What the scriptures said, the Amish believed. Each time they partook of the cup and broke the bread, they were supposed to tell the story of Christ's suffering. Only when they started at the beginning would the story make sense, or the best sense. To them, communion was a time for the best.

Two-and-a-half hours later, Amos arrived at the end of the story and began to pass around the bread and wine. They used one cup, because that was the way Christ served it. Hannah did appreciate that Bishop Nisley used a cloth to wipe the rim after each person handed the cup back to him. Some ministers did not. With her back aching from sitting on the hard benches, she was glad the service had arrived at this point.

After feet washing, when normally they would be dismissed and find relief from the day-long service, Hannah noticed tension in the air. It was only then she remembered an ordination was yet to be performed. Since morning she had not once thought about the coming ceremony, considering the matter none of her concern. There were at least ten married men in the local congregation older than Jake. Several young families were the same age as she and Jake.

Ben and Sylvia Stoll came to mind, but she didn't consider Ben a likely candidate either. A man had to receive at least three votes to be placed in the lot.

With age and experience in mind, Hannah decided on the spot to vote for Henry Wengerd. She would get to vote along with the men, as all the women would. The Amish, for all their traditional norms, are firm believers in equality of the sexes when it comes to voting.

As he announced the vote to be taken, Bishop Amos said it was the Lord's will, not man's ability, that was to guide the voting. What that meant, Hannah wasn't certain. He then instructed them to file into the kitchen, where each vote would be noted. Nothing more, nothing less, just plain instructions whereby some man's life would be altered forever. Amish ordination has little to do with personal calling, the voice of the church being all that is necessary.

The long line of men began, moving quickly, Hannah thought. Apparently everyone was deciding in record time, or perhaps they just wanted to get home. The women started, and Hannah got up when the turn for her bench came. Sylvia Stoll was right behind her and waited outside the kitchen while Hannah went up to the kitchen table and whispered Henry Wengerd's name to Bishop Nisley.

Hannah felt curious as to who was getting votes and wished Bishop didn't have his piece of paper so well covered up. Glad that he couldn't read her naughty thoughts, she went back to her seat while Sylvia walked into the kitchen. Bishop Amos would announce the names in minutes anyway, so it didn't matter.

Sylvia soon joined Hannah back at their bench, as the young girls spoke their choices in the kitchen. Five minutes later Bishop Amos stood up, glancing down at the paper Bishop Nisley gave him. Since there was no deacon in this young church, Bishop Nisley himself had brought along the books to use in selecting the new minister. Three books were placed on the bench, and everyone now knew three men were in the lot. They would come up in turn and make their selection. One book contained the providential piece of paper.

Bishop Amos cleared his throat. "We have three names given to us by the voice of the church. Each of these brethren is to come up and choose a book." Amos motioned towards the books on the bench with his beard. "Will each come forward in the order of these names: Henry Wengerd." Hannah felt a deep stab of guilt in being part of possibly changing a man's life forever. "Jake Byler." Hannah felt ice cold run throughout her whole body. "Ben Stoll." Beside her Sylvia burst out into quiet sobs.

Hannah sat numbly through the rest of the ceremony, seeing men walk in front of her like trees. Henry went first, his step firm, and then Jake, his face as pale as the frost on their bedroom window. Ben followed the two, a great hulking figure, swaying as if he carried a load of logs beyond his strength to carry.

Without a word, Henry took the middle book, Jake took the outside left, and Ben took what was left over, and so their fates were sealed. Amos came forward without hesitation, glancing at the clock as if he were in a hurry to get this over with. Hannah was surprised she could even breathe. What had gotten into these church people to vote for two such young men? Had the world gone mad?

Henry was the one qualified. Surely God would intervene with the peoples' lack of understanding in this matter. This was the only choice that made sense to her, and Hannah clung to the hope until her fingernails dug into the palm of her hands.

Bishop Amos opened Henry's book, flipped through it, and turned it upside down, giving it a little shake. The paper was not to be found. Taking Jake's book, Bishop Amos opened it, then paused. Hannah already knew the paper was there by the look on Jake's face — his eyes wild, as if he saw a vision too horrible to imagine.

Holding the piece of white paper in his hand, Bishop

Amos pronounced, "We have found the will of the church and the will of God. Will you please kneel, brother?"

Jake didn't move for the longest time, until Hannah was sure Bishop Amos would have to repeat the order. Slowly Jake slid to the hardwood floor, his hands clasped in front of him.

"By the will of God and by the voice of the church," Bishop Amos said, laying his hands on Jake's hand, "you have been chosen to the high and holy office of minister. You are to serve in humility, in the power of the Holy Spirit, to rebuke, to exhort, to succor those who are ill in body and spirit, to give warning to the erring, and in all times and seasons to fulfill your calling."

Giving Jake his hand, Bishop Amos helped him to his feet and kissed him, as did Bishop Nisley and the other local minister, Mose Chupp.

Beside Hannah, Sylvia was quiet, her sobs gone. Even in her dulled state of awareness, Hannah was certain Sylvia had pulled away, trying to put distance between them. She, Hannah, was obviously now a minister's wife. So sudden, so abrupt, like a shooting star falling out of heaven on her head. Others would always feel she was different from them, regardless of how much she wasn't.

Hannah heard Bishop Amos dismiss the service, sounding as if he were far away. The bench beside her emptied out on each side, but she stayed seated, unable to move.

Dimly she became aware of her mother, and then Betty, coming in on either side of her. Her senses registered arms around her shoulders. Their tightness gripped her. They stayed that way, the three of them, until the dam broke and the tears flowed. They wept together as one for a life that never would be the same again.

CHAPTER SEVENTEEN

CLIMBING INTO THE waiting van, Hannah felt intensely out of place. She was surrounded by the yard full of Amish buggies, and today of all days, when she was now a minister's wife, they had to climb into a van to go home. Jake's buggy would at least have provided some level of comfort, of sameness. It would have supplied the feeling that she was still one of them. Instead, she felt even more alone, surrounded by black hats and shawl-wrapped women.

Still burning with the intensity of her own feelings, she had yet to look at Jake's face. The driver of the van looked curiously at them as they climbed in. Perhaps, Hannah thought, he wondered if Amish communion services always produced such sober-faced men and tear-stained women.

The driver said nothing, though, minding his own business, whether out of good manners or simply from past experience driving Amish. It didn't matter at the moment to Hannah. She was just glad there were no questions.

The sight of Jake's shoulder beside her on the van seat brought back the memory of his frightened face when the bishop opened the book. With the memory came her first feelings of concern for Jake. If this was hard on her, a mere observer, how must this be affecting him? He was the one who would be doing the work required of a preacher.

Hannah slipped her hand around Jake, finding his arm on the other side and tightening her grip. Jake didn't look at her, but his face became a little less serious, she thought.

Letting her head lean against him, she didn't care how things looked to the van driver, who glanced briefly in his rearview mirror.

At the house and out of the van, Roy stayed behind to speak with the van driver. He was making arrangements to be picked up Wednesday morning, Hannah assumed. She and Kathy followed Jake silently into the house.

The silence was what struck Hannah the most. She had never thought of their cabin as being silent, but it seemed so now, as if it held its breath along with them. She stood for a few moments listening until a sudden pop of moving logs relieved her of the tension.

"You listening for something?" Kathy asked. Jake had simply seated himself on the couch, staring into space.

"It was just silent for a moment," Hannah said. "I'm used to hearing noises."

"I hadn't noticed," Kathy told her, obviously thinking of something else.

"We have to get some supper," Hannah said.

"That's what I was thinking," Kathy agreed.

"You think anyone will be hungry?" Hannah wondered.

"It'll be good to eat. We haven't had anything since lunch. It's later than you think."

Hannah glanced at the clock, surprised. "The whole day seemed long," she said, putting into words her general feelings.

"Same day as always, yet how things change," Kathy said in a low voice, even though they were in the kitchen. Hannah figured Kathy didn't want Jake hearing her mention the obvious.

"What are we going to do?" Hannah asked, the reality of their situation springing up. "We're so young."

Before her eyes passed the things Amish ministers do. Standing in front of congregations, speaking for sometimes an hour at a time. Leaving on Sunday mornings for the upstairs council meeting. Being in on church problems, making decisions on things great and small. Having to provide counseling for any member who needed it. Bringing correction and rebuke to those who disobeyed the church *ordnung*.

Her Jake, nervous in public Jake, who had prayed out loud at home only recently. That Jake would now have to read long prayers in public, stand and speak without any help, and all that in a very short time. How soon, Hannah didn't know, never having noticed such things, but it would be coming quickly.

"We have to get supper ready," Kathy said beside her.

"How soon before he has to preach?" Hannah asked, not able to get the question out of her head.

Hannah thought her mother wasn't going to answer, but then Kathy must have decided to. "About a month, I think. That's how much time they give them. A little time to get ready."

"Ready," was all Hannah could say, more statement than question.

"I know," Kathy agreed. "It doesn't seem very long, now that you think about it."

Hannah was silent thinking about a month, four Sundays, and her Jake would be up there in front of the whole church. The thought made her fingers go cold.

"God will help you," Kathy said, adding, "I guess," as an afterthought, as if she had some question about it.

"Jake is alone in the living room," Hannah said. "Maybe we ought to be with him?"

"Probably," Kathy agreed, and was moving towards the kitchen door when Roy came in. She stopped, waiting for a moment.

"Maybe Dad will talk to him," Hannah whispered, "since supper needs to be made."

"Food will do him good," Kathy suggested.

"Let's just heat up leftovers then," Hannah decided.

While Hannah lit the stove, the flame catching with the first match, Kathy took on the task of going outside to retrieve the meat, gravy, and fruit jello from the spring house. When her mother was gone, Hannah heard her father clear his throat and then begin talking to Jake in the living room.

"I know this was unexpected, son, but such things usually are. We just never know what the Lord has in mind on these matters."

Jake must have nodded, because Roy continued after a brief silence.

"It comes, though, with great honor, this office does. You are one of few who are called to lead our people. Not many receive this good burden. I know in this hour it doesn't feel so. It feels probably the exact opposite, like your world has come to an end."

Again there was silence before Roy continued.

"Yet you must remember. Our forefathers — now over five hundred years ago — needed no special training or gift from God. The first one knelt and asked to be baptized as an adult. The others performed the baptism. That was all they had — just the truth and the support of the brethren."

"But I am one of the youngest ones," Jake said, his voice shaking. "There are others who are much better."

"It makes no difference," Roy told him. "It is God who decides. He is the one who chose David to be king. David was younger than his brothers."

"I don't know," Jake allowed, but his voice sounded a little stronger to Hannah. Behind her the door opened as Kathy entered, her hands full of the leftovers.

"Dad's talking to Jake," Hannah whispered.

"Is he doing any good?" Kathy wanted to know.

"I think so. Anything helps right now."

"Maybe it's good Roy is here. He almost didn't come along for the trip," Kathy said pensively.

"Who would have thought something like this would happen?"

"Not me." Kathy set the bowls down on the kitchen table. "You just never know."

The old stove warm by now, Hannah placed the meat and gravy in the oven. Kathy set the table, the silverware clinking together in the silence of the kitchen. Jake and Roy's voices had ceased in the living room.

"It'll be a few minutes yet," Hannah said, more to make conversation than anything.

"There's bread yet to slice," Kathy said for the same reason.

"We'll wait till the food is warm," Hannah decided, an urge to be with Jake coming over her. "We can sit in the living room."

"You're going to have to learn your German better," Roy was saying as they walked in.

Hannah glanced at Jake's face. He seemed calmer now, his eyes weary, a sadness in them, but the fear was gone.

"Why do you say that?" Jake asked, his voice almost a whisper, as if he were uncertain what lay behind anything.

Silent now, Roy looked like he wished he hadn't spoken, but finally managed, "When you preach. Or will preach. You know — it takes more German words than we normally use."

Jake absorbed the information, his face blank, then said, "I guess I'd better start studying then."

Hannah was sure her father looked relieved.

"Maybe I can send you a German language book when we get back," he said.

"Should you be telling him this stuff?" Kathy spoke up. "Jake's got enough on his mind already."

"I know," Roy agreed, looking contrite. "I'm sorry."

"No. That's okay," Jake said quickly. "The sooner I learn the better."

Hannah marveled at how brave Jake looked, seemingly facing what lay ahead with newfound courage. But then the cloud passed over his face again.

"What's wrong?" she asked him, leaning over in his direction.

"In four weeks," he managed to say, barely getting the words out.

"*Da Hah* will help you," Roy said softly — meaning the words, Hannah could tell, but they held little comfort for her at the moment.

Moving closer to Jake she put her arms around his neck, pulling him against herself, not caring what her parents might think at this display of public affection. They were married after all. She felt useless and helpless to do anything more, but she could love him, she decided. This was easy for her to do, and perhaps it would help.

Jake managed a slight smile, but then looked uncomfortable, so she let him go from her hug, staying close to him though. That he didn't seem to mind.

"The food," Kathy said in a sudden burst. "Oh my."

"Now you burned it," Roy said, a chuckle in his voice.

Even Jake had to laugh as Hannah jumped up. How quickly, she thought in the rush out to the stove, did life come back. Even just hours after their shock, it came back, demanding they go on living.

While she and Kathy were placing the food on the table, Hannah thought of something for the first time. She would not be moving back to Indiana. Any doubt as to that question had been removed as completely as a cleaned kitchen table after a meal. A newly ordained minister did not move except under the most compelling of reasons. None of those reasons existed, she knew. Joblessness and lack of money did not count.

Hannah shoved the thoughts aside for the moment, not wanting to be thinking of herself. It was only after she and Jake were in bed they returned with force. With Jake's arms around her, she wept. She wept for Jake, but also for herself, for the lost dream, for the realization that Montana, cold Montana with its snows and bears, was not going to be parted from her.

Jake thought she was crying for other reasons, she was certain, and didn't feel like enlightening him. This was just something she would have to bear in silence. It would simply not do to make Jake's burden greater than it already was.

"We'll make it," Jake said, stroking her hair, his strong arms tight around her.

"Yes," she said in a muffled voice, because it was the right thing to say. Yet the whole thing seemed one incredible mess with no way out. The sound outside the bedroom wall only confirmed her feelings. It sounded briefly and then was gone.

"That wasn't the bear," Jake said, sounding confident, but Hannah was sure he wasn't.

"It was just a noise," she said, hoping that was true, but knowing it wasn't.

CHAPTER EIGHTEEN

HANNAH WOKE LATE, the sun already risen, its light full in the room. Embarrassed, she dressed quickly and hurried out, finding her fears a reality. Both her parents were already up, and Jake with them. Both Kathy and Roy had coffee cups in their hands.

Too flustered to notice, she missed the looks on their faces until Kathy said, "I guess we get to taste the Montana excitement."

"Like what?" Hannah asked, thinking her mother must be referring to Sunday.

"The bear was here after all," Jake said, a little shamefaced, Hannah thought. "He tore up the spring house."

"Thought we would have heard that much damage," Roy commented, carefully nursing his steaming cup. "At least he left the coffee."

"You would say that. After this mess," Kathy said.

"It is a mess," Jake said, making a face.

Hannah walked over to the living room window to see for herself. She figured they were all just leading her along. One look persuaded her otherwise. The spring house lay torn open, the roof leaning the other direction, Jake's recent work completely undone.

"I said it was a mess," Jake said from the couch.

"He ate all the food," Roy commented. "That's why there's no breakfast. Do you normally starve your visitors in Montana?"

"Roy," Kathy rebuked him, but only halfheartedly.

"By the way," Roy raised his eyebrows. "Who was out last? To the springhouse?"

"You mean last night?" Kathy's hand flew to her mouth.

"Yes. Last night," Roy said. "Didn't I see you go?"

"It was me," Kathy said. "Oh my. Do you think?"

"I wouldn't be blaming anyone," Jake spoke up.

"I'm so sorry," Kathy said. "Do you think I didn't fasten the door right?"

"Could be," Roy told her. "You're not used to such things."

"He would have gotten in anyway," Jake said. "You just never know."

"It's okay, Mom," Hannah agreed with Jake. "It's a wild country in many ways."

"I'm still sorry," Kathy said.

"It could have been me," Hannah assured her mother, turning to look out the window.

Hannah felt a sickening feeling turn in her stomach at the sight of the spring house. This land was dangerous, and now her retreat to Indiana had been cut off. For the first time a grudge against Jake's calling entered her heart, a bitter thought burning through her. Why had God chosen Jake? To torment her? Surely Jake could do something about it. Yet she knew nothing could be done.

Above the fallen spring house Hannah saw the Cabinet Mountains filling the skyline. They seemed to be smirking this morning, proud of the destruction they had produced. Seeming even taller than normal, they were lording it over her and driving home the point as to who was in control.

"Well? What are we doing about breakfast?" Roy asked. "Should a man just blow away because the bear has been here?"

"There's a carton of eggs left," Jake said. "They're on the kitchen table. I found them against the corner of the spring house. Some bacon, too. A little bit."

"But the bear," Kathy told him, her voice full of meaning.

"He didn't touch it," Jake assured her.

Her mother was unconvinced, Hannah could tell, as was she. At the moment, though, the thought struck her how all of this had been handled without someone waking her. *Why hadn't Jake come in and told her? Did he intend to shoulder the responsibility by himself? Didn't he care anymore what she thought about things?*

Then she strove to control her thoughts. Surely he did care. It was just the shock of the bear's destruction and yesterday that had her emotions so torn.

"Will someone make the bacon and eggs?" Roy asked insistently.

"But the bear," Kathy repeated.

"Jake and I don't care," Roy said, to which Jake nodded.

"I have some cold cereal," Hannah offered, bringing her thoughts back to what needed to be done.

Her mother made a face. "That's better than bear slobber, I do declare."

"You're just being dramatic," Roy told her. "No matter. Just more for Jake and me."

Kathy ignored him, getting up to follow Hannah, who was already walking towards the kitchen. Opening the oven lid, Hannah arranged the kindling wood, striking a match to start the fire. The smoke from the small flame curled around in the oven box, then came up the lid instead of going towards the back and the stove pipe. Irritated, Hannah replaced the lid and the fire promptly went out.

"Can't even start the fire," she muttered.

"It's just one of those mornings," her mother said, trying to be encouraging, Hannah knew.

Lifting the lid, Hannah tried again, checking to make sure the damper was open, waving at the smoke as it tried to come up the lid again. Slowly, the column moved sideways and then the draw started, the flames licking hungrily on the wood. Adding several larger pieces, she closed the lid.

With the cold cereal on the table and the bacon and eggs fried, Kathy called into the living room that breakfast was ready. They bowed their heads in prayer, but Jake didn't pray out loud. Perhaps he was too disturbed, Hannah figured, not supposing it mattered either way. Jake would be doing plenty of praying in the future, whether he wanted to or not.

Hannah felt the bitterness again and wished it wasn't there, but what was she supposed to do about it? Jake needed her now more than ever, and help she was glad to give, but why wasn't her heart cooperating?

Kathy still refused to take any eggs or bacon, even when Roy insisted. She settled for cold cereal. "No bear for me," she proclaimed.

"More for us," Roy said with a chuckle, a little too genuinely, Hannah thought, but perhaps her father was as hungry as she was. Overcoming her initial resistance, Hannah took an egg and two pieces of bacon. Jake and Roy divided the remainder between them.

They were still not done when the sounds of a pickup pulling up to the cabin reached them.

"Who would that be?" Jake wondered, getting up.

"Mr. Brunson," Hannah guessed, staying seated. Jake could talk to him.

"His food will get cold," Kathy worried, ever the mother, as Jake walked towards the front door.

"He'll probably be right back," Hannah guessed again.

As if to confirm her conclusions, Jake came back almost immediately, seating himself.

"He's going to wait till we're done with breakfast," Jake said, giving only the conclusion of the conversation with Mr. Brunson.

"What does he want?" Hannah asked.

"He wants us to help him," Jake said, picking up his fork again.

When Hannah kept looking at him he finally offered, "He wants help burying the bear."

"What!" Kathy exclaimed. "Is it dead?"

"Yes," Jake nodded. "Mr. Brunson shot it."

"Shot it?" Now Roy got his exclamation in. "Shot the bear?"

"That's what he said," Jake nodded again.

"But can you do that?" Kathy wanted to know.

"I guess if it's bothering you," Roy shrugged his shoulders. "Don't you think?"

"I don't think so," Jake said. "Don't know much about it. This was a grizzly. From what Mr. Brunson was saying, he seems to think he did something quite illegal. Might even be federal."

"So why are you going to help him?" Kathy was now thoroughly aroused.

"He tore up my spring house," Jake said.

"That's not a good enough reason," Kathy told him.

"Seems so to me." Jake continued eating. "Kind of solves the problem. That is if we help him bury it."

Her mother was now really distressed, Hannah could tell. She didn't know what to say, torn between gladness the bear was no more and a queasy feeling something wasn't quite right about this.

"Jake shouldn't be doing this," Kathy addressed Roy, who wasn't saying anything.

"We'll need his help too," Jake said, calmly enough considering the subject he was addressing.

"How are you digging this hole?" Roy wanted to know.

Jake shrugged. "Mr. Brunson didn't say. Just wanted the horse to drag the bear. I think Mossy can do it." Apparently Jake had a lot of confidence in his horse's strength.

Kathy still looked at Roy, astonishment all over her face. "I can't believe you. They put people in jail for these things."

Roy didn't say she was wrong, Hannah noticed, as the unease grew in her. "Maybe you shouldn't help," she ventured.

"But it tore up my spring house," Jake said, a little heatedly now. "It's going to cost to build again. You know we have to have one."

"I'll help," Roy told him. "Even pay some. Since it might be partly our fault. We're still here for two days. Surely we can do it in that time."

Hannah knew Jake was more worried about the lack of funds than the time required to rebuild, but she said nothing.

"How illegal is this?" Roy wanted to know.

"Why does that matter?" Kathy asked in his direction. "Illegal is illegal."

"I suppose so," Roy allowed, but Hannah could tell he still wanted to know.

"Pretty," Jake told him. "If it's federal as Mr. Brunson seemed to think."

"You're a minister now," Roy said slowly, seeming to think carefully on each word. "You shouldn't be taking chances."

"It's not right anyway," Kathy said. "If it's not right, then it's not right."

"That's right," Roy agreed, but Hannah knew the minister point was carrying a lot of weight with Jake. She could tell by the sober look on his face. A stab of bitterness went through her again. *Were they to be haunted now by this responsibility? Was everything in life now to be weighed by whether Jake was a minister or not? Apparently so.*

"Maybe we should be cautious," Jake allowed, confirming Hannah's conclusions.

"We'd better ask Mr. Brunson in," Roy decided, the last of his breakfast done. Pushing back his plate he got up, and Jake followed him into the living room. Wanting to be in on the conversation, Hannah and Kathy left the dishes until the more pressing matter was resolved.

Jake went out to invite Mr. Brunson in, and he came, seeming hesitant. He took the chair Hannah offered him.

Roy cleared his throat. "About this bear thing. We were just talking after Jake told us."

"Yes, I shot it," Mr. Brunson said. "It has killed the other two of my pigs. Enough is enough. I see it tore up your son-in-law's spring house. I say this situation should just be handled between us."

"Was it legal though?" Roy asked.

"Probably not," Mr. Brunson said. "This is wild country around here. Not like Indiana at all." That went without saying, Hannah thought, but Mr. Brunson continued. "The authorities don't take lightly to having their grizzlies shot. Federal programs, I think. It might be best to bury the thing. Just have it over with."

"I can understand that," Roy said softly enough, "but burying things doesn't always solve the problem."

Mr. Brunson seemed to think on that for a moment. "I guess that's true," he agreed, saying the words with sorrow in his voice, Hannah noticed. She wondered why that should be. Perhaps Mr. Brunson knew this to be true from some past experience, but then most people would, she figured.

"We really are uncomfortable with this," Roy was saying. "With Jake's spring house tore open and your pigs dead, maybe the authorities would be understanding."

"Don't depend on it," Mr. Brunson said, bitterness in his voice now. "They get a lot of things wrong."

"Still...we must do what is right," Roy told him. "Jake just got ordained as a minister yesterday. It might not be good to involve him. If you bury the grizzly, he will be involved."

"Ordained." Mr. Brunson paused, looking puzzled, then let the matter be. "I can't do this by myself. I'm a little old," he chuckled ruefully.

"It might be best just to let the authorities know," Roy suggested. "I'm sorry about that. I know you are the one who shot the bear."

Mr. Brunson snorted in disgust, as if a bitter thought had just passed through his mind, but he answered kindly enough. "I suppose so. What is to be, will be. Didn't Shakespeare say something like that?" He laughed dryly.

Roy didn't say anything, not just because he didn't know anything about Shakespeare, but because he was waiting for Mr. Brunson to arrive at his decision. Such tough choices shouldn't be hurried, Hannah knew her father had always believed.

Mr. Brunson seemed to be struggling with competing thoughts. He didn't wait too long, though. "Let's do it," he said. "I'll go call the game warden."

Hannah felt a deep concern for the old man. *Surely he wouldn't go to jail because of her father's advice.*

CHAPTER NINETEEN

KATHY AND HANNAH watched in a mixture of fear and fascination as the vehicles rolled in. There was, to Hannah, the familiar game warden's truck, then a dozen others with all sorts of markings.

When Hannah thought there couldn't be any more, the area surely having emptied itself of law officers, two more vehicles, dark green in color, came up the dirt road. They had Federal Wildlife Officer written in a half circle on each driver's side door.

"They do take this seriously," Kathy said, awe in her voice. "You think Mr. Brunson's going to jail?"

"He's still there." Hannah motioned towards the yard where Jake, Roy, and Mr. Brunson were surrounded by three officers. The others had already left in the direction of Mr. Brunson's house.

The two federal vehicles pulled to a halt, one officer stepping out while the other remained inside, waiting. After a short conversation with a state officer, the federal officer returned to his vehicle and the two continued up the road towards Mr. Brunson's. Hannah could see them busily talking on their portable radios.

"He probably told them where the bear was," Kathy observed.

"Why didn't they take him along?" Hannah wondered.

"Better staying here than going to jail," Kathy said, as if that explained everything.

The state officer resumed his scribbling on a note pad. Beside him the other two officers seemed to be doing all the talking. A camera was then produced and pictures taken of the spring house.

After more conversation, two of the officers left, driving back to the main road. Jake came towards the cabin and Hannah met him at the front door.

Jake raised his eyebrows at the questions on Hannah's face.

"Well...tell us," Kathy said from behind her.

"Little scary," Jake said. "I thought for a moment there they were taking Mr. Brunson off in shackles. Made me feel pretty bad about the advice we gave him. Then they calmed down."

"So what are they doing with him?" Hannah wanted to know, her concern still not abated.

"The game warden's talking about a big fine at the least. Said there's no excuse for this kind of thing."

"Even with what happened?" Hannah felt indignation fill her.

"Grizzlies come first, I guess," Jake shrugged. "Can't shoot them unless they really threaten life and limb. The game warden said he would have taken care of it."

"Mr. Brunson already spoke to him about it." Hannah felt her feelings growing stronger. "Did you tell the others that?"

"Yes," Jake said. "I said it several times. Don't think the warden wanted it said, especially in front of the other officers. I did anyway."

"Maybe it helped," Kathy offered.

"Maybe," Jake allowed. "We can't help with the fine, though. It sounds big."

"How much?" Hannah wondered, thinking of their small bank account.

"Thousands of dollars, from what it sounds like. Depends on the judge," Jake said.

Seeing her father and Mr. Brunson walking towards the

cabin, Hannah opened the door again. Mr. Brunson looked grim enough, she thought.

"I feel bad," her father was saying. "It's partly our fault. You wanted to bury the bear. I wasn't expecting, well...not this reaction. Figured they'd take it serious, some you know. Not quite like that."

"Sorry for the scare, ladies," Mr. Brunson told Kathy and Hannah. "I guess we lived through it."

"So how are you?' Kathy wanted to know. "It looked bad enough from here."

"Our friendly government at work," Mr. Brunson said smiling. "They think grizzlies are a big concern."

"No jail though?" Kathy asked.

"No," Mr. Brunson chuckled a little. "Will have to go before the judge."

"That's too bad," Kathy told him.

"Better this way," Mr. Brunson said, as if he were trying to put them all at ease. "It wouldn't have been good doing this my way."

"It's still hard," Kathy told him.

"Yes," Mr. Brunson agreed, "as I'm learning. Yet hard is better sometimes."

Again Hannah got the distinct feeling Mr. Brunson was talking about something more than just the decision to disclose the grizzly shooting. She debated asking him what that might be, but decided it was none of her business.

"Expect these folks to stay around awhile," Mr. Brunson shook his head. "What a fuss they make."

As if to accent his words, a large county dump truck rumbled past the cabin, roaring loudly as it started to climb the grade towards Mr. Brunson's place. Moments later a tractor trailer with a backhoe on it followed.

Mr. Brunson shook his head again. "They do take it serious."

"I guess they don't have too many grizzlies," Roy said.

"I guess not," Mr. Brunson agreed. "Well...I must be going. I guess they'll let me go back to the house."

"Surely," Kathy said, sounding shocked.

"I think so," Mr. Brunson assured her. "I just have to take care of this." Taking an official piece of paper out of his pocket he waved it around gingerly.

"His citation," Roy said dryly.

"Next month. In front of the judge." Mr. Brunson looked sober enough. "Lots of money. Just gone," he snapped his fingers.

Hannah could see Jake was thinking about all that money, but she knew they had none to offer.

"At least you're not in jail," Kathy spoke up.

"Of that I'm thankful," Mr. Brunson agreed. "Enough excitement for one day, don't you think?"

"I should say so," Kathy agreed.

"Your spring house," Mr. Brunson said towards Jake. "They are fixing it, aren't they?"

Jake nodded his head.

"Good. Let me know if they don't. Like that would do any good," Mr. Brunson chuckled at his own joke. "See you all later."

"What a morning," Kathy sighed, when Mr. Brunson was out of earshot. "Poor fellow. Brave, too, making the hard choice like he did."

"I'm glad we didn't help bury the bear. Especially after this," Roy said, motioning towards the mountain and the dozen or so vehicles that were still up at Mr. Brunson's place.

"What was this about paying for the spring house?" Hannah asked. "Who are they?"

"The state," Jake told her. "The game warden said the state would pay. We need to wait until tomorrow — that is, before we do repairs."

"Really." Hannah was surprised.

"Yes," Jake nodded.

"But should you?" Kathy asked. "That's government money."

"I think they should," Roy said quietly. "It was their bear. It's not like Jake would be taking anything for free."

"I suppose so," her mother said, not sounding too convinced, Hannah thought. She didn't know how convinced she herself was, but how were they going to pay for the spring house? They did need one. It was all they had to cool food items, and like her father said, they weren't taking the money for free.

"The state's bear did tear it up," Hannah said out loud.

"I'm glad Indiana doesn't own any bears," Kathy said, making a face.

"They probably do," Roy told her. "You just don't know it."

"At least they're not running around my front yard," Kathy told him.

The reminder of Indiana caused a pang to run through Hannah. Tomorrow would be her parents' last day, and the hope of Indiana being her home had left even before they did.

Kathy must have noticed her face. "Did I say something?"

"Just Indiana," Hannah told her, not wanting to explain further. Saying more in front of Jake would just add to his burden.

"I see," Kathy said, understanding. "I guess Sunday did take care of that."

Hannah waited, expecting Jake to ask why, but he must have been thinking of something else.

"I need to get a list of materials together," he said in Roy's direction. "If I take it to the lumber yard this afternoon, maybe they can have it out tomorrow. I can show the state the materials list then."

"I'll be glad to help tomorrow," Roy told him, offering even before Jake asked. Jake got a piece of paper and pen from the desk, and together they walked out to the spring house.

"I am glad Roy came along," Kathy said again. "Funny how he worried about what he would do while he was here."

JERRY EICHER

Two state vehicles came back down from Mr. Brunson's followed by the game warden's truck. When neither stopped, Kathy and Hannah went to prepare lunch sandwiches. Even with the morning's excitement, people still had to eat.

In the kitchen, Hannah felt an overwhelming urge to sneeze and quickly stepped outside. She had quite a little sneezing fit. Out by the spring house, Jake must have heard and looked in her direction. When she smiled and gave a little wave, Jake continued what he was doing. Back inside her mother glanced up.

"A cold?" she asked.

"Just excitement," Hannah said, hoping she was right. She felt no other signs of a cold.

"It could be hard with your pregnancy," Kathy commented.

"Nothing serious though?" Hannah wanted to know.

"You can't take the usual medicines. So you have to live through it."

"I never take much anyway."

"You always were like that," Kathy agreed.

"Just doesn't do much good," Hannah reminded her mother.

Hannah's nose tingled again but quit when she rubbed it.

"Hopefully that's it," she said, sure her mother had noticed the motion.

"You will see a doctor soon though?"

"About a cold?"

"No," Kathy chuckled, "about your pregnancy."

Hannah nodded. "Betty said there is one in Libby. I'll make an appointment soon."

"That would be good. You think the men want dinner early?"

"I suppose. As cold as it is," Hannah said, as outside another state vehicle went by, followed by the lumbering dump truck.

"There goes your bear," Kathy said with distaste.

"He does seem different. Now that he's dead," Hannah said.

"What a way to die. Even for an animal."

"He did tear up my spring house. I'm not shedding too many tears."

"You think he had a mate?" Kathy glanced up from the sandwiches she was making.

"Grizzlies aren't like us," Hannah said.

"If he'd just stayed up in the mountains he would have been safe. Wonder why he didn't?"

"Our spring house would still be up. Mr. Brunson's hogs alive."

"They are awful creatures," Kathy agreed.

"Especially at night," Hannah shivered, remembering the first night Jake's light had found the bear at the edge of the woods.

"Now he's gone for good," Kathy said. "It's just as well, I suppose."

When the sandwiches were ready, Hannah called the news out to her father and Jake, even though it wasn't quite lunch time. There seemed to be no objections as they came right in. Afterwards, Jake hitched up Mossy and left for town with Roy. They took along the grocery list for Hannah, returning with the items and the news the lumber would be delivered that afternoon yet.

Since they were under orders not to work on the spring house till tomorrow, Roy decided that couldn't mean cleaning up around the building. Jake wasn't so sure, but gave in simply from the itch to get started, Hannah believed. She felt nervous for the rest of the afternoon, certain a government official would stop in and fine Jake and her father or maybe something worse. The lumber came just before five o'clock and was unloaded within reach of the spring house. By nightfall, when no one from the state had stopped by, Hannah relaxed a little.

After supper, the noise of gravel under tires tensed her up again. Jake opened the door and went out on the porch before anyone could knock. He said a cheery "Good evening, Mr. Brunson," moments later, so they all knew who it was.

"You want to come inside?" Jake's voice asked.

"Not really," Mr. Brunson said. "Just came to make sure everything was okay."

"Sure," Jake said. "Nobody stopped back by. They all went past. Anything new, though?"

"No," Mr. Brunson said, sticking his head in the door for a quick "Hi" to everyone. "Nothing new. I just have the court date in a month."

"We'll wish you the best then," Roy told him.

"Thanks," Mr. Brunson said. "When are you folks leaving?"

"Wednesday morning," Kathy told him.

"A safe trip then. Good to have met both of you." Mr. Brunson gave a quick nod in Kathy and Roy's direction.

"Thanks," Roy said. "Keep an eye on the children for us."

Mr. Brunson chuckled, "It's more like them keeping an eye on me."

"You're not that old," Kathy told him, smiling.

"Feels like it. Especially after today. But I have to be going." And with that Mr. Brunson excused himself.

"Nice fellow," Roy said when he was gone. "Even if he shoots bears."

"We like him," Jake told Roy, taking his seat on the couch again. "He is a good neighbor. I think that was partly why he shot the bear. He was trying to help us out."

"You think so?" Roy wondered.

"I do," Jake said, to which Hannah agreed.

CHAPTER TWENTY

NOT WANTING TO oversleep on her parents' last day, Hannah had set the alarm. She figured they would have to start the habit tomorrow anyway, with Jake going to work at the hardware. Even so, her mother was already in the kitchen lighting the fire when she came out.

"What are you up for?" Hannah asked, sighing.

"Couldn't sleep," Kathy muttered. "How do you get this thing going? It's been awhile."

"Don't know," Hannah said, because she didn't. "It's got a mind of its own. One time one way and the next the other."

"Now it's going." Kathy replaced the lid, obviously enjoying the conquest.

"It's your last day," Hannah said, the pain of the soon-coming parting starting to sink in.

"I know," Kathy said, glancing at her face. "Where did the time go? I'm so glad we came. My, what if we hadn't? You would have been here all alone through this time."

Not really wanting to think about *this time*, and what it would mean in the days ahead, Hannah changed the subject. "Do we have to take anything tonight?"

"I suppose so," Kathy said. "Betty didn't say. We'll just make something and take it along. Are the men going to get up?"

"I don't know. Jake groaned when the alarm went off."

"Dad will be out soon. Old people can't sleep." Kathy made a face.

"I heard that," Roy said from just beyond the kitchen opening, having walked up in his stocking feet. "Where's breakfast? Is there no service in this house?"

Kathy ignored him as he pulled out a kitchen chair.

"So how's the baby?" he asked Hannah.

"Okay, I guess," she told him.

"You take good care of him. Just remember that," he said, mock sternness in his voice.

"What if the baby's not a he?" she asked him.

"Doesn't matter," he said with a solid smile. "Either way works. Just so he's healthy."

"What if he's not?" Hannah asked, the sudden thought producing a stab of fear.

"Oh," her father seemed startled by the thought. "They usually are. Ours all were. Your mother wouldn't have them any other way."

"Roy," Kathy said from across the table.

"But I may not be like Mom," Hannah told him, knowing she wasn't and wondering if that would give her father pause.

"You're my daughter," he said, meeting her eyes. "That's good enough for me."

"I would hope so," Kathy told him. "It better be."

"You just trust *Da Hah*," Roy said. "He knows where He's leading."

Like with Jake and the minister ordination, Hannah wanted to say, but said instead, "I'll try."

She knew she would, it might just be hard. Jake's ordination had temporarily shaken her confidence in the path *Da Hah* chose for people. He seemed to have a very different point of view.

"Breakfast ready?" Jake asked, his head suddenly appearing in the kitchen opening.

"See," Roy said. "I told you."

"In just a moment," Kathy said with a smile.

"Why don't I get used like that?" Roy asked. "She was really nice to him."

"I thought we'd get an early start on the spring house," Jake stated with a grin, obviously enjoying the attention.

"It's too cold for an early start. I haven't even had coffee yet," Roy stated grumpily. "There's no service around here."

"Maybe they'd get some for me," Jake said, grinning again.

"I'm sure they would," Roy chuckled at his own joke.

"You're both spoiled," Hannah told them.

"You can say that again," Kathy seconded her.

"Maybe we ought to get that early start," Jake said in Roy's direction, "like right now."

"I'm not moving without my coffee," Roy said, pretending he had somehow fastened himself to his seat.

"You're leaving tomorrow," Hannah almost wailed, the suddenness of her emotions overcoming her. "Oh my. What am I going to do? It was so nice you could come."

"Yes it was," Jake added his approval. "It helped in ways you can't imagine."

"We'll be thinking of you. Both of you," Kathy assured them. "Now for breakfast. Did you put the meat outside?"

"On the shelf. When the men came home from town," Hannah told her.

Kathy stepped outside, returning with the bacon and eggs. Hannah started pancake batter, knowing her father would appreciate the gesture on his last morning in Montana.

"Now if we just had some blueberries for the pancakes," Roy said while Hannah was stirring the bowl.

"Talk about being spoiled," Kathy said.

"I wasn't serious," Roy said quickly, but Hannah knew he was.

"We haven't got any," she told him. "Sorry."

"It's okay," he said. "Coffee will do me."

Pouring the batter into the hot pan, Hannah wished she had blueberries, but she didn't. She also wished for some others things, like the hope of a better life in Indiana, only that was gone now. She wished Jake didn't have the burden of being a minister, but there was no choice in that matter either.

"Don't take it too hard," Roy said tenderly, meaning the blueberries, Hannah figured. She felt a tear slip down her cheek even though she tried to hold it back.

"I'll be okay," she managed. "You're leaving tomorrow," she said to explain why she was troubled.

"It's all for a reason," Roy said. Hannah figured he included this parting, and the thought warmed her heart.

"Maybe we could write more," Kathy squeezed her arm. "Maybe that would help."

She appreciated the gesture, but doubted whether writing would quite fill the void she felt in her heart.

"It wouldn't hurt," she said in reply. Perhaps it would help more than she thought it would. Her mother's ideas sometimes turned out that way.

They ate soon after that, then had a short devotion around the kitchen table. Hannah was used to moving into the living room and was surprised when Jake suggested otherwise. He was doing strange things like this since Sunday — sudden and unusual for him. This one was nice, she supposed, but it made her feel queasy in her stomach, as if her world no longer had foundations under it.

Jake and Roy left to work on the spring house, Jake offering Roy an extra coat, which he accepted. Hannah watched them for a moment as they set up, then joined Kathy to work in the kitchen. The sound of the men's hammering and sawing outside came and went all morning.

Kathy suggested they make cherry pie for the evening at Betty's, and Hannah wanted to make donuts. So they did both. The donuts were time-consuming, but Hannah wanted to stay busy. It would make the time go easier, as the day was already going much too fast.

Betty showed up around four with the surrey buggy, earlier than expected. The men were already in the house, relaxing, the spring house in fresh repair. Kathy and Hannah, wanting to get outside, walked out to meet Betty in the yard.

"So you believe in entertaining your visitors, I hear," Betty teased Hannah before she was even down from the buggy.

"What are you talking about?" Hannah asked, pretending not to know.

"Shooting bears," Betty said. "Your parents will never come west again."

"How did you find out?" Hannah wondered.

"You expect news like that to stay quiet? The whole town's talking," Betty informed her.

"Oh, no," Hannah groaned, imagining many eyes looking her way the next time she went shopping in Libby.

"It'll blow over," Betty assured her. "Does around here. Believe me."

"I'm real glad we came," Kathy said. "It was good to be here. For Sunday too."

"I would say so," Betty agreed. "Seems like the two of us are together when crisis strikes these two lives."

"Like not getting married." Kathy made a face. "You want to remember that?"

"Mom," Hannah protested, not wanting to be reminded. "We all get mixed up sometimes."

"I guess so," Kathy allowed. "At least you got straightened out."

"Seems so," Betty said. "Sunday would sure point in that direction. You two have any warning?"

Hannah wished Betty didn't just come out and say things like this, but then she wouldn't be Betty if she didn't.

"No. I didn't," she said, then added, "Jake never said anything either."

"I doubt if he did," Betty sighed. "I expect you wouldn't. Often surprises the people it happens to."

"You wouldn't have been wishing it was Steve?" Kathy asked skeptically. "Surely not?"

"No. Of course not," Betty said emphatically. "Just worried about it. I shouldn't have, I know. I did lay awake the night before thinking about it, not able to sleep. I know I never could handle it."

"You could have if it was the will of *Da Hah*," Kathy assured her.

"Yes, I guess," Betty said, but didn't sound too convinced. "So how are you holding up?" she asked Hannah.

Hannah shrugged, "It's a load for Jake. He took it pretty hard."

"What about you?" Betty asked.

Pondering for a moment whether to tell Betty, Hannah decided to plunge ahead. Betty might as well know. "I had been hoping to move back to Indiana. With Jake's job and all."

"Move!" Betty exclaimed. "Surely not?"

Hannah nodded, "It seemed like the right thing to do."

"Well, I'm glad," Betty said. "I mean…that you're staying here. Then Sunday, too. I think God knew what He was doing."

"Apparently He does," Hannah agreed halfheartedly.

"You'll see in time," Betty told her.

Hannah wasn't so certain about that, but she was glad Betty now knew about her disappointment in not moving to Indiana. Somehow it made her feel a little better for the sharing.

"I'll get Roy, and we'll go," Kathy said, moving back towards the house. "The young folks can come when they're ready."

"Hopefully not too late," Betty said.

"No," Hannah told her. "We're ready. I think Jake got Mossy ready before he came in. Didn't they do a good job on the spring house? The bear tore it up."

"Really tore it up," Kathy added.

"Maybe it was good someone shot it," Betty said. "It's the first grizzly I can remember coming down this far."

"Mr. Brunson will get a big fine for it," Hannah told her. "At least he was trying to help us out."

"Still shouldn't disobey the law, I guess." Betty got back in the buggy. "You two coming?"

"I'll get the pies," Kathy said. "Hannah can bring the

donuts. Unless you don't have room."

"We do," Hannah told her. "The whole back of the buggy is empty."

"What were you two doing baking?" Betty demanded.

"It's my supper."

"Well," Kathy smiled. "You didn't say anything. We couldn't just sit around all day."

"Someone will eat it." Betty made a face. "Shouldn't be me though."

"I'll help you carry the pies out," Hannah offered, as she and Kathy left together for the house. Jake was ready to go. They loaded the pies and then half the donuts in Betty's surrey, after it became obvious there was much more room there.

Jake had Mossy hitched by the time the women were done, and the two buggies followed each other. Pulling in Betty's driveway, Hannah was flooded with good memories from the summer spent here before her marriage. She wondered why the memories should come tonight. Perhaps God was trying to make things a little easier for her.

That thought brought the sting of tears to her eyes, which she hoped Jake wouldn't notice. He did, but seemed to understand, giving her a gentle smile. Again it struck her how fast he seemed to be growing up. His maturity at once was comforting and yet strange, unsettling in a way she would never have imagined.

All evening, no one mentioned Sunday, which was good, Hannah thought. Such mention would have only created discomfort.

They stayed late, considering Jake had to drive into Libby the next morning for his new job. No one mentioned that either. It was simply a night of family, of reveling in the company of loved ones. On the way home, Hannah felt nothing but peace. She thanked God He had comforted her for one evening at least.

CHAPTER TWENTY-ONE

HANNAH WOKE BEFORE the alarm clock went off to the sound of a van motor running outside the log cabin. Dressing quickly, she went out to find the kerosene lamp lit, her parents up, and the suitcases loaded.

"We wouldn't have left without saying good-by," Kathy whispered, giving Hannah a tight hug.

Her father offered her his hand, squeezing it a moment before letting go. "Make it good," he said. "The baby too."

Hannah stood watching from the open cabin door, wanting to be close to her parents for as long as possible, the chilly night air pouring in. The two forms disappeared into the van, the dome light blinked off, then the gravel crunched under the moving vehicle.

Glancing at the living room clock, Hannah figured there was no use going back to bed. She sat down on the couch and cried instead, an awful loneliness sweeping over her. Then she noticed Jake's Bible lying on the floor, the light from the kerosene lamp playing off the black cover, highlighting the gold letters. She thought of reading it.

The realization that Jake had been reading it held her back, for what that meant felt oppressive. He must have been studying for his sermons. They had been thrown into a strange, unknown land, and now Jake was venturing in. He had said little about the matter, but then her parents had been here.

Hannah had the feeling, though, Jake would not be

saying much anyway. He was walking into this new world, and it was up to her to follow if she wished. She felt left out, alone, and ashamed that she felt so.

Jake would be up at five-thirty, and that could serve as her alarm clock. So she lay back and dozed off. A fit of sneezing woke her before Jake came out of the bedroom. He found her blowing her nose in the kitchen.

"They're gone," he said, placing his hand on her shoulder, assuming she was crying. "I didn't hear them leave."

"I was sneezing," she told him. "I did cry earlier. This cold...it's coming back."

"What time did they leave?"

"Sometime before five or so."

"It was good to have them here."

She nodded. "I have to get breakfast ready."

"I'll get Mossy harnessed," he said, reaching for a gas lantern in the closet. Lighting it, he stepped outside and walked towards the barn, the light rising and falling with each step. Hannah took a moment to watch him go, feeling loneliness growing again.

I'll get over it, she told herself resolutely. *I have Jake and soon the baby. Betty. I'll see Mom and Dad again.* Feeling a little better she went back to making breakfast. While they were eating, Hannah was glad for Jake's good mood. It offset what she was feeling, but perhaps that came mostly from the stuffiness in her head. Then Jake left while it was still dark, since he had to be at the hardware store well before it opened.

With the sound of the buggy wheels gone, she gave in to despair and threw herself on the couch. There she lay, feeling guilty, but unable to get up. She awoke just before ten to waves of panic. The dishes were still on the kitchen table and the house in disarray from her parents' visit. Jake had never said anything about her house cleaning, but she didn't want to take any chances. She often had visions of Jake growing up in a house kept spotless by the unswerving diligence of his mother.

By late afternoon, her sneezing had developed into a full-blown cold. She gave in again to tiredness and was sleeping on the couch when an insistent knock awoke her. Thoroughly embarrassed, she saw a buggy in the driveway and hoped it was Betty's. If it was someone else, she didn't know how she would ever live down the shame of having been caught sleeping in the middle of the afternoon. The visitor surely must have seen her through the front window.

"Hannah," Betty's voice came clearly from outside the door.

Relieved, she rushed to open it, sure her embarrassment still showed on her face.

"Hannah," Betty said when she opened. "I have to come in."

"What?" Hannah felt alarm running through her at the expression on Betty's face. "Is something wrong?"

Betty said nothing, pushing past Hannah and sitting on the couch. She motioned for Hannah to be seated.

Numbly, Hannah obeyed.

"There's been a wreck," Betty said simply. "Pretty bad from how it sounds."

"Mom and Dad?"

"Yes...well the van they were in. A driver came across the median."

"How bad?"

"Don't know for sure." Betty shifted on the couch, and Hannah was certain Betty wasn't saying everything she knew. Reaching out, Hannah grabbed her arm.

"You must tell me."

"Someone's dead, I think. The state police wouldn't release the information."

"Who?" Hannah knew her fingers were digging into Betty's arm.

"They said...the state police. They called your cousin's house. The Mennonite."

"Then it's not Mom or Dad?"

Betty shrugged. "You wouldn't think so. Maybe you should come down to the house until we find out."

"Did they say who was hurt?"

"No. Just the hospital number." Betty answered the next question before Hannah asked. "I called from the neighbor's. That's who I use for emergencies. Your cousin called there and left a message. No one at the hospital would give information out, and they said neither of your parents were available."

Hannah's face showed her distress. "Did you ask for someone else?"

"I couldn't think of their names."

"There was Bishop Amos and his wife."

"I know," Betty nodded her head rapidly. "I couldn't talk with them either. I just had to come and let you know."

"So what should we do?" Hannah wondered out loud. "Where is the hospital?"

"In Buffalo, Wyoming. They've been driving all day."

"We can't go there then," Hannah voiced her thoughts.

"I don't know. Depends how bad it is. We may have to."

"I'll leave a note for Jake then," Hannah decided, getting up. "Maybe we can catch him on the way home. He goes right past your place. If not, he can come over afterwards."

"I think so," Betty said, standing up.

"I've got a cold," Hannah said, her running nose demanding attention as she went to write the note. "Bad one."

"Why does everything come at once?" Betty expressed her despair. "They were just here. How can this happen?"

"I don't know," Hannah told her, equally distraught, feeling a general numbness. Carefully she wrote the note to Jake, stating she was over at Betty's waiting for news about a wreck.

Betty now seemed in a hurry to go, so Hannah got her coat. The crisp coldness of the outside air caught her by surprise and provoked another bout of sneezing.

"You shouldn't be out in this," Betty said, climbing in the buggy.

Hannah thought she shouldn't be in any of this, in

the bear trouble and the financial strain and the minister's duties and the loneliness and now the terrible anxiety over her parents' lives, but she didn't feel like expressing the emotion to Betty. God was still in charge, she forcefully reminded herself, even though it didn't feel like it.

"You sure are taking this well," Betty commented, glancing at her when she took her seat in the buggy. "Here, wrap yourself in the blanket." Betty gave Hannah an extra share.

"I don't know how I'm doing," Hannah told her. Maybe she was getting a share of Jake's bravery, she thought, hoping it was true. At least it seemed to be coming from somewhere.

"What if it's them?" Betty asked, fear in her voice as she let out the reins.

The buggy jerked forward as Hannah's bravery fled. Betty drove much too fast towards the blacktop road and her neighbor's house. Hannah used her handkerchief liberally, unable to distinguish between the tears from her cold and the tears from her fears.

"We don't bother Mrs. Emery too much," Betty said, pulling to a stop. "Steve wants to talk with Bishop Nisley about a phone in the barn. Something needs to be done about our phone situation, I've been telling Steve. Otherwise it's the phone booth in Libby."

"We can go into Libby," Hannah said, even with the urgency of knowing her parents' condition. "We might be a bother here."

"Mrs. Emery won't mind. Not in an emergency," Betty assured her, getting out to tie the horse. Moments later they were at the door, but no one answered their knock. Listening, they heard only silence.

"She must have gone to town," Betty concluded.

"We'd better just use the phone there," Hannah said.

"I suppose we have no choice."

The matter decided, they drove into Libby, stopping at the grocery store on the edge of town.

"I could go on down and tell Jake," Hannah observed. "Now that we're here."

"We'd better get some information first," Betty told her.

"That would be best," Hannah agreed. "If someone will tell us anything."

"I'll make them," Betty said resolutely, then her face faltered. "Here's the phone number. Maybe you can call?"

Hannah felt a quiver of fear at what might lie at the end of her phone call, but figured she might as well hear the news straight. She desperately wanted to believe the information wouldn't be too bad.

"I'll get some coins," Hannah said, remembering that lots of coins might be needed. "In the grocery store."

"I have some." Betty reached in her coat pocket.

Hannah wasn't sure how many were needed, but the few quarters Betty produced seemed insufficient.

"I'd better get more," she said. When Betty raised no objections, Hannah went inside. Coming back, she dropped quarters in and dialed the number from Betty's piece of paper. Her fingers trembled in the cold wind swirling around the phone booth, her nervousness only making things worse.

She dropped in more coins as directed by a digitized recording, then a distinct voice answered, "Good afternoon. Buffalo hospital. May I help you?"

"This is Hannah Byler," she said. "I am calling to talk with my mother, Kathy Miller. We had a report of an accident. My parents were involved."

Betty wrapped her coat tightly around Hannah, the wind whipping even harder than it had on the drive into town. Hannah bent away from the blast, trying to use the sides of the phone booth to get a measure of shelter. She expected the voice on the phone to tell her Kathy Miller wasn't available.

"I will page her," the voice said instead.

Silence followed for a few minutes, in which time the digitized voice came back on, "You have fifty seconds before your time expires."

With cold fingers, her nose running furiously, Hannah

dropped in several more quarters. She wished fervently she had obtained more.

"Yes," her mother's hesitant voice came on the phone.

"Mom." Hannah forgot the wind and the cold, gladness leaping into her voice.

"Hannah," Kathy said. "How did you find us?"

"Betty," Hannah told her. She could see Betty waiting anxiously at her elbow. "The state police called Indiana. They wouldn't give us any news, though. Are you okay?" Hannah left the rest of the question dangling.

"Bishop Amos didn't make it," Kathy's voice broke, coming faintly over the phone line.

"Amos." Hannah thought of Sunday, the ordination, the bishop's hands on Jake's head. "He's gone?"

"Yes," Kathy said. "It turned the van on the side. We slid for a ways."

"What about you and Dad?" Hannah could see Betty out of the corner of her eye, following this end of the conversation.

"Dad's got a broken arm. I'm okay. I dropped on him, I think, when the van turned. Everybody else just has bruises."

"Should we come?" Hannah asked.

"No," Kathy said quickly. "That's not necessary. Things are being arranged. We'll get home. There's the funeral, of course, for Amos. You're not close family though."

"Okay." Hannah was thinking quickly, the digitized voice in her ear, *You have thirty seconds in which to conclude this call. Please insert more coins if you wish to continue.* "Will you let us know when you get home then?"

"Through Betty," Kathy agreed. "I think I have her neighbor's phone number at home."

You have fifteen seconds, the voice said.

"Bye," Hannah said, knowing her voice sounded hurried but figuring her mother would understand.

"We'll be okay," Kathy's assuring voice came back. "Please don't worry."

Then the call was disconnected.

"It was Bishop Amos," Betty said, already knowing the answer.

Hannah nodded. "I should tell Jake."

CHAPTER TWENTY-TWO

BETTY STAYED IN the buggy while Hannah went into the hardware to tell Jake. She thought of asking for him at the front desk but decided to simply search. He was working somewhere, she figured. It would give her a chance to see what the hardware looked like.

She found him on the third aisle she glanced down, unpacking items from a large cardboard box and placing them on the shelves.

"Jake," she whispered, approaching him.

"Hannah," he said, standing up. "Why are you here?"

"There's been an accident. With Mom and Dad's van," she whispered, hoping the owner wouldn't see her and think she was taking up Jake's time unnecessarily.

"Your parent's?" he asked, concern crossing his face. "Are they okay?"

She nodded quickly, "Dad's got a broken arm. It's Bishop Amos, though. He didn't make it."

"On no." Jake set the case of batteries he was holding on the floor. "That's unbelievable. He was just here on Sunday."

Hannah saw Jake's face darken then fill with sorrow as she nodded.

"So sudden," he said.

"Yes," she agreed. " Mom didn't know when the funeral would be."

"We can't go," Jake said slowly.

"He's not our relative," she replied, not certain whether Jake wanted to go or not. *Would what happened Sunday give Jake reason to attend?*

"Maybe some of the others will go," Jake seemed to be thinking, then shook his head.

"I'd better be going," she told him. "Stop in for me at Betty's."

"I'll do that," he said.

She turned to go, glancing back at him when she got to the end of the aisle. His back was already bent over the carton again. *So quickly,* she thought, *life can change, and yet it continues on again.*

Back at Betty's place, Hannah got out and helped unhitch. As she took the horse into the barn, the memories flooded her again. Here she had worked that summer, dreaming about what life would be like with Jake. Then she had thought she should go another way. The pleasantness and confusion of those decisions now all ran together in her mind.

She gave Betty's horse a shovel of oats, not certain whether this was normal or not, but figured he deserved the treat after his cold run into town. In the house, Betty got her settled down at once on the couch, bringing out a blanket and then tea.

"I should be doing something," Hannah soon insisted, getting up.

"No. You need the rest," Betty told her. "It's probably a collapse from having your parents here, and now the news."

"I suppose it didn't help," Hannah allowed, settling back on the couch. She had to admit the mothering did feel good. She let the cozy feeling comfort her, protected for the moment from the swirling world of responsibility.

"You can't take anything for that cold. Nothing stronger than tea," Betty hollered from the kitchen, where she was busy working.

"I hadn't planned on it," Hannah told her. "Mom already mentioned that."

"It'll be over soon. Just seven more months," Betty said, apparently trying to supply comfort but succeeding only in making the time sound even longer.

Jake drove in the driveway just as dusk was falling. Hannah got up quickly, wanting to catch him before he started to tie up. But as she was getting her coat, Betty popped out of the kitchen.

"Tell Jake you're staying for supper," Betty said.

"We can't," Hannah replied, though wanting to stay, the loneliness of just her and Jake in the cabin weighing on her.

"Go tell him," Betty said, not taking no for an answer. "He can tie up at the barn. There's a horse blanket inside — you know where."

Giving in, Hannah put her coat on and went to tell Jake. He raised no objections, seeming happy with the invitation. She got the horse blanket for him as he tied Mossy to the ring on the barn door — the same ring she used when she worked here. Behind them Steve's buggy pulled in, and Hannah left for the house as Jake waited.

How Betty made so much food since they got back from town, Hannah couldn't figure out. She insisted on helping Betty set the table, though Betty wanted her to return to the couch. When Jake and Steve came in, the women joined the men in the living room where Betty filled Steve in on the details of the day.

Later, around the table, Steve led in prayer. He thanked God for protection for those who survived the van wreck and asked for grace and comfort for Bishop Amos's family. He prayed in simple words first, then closed out with a more formal prayer that Hannah was sure came from the Sunday prayer book.

"We still have much to be thankful for," Steve wrapped up his own thoughts. "Even with Amos gone."

"You think anyone will go to the funeral from here?" Betty wondered. "It's a long way back east."

"Bishop Nisley might," Steve allowed, then glanced sharply at Jake.

Hannah wondered what the look was about but didn't have to wait long.

"Makes for just one preacher here Sunday," Steve said. "Except Jake."

"You don't think so!" Betty exclaimed. "Not already. It was only last Sunday."

Steve shrugged as it dawned on Hannah what Steve was referring to. She glanced at Jake, but he was paying attention to his food.

"It's way too early," Betty continued. "Way too early. It was only a week yet. Or almost."

"I was just suggesting it might happen," Steve said apologetically. "Maybe Jake could use the warning."

Jake still said nothing, a worried look on his face.

"You shouldn't say things like that. It might not even happen," Betty said to Steve.

"It's okay," Jake finally said. "I'm glad Steve said something. I suppose God will give grace one way or the other."

"I suppose so," Steve allowed.

Hannah glanced at Jake, greatly surprised at what he just said. It sounded awfully spiritual to her. *Was this what lay ahead of them? Jake becoming more and more like this while she remained just herself?* The question caused her considerable discomfort.

"How's the new job going?" Steve asked, changing the subject.

"Okay," Jake told him. "Brings in some money. Not much," he shrugged. "Maybe with the log furniture business later."

"So Mr. Howard is serious then?" Steve asked.

"Seems to be," Jake said. "There's room out back. Heated and everything. Thinks with exposure on the web it should work. We could ship the orders out then."

"Sounds interesting," Steve allowed.

"You won't get ripped off?" Betty wanted to know. "Working with an Englishman like that?"

"I'm not putting any money in," Jake said with a weary

smile. "Don't have any to put in. Guess he could fire me."

"Pretty decent man," Steve said quickly. "At least he's always been with me."

"You let us know if things get too bad this winter," Betty told them. "That goes for both of you. If Jake won't say anything, Hannah can."

"God will help us," Jake said, sounding spiritual again, Hannah thought.

"God will starve you too," Betty told him. "That's what family is for — helping out."

"It's not that bad, surely," Steve said with a chuckle. "God will always help those who obey him. That's what King David said."

"He never had to live through a Montana winter," Betty retorted.

Even Jake had to chuckle at that, and Hannah let herself join in their laughter. She did wonder what Betty meant though. Betty's life had always seemed pretty smooth from what Hannah knew. Later, helping Betty with the dishes, Hannah felt like asking but decided not to. Betty was just being her skeptical self, she figured.

Expecting Jake to be in a hurry to leave, Hannah was surprised when he stayed until after eight. When they finally stepped outside, Hannah had to pull her coat tighter around herself, her eyes watering from the sting of the wind. She hoped the weather wouldn't undo all the good effects of Betty's tea and cozy living room.

On the drive home, Jake seemed lost in his own thoughts. Hannah waited until they were in the living room with the kerosene lamp flickering before she asked him.

"You think you'll have to preach on Sunday already?"

"It could happen," he allowed.

"Are you ready?" she asked.

"How does one get ready for something like that?" he asked wearily. "I've never even spoken in front of people before."

His young face was lined with worry. Hannah leaned

against his shoulder, wanting to give and receive comfort, somehow, all at the same time.

"Do you think this was supposed to happen?" she ventured.

"How would I know?" He turned towards her, his face now in shadows. "We are not to question such things."

"I can't help it," she said.

"There is no choice," he said simply. "No choice at all."

"We can still move to Indiana," she said, knowing she was grasping at straws, but needing to say it anyway. "Maybe it wasn't supposed to mean that."

"You know we can't," he said, the light of the lamp playing on his face. "This is where we belong."

"What about me?" she asked. "I don't know if I can make it. Now you are a preacher."

Jake turned towards Hannah, gathering her in both arms, pulling her close. "That means nothing between us," he said. "We are still the same."

"No we aren't," she said, letting herself sink into his embrace, wanting a closeness to sweep her heart — but the feeling wasn't coming. "You are changing. So fast."

"It's for the Lord's work," he said, letting his embrace loosen. "Can't you understand that?"

"What about us?" she asked, sitting up. "The baby is coming too."

"God will take care of us," he said. "He will."

"I need you," she almost wailed, letting her agony surface. "I need you the way you were. I'm losing you, Jake. You're so spiritual. You're having to preach. Maybe even on Sunday already, in front of all those people. I wasn't made for this. What am I going to do? Now we can't move to Indiana."

"You shouldn't talk like that," he said, gently enough, but the pain wasn't going away.

"I can't help it." She felt the tears coming now. "Our lives are so young. This is all too much. It's not fair — it's not fair of God, it's not fair of the church, it's not fair to ask this of us. There were others much older. Even Steve and Betty could have handled it better. Now Bishop Amos is dead. What if that happens to us? I couldn't stand it, Jake. I couldn't. I don't think I can stand this."

He reached out for her hands, holding both of hers in his.

"We have no choice," he said simply, obviously thinking that was all the answer needed. "There is no other way to go. We cannot turn back. If we do, it's like forsaking God and his church. We cannot do it."

That he was right, she knew, but it did nothing for the pain. To turn back would destroy their lives, much more certainly than going forward. Leaning her head against his shoulder again, and then sliding it into his lap, she wept — partly from exhaustion and partly from sorrow, but mainly from the knowledge that their lives would never be the same again.

He removed her head covering gently, laying the pins beside the couch, letting down her hair. He stroked her and kissed her till she quit crying. She comforted herself that this Jake was still someone she could recognize, and perhaps she would get used to the one he was becoming.

A sob escaped her at the thought, but Jake hushed her. "It will always be just the two of us," he said softly.

"The baby too," she said quickly.

"Yes," he said, "the baby too," drawing her close to him.

CHAPTER TWENTY-THREE

HANNAH SAT ON the hard bench, afraid the women around her might notice her discomfort. From how several had acted this Sunday morning, she knew they already felt the difference. She was now a preacher's wife, and Jake was about to leave for his first Sunday morning ministers' conference.

Seeing Jake sitting up front, away from his usual seat among the other men, had been hard enough. Her first sight of him, what now seemed years ago, had been at church, so young and good looking, about to get picked to sing the Praise Song.

Thinking of that moment almost brought a smile to her face, but it vanished before its birth, lost in the thought that now Jake had been chosen again, only not just to sing the Praise Song. He had been called to preach and might have to after he came back down from upstairs.

Steve's prediction had come true. Bishop Nisley had left for the funeral in Indiana, leaving his only minister, besides Jake, to conduct the Sunday morning service. In Amish tradition, one man never was in charge of anything, if it could be helped. Perhaps if this had been the Sunday school Sunday, things might have worked out, but it wasn't. Today was the regular preaching Sunday, and two ministers must preach.

The first song started, and at the second line Minister Chupp stood up, solemnly leading the way. Jake followed, her Jake standing to his feet and following. In slow motion she watched them leave. Jake carefully lifted his black Sunday shoes on to each step of the stairs, shoes she had freshly polished for him, hoping it wasn't vanity.

The upstairs bedroom door closed behind them, shutting her out, driving home the point that Jake now went where she could never go. Around her the singing rose and swelled, and Hannah followed along, forcing her mouth to move, but inside the fear gripped her.

In what seemed like forever, but was really only thirty minutes, the black shoes came down the stairs and the singing soon stopped. Absolute silence filled the house.

Jake slowly got to his feet, his hands trembling, Hannah could see, as she tried unsuccessfully to look away. Her eyes seemed fixed on Jake's face, on every line she knew so well. His jaw muscles were tight, his eyes on the floor.

Hannah wished she wasn't here, wished Jake wasn't here, wished last Sunday had never happened, wished this Sunday was not happening...but it was. Jake lifted his eyes, letting them move slowly around the room, but they never got to Hannah before he dropped them again.

Slowly he started speaking, haltingly at first, each word causing an ache in Hannah's heart. She had never heard him speak in public before. He was quoting something that sounded like scripture, but she wasn't sure. He then began telling the story of the van accident this past week, how he had received the news about Hannah's parents being involved and about Bishop Amos's death.

Jake then spoke about Amos, how he had been a father to many, how he had been here only last Sunday and had spoken to him in private after church. This Hannah didn't know but figured she might as well get used to such things. Jake apparently now did a lot of things she wouldn't find out about.

Jake said what a great encouragement this conversation had been to him, confused as he was with the sudden turn of events. Bishop Amos had said God did not call to a duty without providing the strength to fulfill it.

Then Jake told the story of the shepherd who left the ninety-nine sheep safe in the sheepfold to find the one lost in the mountains. Hannah had heard the story before, but Jake told it a little differently, concluding that the task of helping the lost and hurting belonged to each one of us, not just to ministers. The Good Shepherd greatly cared for the lost and wanted us to care.

Hannah found herself listening, forgetting for a moment that it was Jake. Then he was done, calling for prayer. Together the whole congregation knelt as Jake led in a prayer out of the prayer book. From how well he read the prayer, Hannah felt certain he had read it before, but she had never seen him do so.

Minister Chupp then read the scripture and preached the main sermon, closing as usual by asking for testimonies. Hannah tensed for a moment, thinking someone might say Jake had preached error, but no one did.

After church dismissed, the tables were spread and lunch began. In Bishop Nisley's absence, minister Chupp announced the prayer time. Hannah realized this might be another public thing Jake would soon be doing. She suddenly felt old and haggard, certain her face betrayed her emotions.

Apparently Betty saw and took Hannah's arm, pulling her along to sit with the older women at the first table. It only made Hannah feel worse, since she now looked out of place as well. But the women asked ordinary questions that soon put her at ease. They saw her not just as a minister's wife, as she had feared, but a person, and she felt their concern. Clara, minister Chupp's wife, asked about her mother and father. She answered as best she could and then Betty took over.

"Kathy called the neighbor's house a day ago. Friday, I think. Roy can't work for awhile with his broken arm. I can't imagine that. Steve would have a fit too. She's okay, though. Then there was the funeral on Saturday. Amos wasn't from their district though. I think from around Shipshewana."

"When are the Nisleys coming back?" Clara asked.

"I don't know," Betty told her.

"Probably later this week," Ruth Yoder said from where she was sitting at the end of the table. "They'll take some time to visit. We would. Once you're in the east."

"Everyone usually does," Betty agreed.

One of the younger girls brought new bowls of peanut butter and red beets, making Hannah feel really old and weird, since she often served the older women.

"I'm not used to sitting here," Hannah whispered to Betty.

"You'll get used to it," Betty whispered back without much sympathy in her voice.

The flow of conversation shifted, leaving Hannah to her own thoughts. She thought of Jake and his good preaching that morning. Suddenly a memory came to her from years ago. She wasn't sure the occasion, but her father had said, *Preachers who preach good have extra temptations. For many of them it goes to their head. Some even leave for more liberal churches. Can't stay humble enough, I guess.*

Hannah remembered the words just like that, as if they had been dropped in her mind all in one piece. Would her father say that about Jake? Jake had preached well, had he not? Was that not what a good preacher did? That on his first sermon, too. Who could tell where he would go with some practice?

The thoughts sent strong emotions throughout her body, from extreme hot to cold. She thought of whispering a question to Betty, so strong was her distress, but someone around the table might hear and this was not a matter for others. It might not even be something Betty should discuss.

Hannah wished her mother were here. She would be one safe place to go with thoughts like these.

Her thoughts were interrupted by Minister Chupp's announcement of the closing prayer. Hannah bowed her head along with the others, convinced she must talk to someone, even if it was Betty.

The prayer done, Betty whispered as if on cue, "I need to talk to you."

It was obvious to Hannah that Betty intended a private conversation. Getting up with a glad heart, she followed Betty into the back bedroom without either of them drawing attention to themselves.

"I just have to tell you," Betty whispered once they were inside, leaving the bedroom door open.

"Yes," Hannah waited. This would take just a moment, she thought, as Betty would mention plans about some coming event and then she could ask if her concerns about Jake were valid.

Betty's face got sober instead as she glanced around the room. Two sleeping babies lay on the bed, but no mothers were apparent.

"After today..." Betty began, keeping her voice low. "My, can Jake preach! And his first time. I just had to tell you something. It's been bothering me for years, heavy on my heart. I have never told anyone. Not even your mother, and she was the sister I was close to." Betty glanced around the room again.

Hannah's heart sank as she realized what Betty was saying and the implications of it. She was now the minister's wife, and her only aunt who lived here was using her for confessions.

A tear hung on the edge of Betty's eye. "I wish I had said something, even to Steve, but I couldn't bring myself to tell him. We married and still I couldn't tell him. I don't think I ever can either. Today, though, for the first time, Jake gave me the courage to say it. I just have to tell you, Hannah. It hurts so inside. Keeping it here," Betty pressed her hand against her heart.

Hannah swallowed hard. There would be no sharing her own concerns with Betty today or perhaps ever. That was quite obvious.

"The other night at supper, when you and Jake were there — what I said about King David and God. I shouldn't have."

Hannah felt relieved. If this was all her aunt was referring to, then perhaps there was nothing to fear. Betty was always one to get overworked about things. There would be time yet to ask about Jake.

"It's okay," she said as she squeezed Betty's arm. "You didn't mean it."

"No," Betty shook her head, two tears now moving down her cheeks and obviously many more getting ready to follow. "It's not just that. It's the reason I say things like that. See, it's just easier to blame God sometimes, even when I know it was my own fault."

Betty clutched Hannah's arm now, seemingly unaware where she was. Hannah was deeply grateful no one else had walked in on them yet. She doubted whether she and Betty could pass this off as a normal conversation.

"I was wild once. Your mother was too," Betty continued. "I was the bad one, though. Much worse than the others, only no one really knew. I was good at hiding things. Then too... see, Hannah...." Betty's eyes filled with pain. "I had an English boyfriend. In secret. For a long time. I thought I would die when he left me, because I wouldn't go with him. Only I had wished to go. Wished it with all my heart. Oh, Hannah, I thought God would never let me love again. That is what I almost told Steve so he would know. Now that I married him, I thought I could forget about it."

Hannah, completely overwhelmed, didn't know what to do. Her feelings came not just from her aunt's confession, as she had known from her mother about the *rumspringa* days of her parents' youth, if not this much detail. Rather, she felt the burden of the confession itself, the unexpected weight confessions place on those who receive them. She felt sorrow that she had to be the one to bear it.

"Oh, Hannah," Betty was saying, wiping away her tears. "I'm so glad I could tell you that. God has sent us such a good minister in Jake."

Not knowing what else to do, Hannah gave Betty a hug. It felt strange, but Betty responded with a squeeze back, and then someone came in the door. They both smiled as if it were a perfectly normal Sunday morning.

On the way home in the buggy, Hannah asked Jake, "You're not going liberal are you?"

"Liberal?" he asked, a perfectly puzzled look on his face.

"Nothing," she said with a shake of her head, her thoughts fuzzy. "I was just asking."

"You don't want to?" he asked with a note of horror in his voice.

"Of course not," she said.

"Good," he said, shaking Mossy's reins, urging him up the incline towards their cabin.

CHAPTER TWENTY-FOUR

THE FOLLOWING WEEKEND Jake went elk hunting with Steve in the Cabinet Mountains. They took along white-tailed tags too, just in case there were no elk. Hannah felt certain they were driven by the joy of the hunt more than the desire for fresh meat.

She was relieved to see a smile on Jake's face. For that reason alone, the plans served a good purpose, Hannah figured. Jake had been sober long enough, between his new preaching responsibilities and his new job at the hardware store. He was bringing in little enough money for the hours he worked, and she knew the matter weighed on him.

The hunters left before dawn on Saturday morning, going with two English men, friends of Steve — an organized affair of sorts. It was better not to be alone in the mountains, Steve had said. Plus driving with the English men supplied the easiest way to the jumping off point, where they would then hike into the mountains.

The day went by fast enough for Hannah, but by four, with darkness threatening and what looked like snow clouds on the peaks of the mountains, she began to wonder if something had happened. She went out on the porch to look towards the mountains when the pickup truck pulled in.

Jumping from the back, Jake stepped aside and held his gun while he waited for the two English men to leave. He waved and said thank you as the pickup truck pulled out the driveway. She watched him expectantly, curious how the time in the mountains had affected him.

Jake seemed happy enough as he walked towards the house after putting his gun in the barn. The success of the hunt was not exactly on her mind as he came in the door.

"Got something," he said cheerfully, bringing her back to the subject.

"An elk?" she asked.

"No, just deer," he told her. "We need to go over to Steve's tonight. He's going to keep part of it."

"Your deer? So you got one!" Hannah said, remembering that work would be involved in its preparation.

"We need to go cut it up," Jake told her. "Steve said to come right away. He has a much better facility to work in, and Betty will get supper up. Maybe if we hurry, we might get most of the meat worked up before too late."

"It's Saturday night," she said, the implications of his proposal sinking in.

"I know. That's part of the fun."

"Well," she told him, letting his enthusiasm infect her, "sounds so."

"I'll get Mossy then," he said. "We need to go."

"I'll get some pans and knives," she said, already walking towards the kitchen.

Hurrying Mossy, Jake made a quick drive over to Steve and Betty's, the pans and knives rattling in the back of the buggy. Steve already had one deer strung up in the barn when they got there. Having forgotten an apron, Hannah ran into the house to see if Betty had an extra.

"What a mess," Betty proclaimed when she opened the kitchen door. "On a Saturday night to boot."

"Jake seems to have enjoyed himself," Hannah told her. "That's worth a lot."

"I think Steve did," Betty said wryly. "There's something about men, guns, and mountains."

"You have an apron for me?" Hannah asked. "I forgot mine."

"Think so." Betty dug in the kitchen cabinet drawer, producing two dark blue full-length aprons. She held them up. "Good butchering aprons. Saturday night's just not good."

"Just think fun," Hannah told her with a grin, Jake's feelings still affecting her. Outside, carrying Betty's aprons with her, Hannah noticed the snow clouds seemed on the verge of dumping their load. The heavy air wrapped itself around her but was not about to dampen her spirits.

Jake and Steve were already busy cutting up the first deer, spreading the meat out on a card table covered by clean plastic. It began snowing just after Betty came out, thick heavy flakes that fell gently towards the ground.

"Looks like it's good we didn't get lost in the mountains," Steve said teasingly.

"You didn't get lost?" Betty still asked, horror in her voice.

"Not really," Jake said quickly. "We just thought so for a moment."

"That's what I don't like about mountains," Betty declared. Hannah gave her a quick glance of agreement, glad to learn that others shared her recent suspicions of the towering heights. They looked so innocent, so friendly, and yet harbored dangers one would never notice at first glance.

Betty filled several bowls with water from the barn spigot, and Hannah set to work washing the meat. Separating the types of meat in different piles, as best she could, Hannah soon had the table half full. Betty then went even further, cutting the slabs into smaller pieces and bagging them. Two plastic tubs on the barn floor took the finished product.

A little after eight they were done. Steve and Jake hauled the unused portions back into the woods with flashlights.

"Something will take care of it," Betty muttered to Hannah.

"At least you don't have bears around," Hannah said.

"Not yet," Betty replied, still not in a very good mood. "At least it's stopped snowing."

"You think it will be a hard winter?" Hannah wondered, dreading the approaching season.

"You never know," Betty shrugged, putting lids on the plastic tubs. "Snow's early enough, I guess. You think this tub's got enough meat for you?"

Hannah lifted the lid on the smallest tub, calculating before replying. "Too much," she said.

"You sure?" Betty wanted to know.

"I'm sure," Hannah assured her. "We can't use that much in the next few weeks."

"I guess you don't have a freezer," Betty agreed, taking several bags back out. "You know how to marinate this meat? Makes a real tasty meal using the steaks."

"Don't have a recipe," Hannah told her. "I'm sure you do though."

Betty nodded, "Don't let me forget to give it to you before you go. You're staying for supper."

"If it's not too much bother," Hannah said hesitantly, remembering Jake said they were staying but still not wanting to barge in.

"There's no sense in you going home to the cabin still having to fix supper. I've got plenty."

The men came back in, stamping snow from their feet.

"Enough meat for a little bit," Steve pronounced. "Now for supper. Looks like we didn't even go too late."

Following Betty to the house, Hannah helped set the table while Betty's oldest daughter heated the soup prepared earlier. Betty went to put her share of the meat in the deep freezer in her basement. It was propane powered, legal by the church rules. Hannah knew she and Jake would have one someday when they had enough money, but for now the spring house would have to do.

Jake and Steve came in, having put Jake's share of meat in the buggy, and soon supper began. When it was over, Hannah had just risen to help Betty and the girls clear the table when a clear, unearthly scream rent the air from outside. Hannah stopped in midair, several dirty bowls balanced in her hands.

"What was that?" Betty asked, her voice rising with fright.

Steve and Jake jumped up from the table at the same time, two protectors ready for battle.

"It's just an animal," Hannah told them, remembering the bobcats she often saw on the edge of the cabin woods. "You did drag the deer parts into the woods."

"I knew they shouldn't have done that," Betty said from the kitchen, her voice still high pitched.

"You think so?" Steve asked in Jake's direction.

He raised his eyebrows as another scream rent the air.

"It's more than a bobcat," Steve answered his own question.

"We'd better look," Jake agreed.

"No you don't," Betty told them, coming in the dining room.

Steve and Jake ignored her, Steve going to get his flashlight in the bedroom.

"You'd better just stay inside," Jake said to everyone.

"It's just a bobcat," Hannah told him, more hesitantly now that she had heard the second scream. That was an awful lot of noise for the size creature she had seen near the cabin.

"I think it's something bigger," Jake told her. "We'll be careful," he added to her look of concern.

"I'm going with you," Hannah announced, producing a look of astonishment on Jake's face.

"Going with them," Betty whispered, her face pale. "I'm not."

"Ready?" Steve asked, heading for the front door with his flashlight. Jake followed, making no objection as Hannah went with him.

Outside the snow covered the ground, making no sound when they stepped off the porch. Steve's torch was almost as good as Jake's, searching the darkness with a stream of brilliant light.

"I don't see anything," Steve said, now at the edge of the woods.

"We left the deer parts deeper in," Jake told him, apparently not afraid of proceeding.

"We should have buried them," Steve said, regret in his voice. "I was thinking small animals."

In answer to his regret, the scream sounded again, very near. Hannah involuntarily grabbed Jake's arm.

"We'd better get out of here," she whispered, not sure if Steve could hear.

Jake shook his head, its outline faintly visible in the backside of Steve's light. "It's too big to leave here."

"I think it's a mountain lion," Steve voiced his conclusion, moving deeper into the woods. Jake followed, and Hannah wasn't about to stay by herself.

Flashing eyes came up in the stream of Steve's moving light, the two points low on the ground with a faint outline of a long body behind them.

"Get out of here," Steve shouted, bending down to search for something to throw.

The answer was another scream from the cat, its tail now violently slamming against the ground.

"Maybe we'd better go call the game warden," Jake suggested, hanging back now as Steve advanced even closer.

"A lot of good that did with your bear," Steve retorted, finding what he was looking for. He lifted a good-sized branch from the ground, and waving it above his head he charged the two eyes.

Hannah stifled her own scream, hearing it come out as a muffled cry of horror. In her mind's eye she saw flashes of charging cat and Steve falling to the ground. Instead, the cat retreated slowly, its tail thrashing wildly, low growls coming from its throat.

"Get," Steve said even louder. "Leave."

Jake seemed to gather courage and moved closer.

"Get a shovel," Steve told Jake. "We need to bury this. I can't have cats like this hanging around."

"Where is it?" Jake asked.

"In the barn. Hannah knows."

Thinking fast in her fear, Hannah followed Jake to the barn and showed him where the tools were kept. They went back and found Steve had somehow succeeded in completely getting rid of the cat. Taking turns, Jake and Steve dug several deep holes, the digging going better once they were through the frozen surface.

"That ought to do it," Steve concluded when they were done pushing the deer parts into the holes.

"Should," Jake agreed, throwing on another shovel of dirt and tamping it with his foot.

"What if the cat digs it up?" Hannah asked, the thought occurring to her.

"Then I guess we have to call the game warden," Steve said. "Something has to be done anyway. Hopefully this will work for now.'

Back in the house, Betty looked as though she expected them to be torn to bits.

"We're alive," Steve told her, chuckling.

"Don't do things like that again," Betty told him. "My heart can't stand it."

"I'll try not to," Steve said, sounding genuinely regretful.

"We'd better get going," Jake said, moving towards the door.

"Thanks for supper," Hannah told Betty, following Jake.

"And for help with the meat," Jake added as he turned at the door.

Arriving home, Hannah helped Jake stash the meat in the spring house, making sure the door was securely fastened. One animal disturbance for the night had been enough for her.

CHAPTER TWENTY-FIVE

THE NEXT DAY Jake didn't have to do anything in church since Bishop Nisley was back. He sat in front on the ministers' bench, which still bothered Hannah but less so than the previous week.

On Monday, she reminded Jake about the need for a doctor's appointment. Betty had told her Sunday about a woman doctor in Libby, Dr. Lisa, who came highly recommended. That was good enough for Hannah, as neither she nor Jake had a regular doctor since moving to Montana.

When Hannah suggested the possibility of using the woman as their family doctor, he made a face, so she dropped the idea. When the time or need came, Jake could look for his own doctor.

Getting Jake to call for an appointment wasn't too difficult. He had hesitated a bit at first but soon warmed to the idea, calling from the hardware store. Hannah was concerned about the money but left it unmentioned for now. She needed to see a doctor for the baby's sake, and Jake likely had no doubts about that either.

Jake came home with news of an appointment in two weeks, on Thursday. Hannah then raised the question of how to pay. Jake didn't say anything for awhile, then simply said the money would have to come out of his paycheck. They were starting the log furniture this week, he added, and perhaps there would be more income then. Hannah didn't think Jake sounded at all certain.

That evening, Hannah served the first of the deer burger and asked if Mr. Brunson could be invited for supper on Friday night.

"I'm marinating steak," she told Jake. "Thought he might enjoy it."

"What about the burger?" Jake asked. "Wouldn't that be good enough?"

"You'll be good and tired of deer burger by then," Hannah assured him. "Trust me. We will be depending a lot on hunting this winter."

Jake solemnly nodded. "I should go again before too long. The white-tailed deer licenses are easy enough to get."

"You wouldn't even have to go back to the mountains," Hannah told him, figuring this would make things easier.

"I guess we're stuck with wild meat for awhile." Jake didn't look all that happy about it.

"Maybe we'll learn to like it as good as hamburger," Hannah said, feeling cheerful enough, not quite able to believe her own attitude. Maybe she was maturing, she thought.

The following day a long letter from her mother arrived, full of news. Her father was about to climb the walls wanting to get back to work. The funeral had been a sad one, Kathy said, and large, as it often was when a tragic, sudden death occurred. She and Roy had attended even though Bishop Amos did not live in their district.

Towards the end, Kathy said the trailer factories were on a fresh hiring plan with many new openings, if one liked that type of work. Why her mother should mention this Hannah was uncertain; it felt like salt poured into her still open wound. Did her mother think there was still a chance they could move?

Maybe her mother had forgotten about Jake's ordination, but that seemed hardly possible either. Hannah sighed, figuring her mother meant well. Likely she just wanted all the options out in the open. There then followed some baby news, and who was dating whom, as if her mother were really interested in such things. *She must be trying to satisfy my interest,* Hannah thought, *since these are people I know.*

At the end there came a little mention, a mere dropping of words on the page, that Hannah was to tell Jake the district next to theirs lacked a minister, one short of the usual number.

This stirred emotions Hannah thought she had forgotten. Possibilities raced through her mind until she had to calm herself down. It seemed unlikely Jake would consider this, and she decided not to tell him. At least for now she wouldn't. If an appropriate time ever came, then perhaps.

Jake came home on Wednesday night grinning with the news that Mr. Wesley had set up the first tools in the shop.

"I started my first attempt," Jake informed her. "Not bad, if I have to say so myself. Mr. Wesley said things should really sell."

Hannah sat on the couch to listen, glad Jake was happy.

"I nicked my finger a little." Jake showed her the bandage.

"Surely you're not starting that!" Hannah imagined future injuries, even missing fingers. Jake laughed at the look on her face.

"I'll learn to be careful," he assured her.

"Please," she said, looking beseechingly at him, glad at least he seemed to take her concerns seriously.

"Supper ready?" he asked.

"Yes."

"Deer burger again?" He made a face.

"I have cherry pie," she told him, delighted when his face lit up.

"Can we afford it?" he asked, his face falling a little.

"It's leftover pie from when my parents were here. Maybe I shouldn't buy such extras for a while, though."

"Maybe," he said.

"Did you invite Mr. Brunson yet?" she asked him.

"Yesterday. He said he'd come."

"I still have cherry pie filling left," she told him, hoping it would help him enjoy the pie she served tonight. Considering she was not used to such tight grocery spending, she surprised herself at how well she was taking it. Maybe the downer would come later, she thought, sometime when Jake wasn't around.

A buggy rattled into the driveway soon after they finished supper. Jake went to the door, stepping outside on the porch to wait. Hannah wondered who would be coming this time of night, unannounced. Betty would, she knew, but had no reason at present unless bearing bad news. Hannah pushed the thought away, staying in the kitchen until she knew this involved her in some way.

〰️

When the door opened, Hannah could hardly believe her eyes. Bishop Nisley came in followed by Elizabeth, his wife. Jake closed the door behind them, a concerned look on his face. Hannah instantly knew this visit could not be for social reasons.

Bishop Nisley took off his hat, holding the black rim in his hands, looking friendly enough as he took the seat on the couch Jake offered him. Hannah felt frozen to her spot in the kitchen. She saw Elizabeth glance towards her, obviously on the verge of moving in her direction even as Jake was offering her a seat beside her husband.

Hannah knew she must face this, whatever it was. It might only be a church matter—perhaps this was Bishop Nisley's method of handling such things? Though why it couldn't wait for their regular Sunday morning meeting, she couldn't imagine.

Forcing a smile on her face, Hannah stepped forward to greet Elizabeth. Normally the smile would have come with no effort, as she had always felt close to the bishop's wife, ever since the summer she spent keeping Betty's riding stable. Now, Hannah knew, she was faking the smile. Was this her destiny as a minister's wife, faking her expressions while she tried to feel what she ought to feel? That's what she had to do when Betty made her confession, and now she was doing it again.

"Good evening," Elizabeth said. She was all smiles. "I hope we aren't interrupting your supper?"

"No," Hannah forced the smile again. "It's over. Just. But over."

"Can I help with the dishes?" Elizabeth moved past Hannah and glanced into the kitchen.

"I can get those later," Hannah told her quickly.

"No, I'm helping." Elizabeth obviously had made up her mind. Her help meant this visit was going to be lengthy, whatever its purpose. It seemed unlikely she would be helping just to earn a five-minute chat afterwards.

Elizabeth purposefully turned the spigot in the kitchen sink to the left, but succeeded in getting only cold water.

"We have to heat water," Hannah told her, motioning towards the bowl of water already warming on the stove. "We only have a spring."

"Oh, that's different," Elizabeth said. "I didn't know that. I guess this is a log cabin."

"Well...." Wild thoughts ran through Hannah's head. *Did Elizabeth think her new minister's wife completely strange for how she lived? Was she disappointed in how poor they were? Did she think Jake ought to own a gas water heater?*

Elizabeth must have noticed her face, "Oh," she laughed softly, "I didn't mean anything bad. There's nothing wrong, really. We didn't always have everything just right either."

"Oh?" Hannah tried to feel normal again.

"That was in Indiana, I guess," Elizabeth shrugged. "John could afford a water heater when we were married. There were other things, though."

"I suppose so." Hannah felt worse now, as she could well imagine the *other things* Elizabeth referred to were probably furniture—new furniture items she didn't even dream of owning. She was still stuck on a gas water heater. Shame filled her and she found herself wishing she could disappear.

"What can I do then?" Elizabeth asked, glancing around. "John probably wants us back in the living room before too long."

"I'll put some more wood on the fire," Hannah told her, feeling like an inferior country bumpkin who must stoke her smoky fire before she could even wash the dishes.

Perhaps it was the light from the fire, as Hannah bent over the stove, that gave Elizabeth a good look at her face. Hannah was making no attempt at hiding her feelings now.

"I'm so sorry," Elizabeth exclaimed. "Did I say something? I really didn't mean to. Here I am barging in, disrupting your evening and your kitchen."

When Hannah didn't say anything, standing there beside the stove, Elizabeth gently took her arm and guided her to a chair beside the kitchen table.

"I'm sorry. This must all be so sudden. You're both so young. Now John thought he had to come over tonight, though I tried to tell him it wasn't that serious. He just thinks things should be taken care of before they get serious."

"Elizabeth," the bishop's voice called from the living room. "We shouldn't be staying too late."

Hannah felt deeply grateful she wasn't crying. What had she and Jake done already? It must be something terrible. She felt frozen in place and wasn't sure she could have stood up if Elizabeth hadn't helped her.

"It's nothing serious, really," Elizabeth whispered, as if she were afraid someone might hear. "John just wants to talk to Jake."

Numbly Hannah followed Elizabeth into the living room, all attempts at faking smiles gone. She knew the bishop was looking at her but didn't care at the moment. What she was they would just have to see.

"Ah," John cleared his throat, seeming to search for

words, no preacher tone in his voice. Hannah dared glance at his face and was surprised to see it soft and tender. Jake had his head bowed, as if he already knew what was coming.

"Mose Chupp told me about the other Sunday," John said, tightly clasping his hands. "I knew you would have to preach, and that so soon."

Hannah glanced at Jake, who still had his eyes on the floor.

"From what he told me you did quite well."

No one said anything.

"I know this may sound strange," the bishop continued. "I just had a concern about that. I know it's soon, but perhaps it's best to say it now rather than having to say something more important later."

"He's just trying to help," Elizabeth spoke up. "I told him Jake meant no ill. He was trying so hard, they said."

"What did I do?" Jake managed. Hannah saw his eyes were still on the floor.

"You preached pretty good," the bishop said, as if that explained things. "I'm just concerned about that. So good, so quickly. It can do things to a person. I don't want you spoiled, Jake. I really don't."

"He's just trying to help," Elizabeth said again. "He really is."

"So what am I supposed to do?" Jake sounded puzzled.

The bishop cleared his throat. "Apparently you are one of those to whom preaching comes natural. You are good at this, Jake. That is a great danger. I don't want to lose you."

"How would you lose me?" Jake asked.

"I don't want to put things into your head," the bishop shrugged. "A lot of churches are looking for good preachers. Liberal ones. Things get around. I hope you don't go down that road."

"I don't plan to," Jake told him.

"Temptation is a strange thing," John spoke slowly. "It comes when we least expect it. Comes in ways we hadn't thought. I just wanted to warn you right away. Walk humbly with God, Jake. We need you around here."

Jake nodded.

"We'd better be going," the bishop said, glancing towards his wife.

"We haven't finished the kitchen," she replied. "We were just going to start."

"I can manage," Hannah spoke up. "I really can."

The Bishop waited a moment before he said, "We really should be going. Good night then."

Jake rose and opened the door for them, and they stepped out into the brisk night air. Numbly Jake sat back down on the couch, while Hannah went back to the kitchen. The water was boiling furiously in the bowl. She dipped some out to fill the sink, adding soap. Her tears soon joined the dishes in the bubbling suds. She didn't hear Jake until his arms came around her shoulders.

"We have to move back to Indiana," she whispered. "We have to."

"No," his answer came, as if from far away. "God wants us to stay here."

She laid her head on his shoulder and wept, till he gently joined his hands with hers in the kitchen sink. They washed dishes. Together.

CHAPTER TWENTY-SIX

THE SUN SHONE with full vigor, not allowing any clouds to cross the sky. Hannah felt a little better, busily preparing for the Friday night meal with Mr. Brunson. She had been marinating the deer steak since Wednesday, using Betty's recipe plus adding a few touches of her own.

Kathy had always told her a good cook must allow intuition to guide her, not just the recipe. If things went wrong, it was just food that was wasted. That might be true for Indiana, Hannah thought, but here, for Friday night, she couldn't afford to be wrong.

She had thought for a moment of inviting Steve and Betty but decided against it, since Betty would wonder if her recipe had been followed to the letter. If the new formula worked, then things would be okay. If not, then Hannah knew she would feel thoroughly embarrassed. She didn't want the pressure.

Boiling the potatoes early, she let them cool by the stove while preparing the cherry pie. The crust turned out satisfactorily — not quite like her mother's, but good enough. Who could be like her mother, she thought. Perhaps later in life, if she survived what she was going through now.

Feeling waves of self-pity rising, she told herself to grow up. Jake loved her, and that fact brought comfort, even if she didn't always understand him.

Why didn't Jake want to move back to Indiana? The thought puzzled her as she peeled the still steaming potatoes. He never really mentioned why. He just said God wanted them here. *Was it something deeper? Some reason he was not telling her?*

Remembering the comfort of his presence as they washed dishes last night, she couldn't imagine he would be hiding anything. *Yet was he?* The thought wouldn't go away, and she gave up trying to dislodge it. It would just have to stay until it answered itself, she figured, continuing with her supper preparations.

Jake came home on time and offered to help. She told him he could set the table, which he did — not perfectly, but the dishes were in the vicinity.

Their first log table was finished, Jake announced as he jerked on the tablecloth to straighten it out. A customer had stopped by, taken a look at the still unvarnished product, and placed an order for two.

"Just like that," Jake said, with a huge smile on his face. There would be a bonus next week, Mr. Wesley had said. Just in time for the doctor's bill.

Mr. Brunson arrived on time, his tires crunching on the gravel in the driveway. Jake lit the gas lanterns, hanging one in the kitchen, as he usually did with company.

Sitting down, they bowed their heads for prayer, Jake not offering to pray out loud tonight. Then Hannah produced her steak from the oven. She knew her hands shook as she set the steaming bowl on the table. Earlier she had sampled the meat, liking what she tasted, so that was some comfort.

The test still was whether Jake and Mr. Brunson would. She knew men did not always agree with a woman's taste on such matters. Jake served himself gingerly, she noticed, while Mr. Brunson seemed to have no such qualms, piling his plate high with meat.

Jake noticed, clearing his throat. "You might want to go slow on that," he said. "It's Hannah's first time marinating deer meat."

"I have full confidence in her," Mr. Brunson announced, smiling. "She's a good cook."

"I might not be," Hannah said quickly, hoping Mr. Brunson was right but not quite believing until she saw Jake eat and pronounce the meat satisfactory. Mr. Brunson might just say so to be kind.

Mr. Brunson was busy chewing when Jake put a piece in his mouth, biting down thoughtfully. For a full minute both men chewed, then looked at each other and burst out laughing.

"It's awful," Hannah cried, her hands flying to her face as red crept up her neck. The supper was totally ruined, she was certain.

"I've never tasted better," Mr. Brunson pronounced, solemn-faced now. "Not even in the best restaurants Boston has to offer."

"Agreed," Jake said. "Although I've never been to the best in Boston."

"You're just saying so," Hannah whispered, feeling a need to sit down. "Is it good?"

"It is," Mr. Brunson said.

Jake just nodded.

"Have some yourself," Mr. Brunson said.

"I'll get the cherry pie first," she said, wanting to savor the moment fully.

"So how's the furniture business coming along?" Mr. Brunson asked Jake.

Jake brought Mr. Brunson up to date, going into great detail about log furniture making.

Later, Hannah cleaned the kitchen while the two men took seats in the living room. When she joined them there, she expected a quiet evening of conversation until Mr. Brunson left. He usually didn't stay too late, at least from what she had seen on his earlier visits.

"I heard you were ordained," Mr. Brunson said, clearing his throat.

Jake grunted something unintelligible from his seat on the couch.

"Heard it in town," Mr. Brunson added. "Remembered

your father-in-law said something. Didn't make sense then."

Silence hung heavy in the room. Hannah wondered if conversation on the subject would always be like this, his ordination clouding their lives with uncertainty.

"I hope I'm not imposing," Mr. Brunson continued. "I've just wanted...for some time to talk with someone."

Hannah had an instant flashback to Betty's drawn and sober face in the bedroom. *Had people nothing but confessions to make? Was everyone hiding secrets? Was she to bear this burden all her life now?* Jake, sitting beside her on the couch, was listening intently.

"It's been many years," Mr. Brunson began with sudden tears in his eyes, softening Hannah's heart to listen. "You will think me crazy, as I no doubt am. A crazy old man stuck here in the mountains. Alone and crazy. Yet there is a reason for it."

Mr. Brunson took a big blue handkerchief out of his pocket and blew his nose. Jake was saying nothing, just listening.

"There is the court date coming up soon," Mr. Brunson continued. Hannah hoped this wasn't about money, since her and Jake's checking account would supply none. She felt some of her sympathies slipping away.

"We would be glad to help," Jake said, to which Hannah felt like jerking on his shirt sleeve, reminding him of the realities. Mr. Brunson, though, waved aside the implied suggestion.

"No son. It's not money I need. I need to confess my sins. I'm sorry to impose on you two." His eyes went to Hannah's face and then dropped to the cabin floor.

"Your sins?" Jake managed.

"Yes, my sins," Mr. Brunson said simply. "They are about to find me out, I think, as the good book says. See, I have money. The fine will be big, but that's not the problem. It is what will happen when I draw the money to pay the fine."

Jake looked puzzled.

"I am not a criminal, at least not in the eyes of the law. In here, I am...." Mr. Brunson laid a hand on his heart. "Let me start from the beginning. Is that okay? Have you got the time?"

"Sure," Jake said, and Hannah nodded.

"I'm a businessman. Or I was," Mr. Brunson said. "Back east, as you know. Beyond that, you don't know. See..." — Mr. Brunson brushed away another tear — "I am also a family man. Or I was. I have a son; I had a daughter and a wife."

There followed a long silence, in which no one seemed to move.

"One night I was driving home from a social function — a business Christmas party, a busy season for the company — with my wife and daughter, whom I had hardly seen for weeks. I slid off the road, or the car did. It was raining. The officer said it could have happened to anyone, but I knew, knew with certainty — this was my fault. It would not have happened if.... My wife, Bernice...well, we were arguing. It doesn't matter about what. Some little thing. I wasn't paying attention."

"Your wife and daughter?" Jake asked.

"They were killed," Mr. Brunson said, his face a picture of agony. "Why should I have survived? I was the guilty one."

"Your son?" Jake asked.

"He doesn't know where I am. I left. Suddenly. With enough money for what I wanted to do. I never planned on going back."

"Would he be looking for you?" Jake asked, obviously perplexed.

"I don't know," Mr. Brunson said. "That's the problem. I didn't want him to find a trial. That's why I left none. Now... do I want to know? Will he try to find me? If I draw out the money from the accounts. I will leave the trail."

"How was your son feeling when you left?" Jake asked.

"Very bitter," Mr. Brunson said softly. "He and his sister

were close. It's been easier this way. I shielded myself from the pain by forcing distance between us. Now I will know if he hates me."

"Perhaps your son doesn't hate you," Jake offered. "Maybe this is God's way…of mending the past."

"It could be," Mr. Brunson allowed. "Maybe that's why I'm telling you this. In your world it seems possible. In mine, it doesn't. I wasn't the father I should have been."

"Your son's name?" Jake wondered.

"Eldon," Mr. Brunson said. "A fine boy."

"I'm sure he is," Jake said quickly. "Perhaps he will contact you. God looks at all of us the same."

"I guess we'll find out," Mr. Brunson said, seeming to collect himself. "I really appreciate your time." He nodded to both Hannah and Jake. "I won't bother you anymore. Thanks for the supper. The meat was the best."

"You are welcome," Hannah said, wishing she could think of more to say, but nothing came to mind.

"We will hope for the best," Jake told him, going to open the door. "Your son, I mean. God has His own ways of doing things."

"Thanks," Mr. Brunson said, as he left quietly.

Jake shut the door and came back to his seat on the couch. He silently stared at the log cabin ceiling.

"So that's what's been bothering Mr. Brunson," Hannah mused. "He often seemed sad."

"I guess so," Jake said, offering nothing more.

"Is this why you want to stay here?" Hannah asked, the question crossing her mind suddenly.

"What do you mean?" Jake asked.

"Not move to Indiana?"

"I don't understand." Jake looked at her closely.

"This…." Hannah tried to put the vague feeling into words. "You are getting a lot of attention. Now Mr. Brunson comes over. You wouldn't get this in Indiana, would you?"

"I have no idea what you're talking about." Jake still looked at her.

"Is this what you mean by God wanting you here?"

"He just does," Jake said. "I can't explain it."

"Are you sure?" Hannah wished she wasn't asking these questions, but they just bubbled up.

"I think so," Jake said. "I'm not trying to get attention."

"I'm sure you're not," she assured him, but in her heart she still wondered. Finally she chased the question away.

"I'm just trying to do my duty," Jake said, sounding sincere, she thought.

"I believe you," she said, but in the shadows the pesky question still lingered. She leaned against Jake's shoulder, seeking shelter in this whirling world that now seemed to be her home. Outside the cabin the night settled in, seeming to have dark things on its mind.

CHAPTER TWENTY-SEVEN

THURSDAY CAME SOON enough, since Hannah wasn't looking forward to the doctor's appointment. But if she was to continue having children as she hoped, doctors were to be a part of her life.

Betty had said there was a midwife in Bonner's Ferry, but she didn't like to be contacted until after a doctor was involved. She worked with doctors not against them, Betty had emphasized.

Hannah hoped Dr. Lisa would be sympathetic to these plans. Since expense was the primary consideration, Hannah wasn't certain. Doctors and midwives in Indiana usually stayed out of each other's way. There, most of the Amish went to the hospital — but they also worked in trailer factories, Hannah reminded herself, not without a little bitterness. Here, she lived in a log cabin.

Jake needed Mossy to get to work, so Betty was coming to drive her into Libby. They had coordinated the time, allowing enough for a relaxed drive. Hannah wanted to be ready when Betty came.

Trying to think what questions the doctor might ask, she prepared herself mentally. She had developed another bruising cold the past few days, apparently a relapse. It took a puzzling form with no sniffles, but pain in her neck glands. The thought of calling off the appointment had crossed her mind, and if this were the second or third appointment she would have. But she wanted to get the first one over.

Betty came a few minutes early, which didn't surprise Hannah. She met her out by the driveway before Betty had time to tie up.

"Good morning," Betty said cheerfully. "How is the baby girl?"

"How do you know what it will be?" Hannah asked, hopping in.

"I meant you, silly," Betty replied. "How would I know what the child will be?"

"That's what I wondered."

"How are you?" Betty looked suspiciously at Hannah as she shook the reins to get going.

"The cold came back," Hannah told her.

"You think you should go?" Betty questioned. "You look like you have a fever."

"Checked it," Hannah assured her. "No fever. Just swollen glands."

"Doctor might not like that."

"She can look at me anyway," Hannah said, feeling stubborn. "I want to get the first time done."

"That's understandable." Betty shook the reins. "Next ones are easier, though."

"How bad is the first time?" Hannah wanted to know.

"Bad enough," Betty told her. "It's worth it."

"Figured," Hannah said as she settled back into the buggy seat.

"Jake excited?" Betty asked.

"I think so. He's busy working and being a minister."

"Yeah, I suppose. You two do have your hands full."

"I still think we should move back to Indiana."

"I don't," Betty said firmly. "I need all the family here I can get."

The horse suddenly jerked his head into the air, shying sideway. Betty pulled sharply on the reins.

"What was that?" Hannah wondered, looking back

while Betty brought the horse back under control.

"Can you see anything?" Betty asked, too busy to look back herself.

"Just fence posts," Hannah said, puzzled.

"He's usually pretty good." Betty relaxed as the horse settled down to a steady pace again. "Something must have gotten into him."

"You did pretty good, though."

"Good thing nothing was coming," Betty said, turning around to look back. "One of those posts does look a little scary."

"Maybe that's what it was," Hannah agreed.

"How's Jake coming along with his job?" Betty asked, her hands firmly on the reins.

"Pretty good, from what he says. Things are still a little tight money wise."

"I suppose so. Remember to tell us if things get too bad."

"I don't think I'd like that," Hannah told her.

"You're family." Betty gave her a look.

"Well, anyway...." Hannah left the subject there as the edge of town appeared. Her thoughts went to the doctor's office ahead of them.

When she walked in, Hannah was directed to wait, and then taken back while Betty stayed in the waiting room. Most of the examination went as she expected, with the weighing, the blood pressure test, and then a blood test.

"Just standard procedure for us," the nurse told her, confirming her feelings. "Nothing really has to be wrong. Doctor Lisa will be right in."

Hannah was pleased she didn't have to wait long. The door opened and Dr. Lisa greeted her warmly. She was a middle-aged woman, her skin brown and weather-streaked, not at all like Hannah had expected a woman doctor to look.

"So what will it be?" Dr. Lisa asked with a smile, beginning her examination. "A boy or a girl?"

"Doesn't matter," Hannah told her, holding her breath as the cold stethoscope touched her skin. Dr. Lisa listened intently and didn't comment for a moment.

"That's a good attitude to have," she then smiled. "You're Amish?"

Hannah nodded, wondering what that had to do with her coming child.

"Just asking. I'm a doctor part-time. My husband and I keep a ranch down by the other mountain range and try to stay out there as much as possible. As if that happens often." Dr. Lisa made a face.

So that explained the outdoor appearance, Hannah thought.

"You looking for a midwife?" the next question came.

Hannah stiffened, having anticipated this. "My aunt suggested it. Yes."

"Most of the Amish do." Dr. Lisa didn't seem offended. "I'm starting a little birthing clinic right here at the office. Why don't you let me see if I'm competitive with your midwife's fees?"

"Oh," Hannah said, letting the delight show on her face. "I would like that. We can't afford much, though."

"We'll see what we can do then." Dr. Lisa placed her hands on Hannah's swollen neck glands. "What have we here?"

"I think my cold came back."

Dr. Lisa looked skeptical. "No sniffles?"

Hannah shook her head.

"Where do you live?"

"Outside of town a few miles."

"I mean — the kind of house?"

"Log cabin," Hannah said, thinking a lot of people probably did in this area, so why should she be ashamed.

"Animals around? Cats?" Dr. Lisa's hand went back to her glands.

"Just the driving horse."

"You sure?"

Hannah nodded, sure the grizzly didn't count.

"Eating deer meat lately?" Dr. Lisa raised her eyebrows.

"Yes," Hannah told her, but that shouldn't be strange either. It was hunting season.

"Much?" came the question.

Hannah made a face. "A lot. Jake and his uncle got a deer. We can't afford a lot of other meat."

"You've been cooking it well?"

"I thought so. Frying usually."

"Let me take a look at that blood test," Dr. Lisa said. "I'll be right back."

Hannah waited, feeling fidgety, ready to get back home and out of this place, but there was nothing to do but wait.

"Well," Dr. Lisa said matter-of-factly when she came back. "I don't like the looks of this."

"Is something wrong?" Hannah asked, her first feelings of fear coming.

"There might be. I'll need to send the blood test to the lab in Kalispell."

Hannah knew she was staring but couldn't help herself.

"I'm sure enough to tell you," Dr. Lisa finally said. "It looks like a toxoplasmosis infection. Parasites really. That's why your glands are swollen. It doesn't happen too often and is usually not that serious. The body fights it by producing an antibody. You're pregnant though."

"Are you sure? About the disease?" Hannah asked, trying to act normal.

"I'll know by tomorrow. Can you check back then?"

"My husband can."

"I'll give you a full dose of this prescription—as much as I can, considering you're pregnant. You should begin taking the drugs right away."

"Before we know for sure?"

"I'm sure enough," Dr. Lisa nodded her head emphatically. "Thankfully you're still in the early stages of your pregnancy."

"What will happen with the baby?"

"Hopefully he won't get infected. It seems early in the infection, plus, as I said, you're early yet. I need an ultrasound too, maybe in a few weeks."

"Will that cost a lot?" Hannah couldn't help asking.

Dr. Lisa shrugged. "Maybe we can pass on the ultrasound. We'll see. It's not always conclusive anyway. I can do another type of test after you're twenty weeks. That one we can be sure of."

"The baby?" Hannah tried again.

"Hopefully there will be no transmittal." Dr. Lisa was trying to keep a hopeful face, Hannah felt certain.

"If not?" Hannah asked, planning to insist on the information if necessary.

"Not good," she said simply. "There could be a miscarriage, or stillborn. If not, infected babies usually seem normal at birth, then serious problems follow — mental disability, vision loss, possibly even seizures."

Hannah knew she was not taking this well. The suddenness hit her hard, but then so had a lot of things of late.

"You okay?" Dr. Lisa put an arm on her shoulder.

"No," Hannah said, knowing she was about to cry.

"I'm sorry. It's usually best to know details right away. At least I like it better." Dr. Lisa gave her a quick hug. "You can get dressed now. The prescription will be at the front desk. Start taking it right away."

"I will," Hannah said, her voice trembling.

Betty looked strangely at her when Hannah came into the waiting room. Hannah knew she couldn't hide her red eyes. Yet she controlled herself while writing out the check to the receptionist and taking the white piece of paper. Outside in the buggy she no longer tried to hold back, sobbing hysterically.

Betty held Hannah close and didn't ask any questions until the sobs died down. The horse waited at the post.

"There, there," Betty said gently. "My, my, the Lord must really have it in for you two. Is the baby dead?"

"No," Hannah managed before bursting into fresh tears. "It's just everything. Jake, and the ordination—he's so strange now. I can't move back to Indiana. Now I have horrible parasites."

"Parasites?" Betty asked.

"Yes," Hannah choked. "From that deer meat we've been eating. I was trying so hard to save money. Jake was, too. Now we might have destroyed the baby."

"You sure you know what you're talking about?"

Hannah nodded vigorously. "The doctor just told me."

"Did she give you any information? Something on this infection? Papers?"

"Just told me," Hannah said.

"I'll be right back," Betty said, stepping down from the buggy.

It seemed a long time, sitting there in the cold. Hannah began to think of going inside herself when Betty returned.

"They gave me this," Betty said, waving some papers around. "It doesn't look good."

"That's what the doctor said." Hannah sank back into the buggy seat.

"We should go tell Jake about this," Betty said.

"Don't think so," Hannah shook her head. "He has work to do. I don't like going into that hardware anyway."

"Maybe not," Betty agreed. "Let's get your medicine then."

"That's going to cost more money," Hannah groaned. "I can't believe this."

"Believe it," Betty said. "It's part of life. Just remember the church is here to help you."

"Jake's a minister," Hannah said, with no idea why she was saying it. The thought just pushed into her mind.

"See," Betty said, as if the words made perfect sense. "All the more reason."

They drove towards the drug store on the main street.

CHAPTER TWENTY-EIGHT

When Jake arrived home, he found his wife weeping on the couch, clutching the crumpled papers Betty had gotten from the doctor's office. The words now looked like the spelling of doom to her, accenting what Dr. Lisa had said. Hannah waved the pages weakly in Jake's direction.

Jake took them but didn't read anything. Instead he sat down and drew Hannah close. "What's wrong?" he asked, smelling of wood shaving and winter air.

"The meat gave me an infection." Hannah sat straight upright. "It tells about it in those papers. If the baby gets it, terrible things will happen."

After glancing briefly at the pages, Jake's eyes found her face again. "What about you?"

"I'll be okay," she told him. "Just the baby's in danger."

"We'd better stop eating meat then," he said with resolution in his voice.

She shook her head. "It was my fault. The meat has to be cooked well."

"When will it stop?"

"I have medicines here." She pointed towards the desk. "They cost money. Too much."

"Will it happen again?"

"Don't think so. I didn't read all the paper. The infection is only once, from what I understand. Then your body takes care of it. Dr. Lisa didn't mention anything about another infection either."

Jake lifted the pages in his hand, scanning them for a few minutes. "We had better pray," he said softly.

Hannah felt hopelessness run through her. "I'm infected already."

"The baby isn't."

"How do you know?" She looked him in the face, searching for what, she wasn't certain. For hope or strength maybe? Neither seemed to make a difference at the moment. The feelings all ran together inside of her.

"I don't," he said. "Only God does."

What she wanted to say was, *so that leaves us in a real pickle. From what He's been doing, anything could be coming. We could have a completely crippled child.* Instead she said, "Maybe He knows what He's doing."

"He always does," Jake nodded solemnly.

Outside it had begun snowing, but neither of them noticed.

"I have to get supper," Hannah suddenly remembered, her face darkening.

Jake must have read her attitude, because he said softly, "We can't back down. You just need to cook it well."

Hannah saw his face set and wasn't sure she liked it. Was he being stubborn? It reminded her too much of his refusal to move to Indiana.

"It's dangerous," she said.

In response he studied a section of the paper in his hand. "We can't be afraid. It says right here — only one infection, and the meat must be well prepared. You can prepare it well from now on."

"It's just the money," she managed finally.

"No, not really," he said, then seemed to change his mind. "Maybe it is. Either way we'd better use the meat when we can."

"I'll burn it black," she told him, knowing she wouldn't.

He smiled, "I don't think I could eat any tonight anyway. Just do what you think best."

"I'll make soup," she decided, glancing at Jake, but he had already picked up the Family Life and was shaking his head as she left him for the kitchen.

Hannah noticed the snow through the kitchen window coming down in large flakes that hung close to the glass pane. So like life, she thought — lovely and light till you handled it, but then it left you cold inside.

I must be cried out, she thought as she prepared the soup for Jake's supper.

Jake said a simple prayer when they bowed their heads before eating. He asked God to help them, to give them grace for the trials of life and light from his word to guide the way. He asked for protection for the baby, so tenderly, that it seemed he already held it in his arms.

When he was done Hannah knew there were tears still left in her, as they rolled freely down her cheeks. Jake noticed, touching her arm from across the table and waiting until she calmed down before dishing out his soup.

"It's snowing," he said matter-of-factly.

"I know," she replied as she reached for the soup bowl. "It looks serious."

"God will help us," Jake said calmly. "It will soon be Christmas."

"What has that got to do with it?" She looked at him, puzzled.

"That's when the Christ child came — in the manger."

Hannah waited, wondering what Jake meant.

"The angels came close to earth that night. Maybe they come near every Christmas."

Hannah glanced sharply at him. He was changing faster than she could keep track of. *No wonder he could preach on Sundays if he could say things like this. Did he mean it?* "You think so?" she asked.

"I don't know." Jake looked out the kitchen window, seemingly studying each passing snow flake. "If they do, perhaps they will protect our child. It's not in a manger, but it's still in sort of a manger."

"It's just our baby," she said, wanting to be sure Jake understood. "That's not the same."

"Maybe to God it's enough," he said. "He has cared for little children ever since then. Has he not?"

"You must be careful what you say," she warned, the emotion strong in her voice.

Jake didn't seem to mind. "I know," he said, nodding slowly.

"You must be careful too with your preaching," she told him, remembering the bishop's visit.

"Yes," he said. "It's still the will of God in everything. I know that."

"What if the baby is born with the infection?" Hannah heard herself ask.

"Then we must bear the burden," Jake sighed, watching the snowflakes again. "It will be His will, and the best for us."

As Hannah got up to do the dishes, she felt exhaustion creeping over her. When she finished, she found Jake reading in the living room and told him she was going to bed. She never heard him come in but noticed he was there when she woke late in the night from her tossing and turning.

She had been dreaming she was back home again, the house so familiar and comforting, so strong and protecting. Each day went by normally — and yet not quite. A hidden danger seemed to follow her every move. When she hung out the wash or did the dishes it hovered over her. In both thunderstorms and sunshine she felt its presence.

She tried to tell her mom, to get words out of her mouth, but they wouldn't come. She tried once to meet her father at the door when he came home from work, but no matter how fast she walked or how hard she strained she couldn't get there in time.

Even on Sunday, sitting among all the usual people from her growing up years, she tried to scream that danger was coming, but no one could hear her.

Her face was sweaty and her arms cold when she finally

woke. She found relief in the familiar darkness of the bed-room. Holding still, she listened for Jake's even breathing, thankful she hadn't wakened him with her restlessness.

I have to write Mom, she thought. *I should have done it yes-terday.* Then she realized there had been no time yesterday, even if she had thought of it. Knowing she wouldn't be able to sleep now, at least for a while, she got out of bed, careful not to waken Jake.

Wrapping herself in a blanket she went into the living room. The snow continued to fall against the window. She lit the kerosene lamp, pulled the drawer open, got the paper tablet, and started writing.

Dear Mom,

It now seems like so many years since you and Dad were here. I would so love to hear your voice again, to see Dad sitting on the living room couch. If not here, then in Indiana, but it seems like it will not be. Jake thinks we are to stay in Montana, and I feel as if it will be forever.

We seem to be having nothing but troubles. I don't understand why this should be, but I know what you would say. Trouble makes us grow up. Well…I feel like I am about as grown up as I can stand. Things are happening so fast, I can hardly take it.

That my Jake, my good Jake, now has to stand up and preach in front of church — who would ever have imagined such a thing? I must say he did a good job the other Sunday. I wish you had been here, although he really did scare me.

Do you think I should have been scared? You really don't think Jake will think about going liberal? Do you? You can't imagine the kind of thoughts that go through my head. There seem to be new ones everyday now.

Then the worse thing is that I am now sick with

an infection. Betty told me about a good doctor in Libby, Dr. Lisa. I went there yesterday for my first baby checkup. She found the infection. I thought it was just a normal cold, like I got soon after you left.

It's not, though. It's parasites that could infect the baby, too. They won't hurt me, but will the baby. Dr. Lisa was hopeful about it. She has tests she can do later, to see if the baby has been infected. Not much help for the baby, if and when it should be infected.

I completely broke down crying with Betty while in the buggy and then here at home again. I suppose Jake wonders what to do with his wife sometimes, but he's bearing up. Did you ever have this much trouble?

One good thing, though. Jake really likes his job. I think there will even be extra money for the doctor bills and all. I hope so, at least. It's the one bright spot in our lives.

I had Mr. Brunson down for supper the other Friday night. Seems he heard Jake is a preacher, and shared his sad story with us. I can't tell you everything here, but it might not be over with yet. He seems to think his son may contact him. He was involved in an accident that killed his wife and daughter. That is why he lives out here all by himself. Now I know why he appeared so sad at times.

Jake says God will surely take care of us through all this, but I'm ashamed to say I wonder sometimes. I suppose Jake does too, but he never shows it.

It's snowing outside, and I couldn't sleep. Had some nightmare. You know the usual, but feel sleepy now. Kiss Indiana for me. I could cry about that too, but I'll have to be a big girl now. Isn't that what you would say?

With love, Hannah

Folding the paper carefully, Hannah watched the light from the kerosene lamp dance on the log cabin ceiling. *What if her child was born, perfect and wonderful, only to be doomed to life as a cripple?* It was too horrible a thought to entertain long, and she pushed it away.

Back in the bedroom, she carefully slipped under the covers without waking Jake and succeeded in dropping off to sleep.

Chapter Twenty-Nine

Jake came home the next evening with the news. His call from the hardware store to Dr. Lisa's office confirmed the diagnosis—Hannah had the toxoplasmosis infection. As if Betty knew Hannah needed support, her buggy came rattling into the driveway the next morning.

Hannah thought of throwing on a coat and meeting her outdoors, but the chilly morning persuaded her otherwise. By the time she bundled up, Betty would already be at the door.

"Good morning," Hannah said, opening the door, her face showing her delight in the visit.

Betty, not yet to the porch yet, called out, "You shouldn't stand with the door open. It's too cold this morning."

"I guess I'm glad to see you," Hannah told her, making no effort to move away.

"Has there been news?" Betty gave Hannah a quick sideways hug, pulling her tight with one arm. "Let's get you inside where it's warm."

"Jake talked with the doctor's office yesterday. It's confirmed."

"Oh, my." Betty's voice sounded dismayed. "I guess we already knew."

"I know," Hannah assured her.

"Have you let your mom know?" Betty took a seat on the couch.

"Wrote her yesterday. I couldn't sleep, so I got up during the night."

"To write the letter?"

"Yes."

Betty shrugged. "Can't say I blame you. I've never written letters at night, but I've walked the floors plenty."

"Mr. Brunson has his court case this week," Hannah volunteered, feeling like talking about someone else's troubles.

"That bear thing!" Betty exclaimed, apparently having forgotten.

Hannah nodded and thought about telling Mr. Brunson's family troubles but decided that wouldn't be appropriate.

"The game warden did come out about the cat," Betty said, adding with a chuckle, "They tracked it down right away and removed it from the area."

"Maybe they don't want another bear situation?" Hannah ventured.

"I'm sure you're right. You have any coffee?" Betty half rose from the couch. "I can make some. Still haven't had mine, rushing around to get the children off to school."

The mention of children brought a cloud across Hannah's face.

Betty noticed and told her quickly, "I'm so sorry about your situation."

"Let me get your coffee," Hannah said, glad for the distraction, knowing it helped keep back the tears. "The water is already hot."

"You think there's any hope? Of the child not being… you know…infected?"

"We don't know any more than we did," Hannah shrugged.

"I think the Lord will take care of you," Betty said, as Hannah left for the kitchen.

Coming back with Betty's steaming cup of coffee, Hannah asked, "Why do you think so?"

"Oh, Jake…." Betty said. "I just think so. Preaching like he does."

Was this what Bishop Nisley was concerned about, Hannah wondered? People making special things out of men because they could preach well?

"You only heard him once," Hannah said out loud.

"I know. It's about his turn again," Betty said. "Bishop might even let him have the main part before too long."

"I don't know," Hannah said, not wanting to consider it.

"God is so kind to this church," Betty said, her head over her coffee cup. "Giving us a real interesting preacher. Who would have thought of it? Jake Byler — I never did. He can sing of course, but that doesn't always carry into speaking. So young."

"The other ministers are good, too," Hannah felt the need to say.

"Of course," Betty was quick to agree. I wasn't saying that — just another one."

Hannah, though, knew she meant otherwise. At the very least Betty thought Jake was better than the others.

"I've really come to invite you for Thanksgiving." Betty put on her cheerful face. "I know we're all the family you have around here. Me too...not counting Steve's side. His family has so many gone, they aren't having anything till Saturday. I thought it would be my chance."

"Thanksgiving dinner," Hannah more stated than asked.

Betty nodded enthusiastically. "I could have Elizabeth and John over too."

"Really," Hannah said, feeling excitement rise in her. Then she remembered the last visit with Elizabeth and John.

"Surely you would like that?" Betty was looking at her strangely.

"Of course," Hannah assured Betty, telling herself that it would be okay, that Bishop Nisley had only done his job, and Jake had received the correction well. Things were as they should be now.

"It's decided then," Betty declared, finishing the last

of her coffee. "I really must be going. The wash is still not done. Really...not started." Betty got to her feet.

Sudden inspiration hit Hannah. "Why don't I come over for the day?"

"You would?" Betty smiled broadly, then her face darkened. "Oh my, but I'd just work you, like a hired hand...if you came now. There's work all over the place."

"Then all the more reason to come," Hannah declared. "I'll put some things away. Then I'm ready to go."

"Oh, this is so good," Betty gushed. "I'm really glad I came now. Didn't think I could spare the time. Now...I actually gained time."

"Jake would say you're right. Helping others adds to ourselves," Hannah added without thinking, never having heard Jake say so, but it sounded like something he would say.

"What a good preacher," Betty proclaimed.

Hannah reminded herself not to compliment Jake again, around Betty at least. Bishop Nisley apparently did have a point.

Seated beside Betty in the buggy as it rattled out the driveway, Hannah took deep breaths of the crisp air.

"Better than Indiana air," Betty had to say, spoiling the moment.

"I suppose so," Hannah acknowledged grudgingly. "At least Jake still has work."

"The Lord is looking out for you. Both of you," Betty said firmly. "He really is. The baby, too."

Hannah was about to say, *That's what Jake would say,* but remembered in time. "It's in the Lord's hands," she said instead, sounding all grown up, she thought. Perhaps she was changing too, changing right along with Jake in this land of mountains and rivers.

"Yes," Betty said from beside her.

As they turned right on the main road, the view of the mountains rose on both sides. The early morning fog had lifted to nearly the top of the peaks, adding a shine of white to the wooded slopes. Sunlight poured out of the fog in sheets of blinding light.

"It's angel country," Hannah said, not able to help herself.

"Cold right now," Betty replied without taking her eyes off the road. "More to come, too."

"You think it will be a hard winter?" Hannah asked.

"No doubt," Betty nodded. "Steve thinks so."

"You should know. You've lived here long enough." Hannah shifted on her seat, thinking of this road and how it might look come January with snow banks on either side. "Can you still get around?"

"Main roads, yes," Betty assured her. "It's not that bad."

"I hope not," Hannah said, not feeling too much comfort from the words.

They pulled into Betty's familiar driveway. Hannah helped unhitch, then waited while Betty took the horse into the barn.

"I'll leave the harness on," Betty shouted over her shoulder.

"Don't," Hannah said quickly, knowing Betty meant to keep the visit short. "I'll put the harness back on when I leave."

"The horses are used to it. They stand all day at church," Betty said, opening the barn door. "You can't stay too late anyway."

"I guess not," Hannah agreed, knowing she needed to be home in time to get Jake supper.

"You still eating that deer meat?" Betty asked when she came back out.

"Jake is." Hannah made a face.

"I don't blame you," Betty agreed. "If you can't eat all of it, we'll take it. That is, before you throw it away."

"I'll keep that in mind. Jake still wants it for now. Comes home pretty hungry. I guess he works hard in the furniture shop."

"We need to see what Jake's doing sometime," Betty said as they walked towards the house.

"I suppose so," Hannah said without too much enthusiasm, wondering why Betty wanted to see Jake's furniture. Was Jake's ordination now going to color all their relationships with people?

"It's probably as well done as his preaching," Betty said with a smile, confirming Hannah's suspicions.

"Probably is," she agreed because she knew it was true, and there was no sense in being mad at Jake. He had not chosen to have that piece of paper put in his book. Yet he was falling right in line, she told herself, like he kind of liked it.

"Now my work...." Betty drew in a deep breath. "My, my...here I am with the house all in a mess, and so much to do."

"That's what I came for."

"Yes...I know. It just feels so...well, wrong. Like I'm just using you."

"I didn't have much to do anyway. Just the cabin to take care of," Hannah assured Betty. "I need the company anyway."

"I imagine so...calm down then," Betty said, obviously speaking to herself. "Let's see. If I start the wash, maybe you can do the kitchen?"

"That would be okay." Hannah suited her words with actions, turning to the kitchen sink. Turning the knob to the left brought warm water and a feeling of surprise. She forgot how it was to have warm water without heating it on the stove. So quickly, she told herself, she was becoming a savage, losing the finesse of civilization she had known all her life.

"Warm water," she said, without thinking about it.

"I guess you don't have that," Betty said. "When's Jake going to install a water heater?"

"We seldom talk about it," Hannah said. "It costs money."

"That it does," Betty agreed. "Maybe with the furniture making you can soon afford it."

"It's not a big deal," Hannah shrugged. "I think Jake said the plumbing would have to be changed, too, if hot water was installed. The owners who built the place liked things rough, I guess."

"Well, I'll be at the laundry," Betty said, disappearing towards the bedrooms.

Moments later the gas motor, which Hannah knew ran the Maytag washing machine, started up in Betty's laundry room. Hannah finished up the dishes, then followed Betty as she carried out the first basket of wash.

"You don't have to help here," Betty told her when she saw Hannah coming.

"Your hands are cold already," Hannah replied, blowing on her own.

"They are," Betty agreed, hanging the first piece on the line, her hands red from carrying the basket.

With ⌐ ⌐nah helping, the wash went up quickly, the woode⌐ ⌐s holding things in place.

"⌐ ⌐ ⌐ ⌐ink it'll freeze?" Hannah asked, meaning the

"⌐ ⌐on't think so," Betty said, her teeth chattering. "My, ⌐ cold though. Don't know why it bothers me — guess I'm ⌐etting older. The sun will hit the line soon."

They continued the routine until all the wash was on the line. After lunch, the sun did do its job, and Hannah helped bring in the baskets of clothes. Betty insisted on taking her home as soon as the last piece was in.

"I'll help you with the folding," Hannah told her, but Betty would hear nothing of it.

"You have things to do, I'm sure."

Hannah agreed and went to get the horse. The drive home turned out pleasant enough, though Hannah could tell it would turn cold again that night. Mr. Brunson's pickup rattled past as Betty dropped her off in front of the cabin. She wondered how he was doing and whether his son would make contact anytime soon.

"Thanks so much," Betty said without getting out of the buggy. "I have to be getting back."

"Thanks for picking me up," Hannah told her. "I needed the company."

"We all do," Betty said, closing the buggy door and driving off.

Hannah watched her leave before entering the cabin. The fire had gone out in the stove, and she stoked it back to life, reaching for its warmth as the flame flickered and then burned brightly.

Chapter Thirty

J AKE CAME HOME cheerful enough, Hannah thought. She met him at the door, feeling well herself from her day at Betty's place.

"Betty had me over," she announced as a greeting, thinking Jake wanted to know why she was in such a good mood.

"We are blessed to have some family close," he smiled broadly. "I have good news, too."

"Yes." she tilted her head back, reveling in the closeness of his presence.

"Mr. Howard sold our first table and chairs. A full set. Brought a pretty good price, and the customer loved it. It's being shipped back east."

"Who was it?" Hannah wondered.

"Don't know. Some party hunting in the mountains, I think. He purchased it for his wife's dining room." Jake's smile lit his face again.

"Sorry I have to spend it on doctor bills," Hannah said as her face darkened. "I'm glad, though, it's working out. I guess God knows we need some good news."

"There will be more good news. For us" — Jake shut the cabin door, drawing her close — "and for the baby, too."

She smelled the scent of wood on Jake, his growing beard brushing her cheek. That was another thing, she thought, laughing softly as Jake let her go. If he didn't trim his beard soon, it would be down past the first button on his shirt. She reached up to playfully run her hand down its length.

"You need to trim the edges," she told him, laughing again, wondering if this was a preacher thing, too.

"I guess," he said. "Just didn't get around to it."

"Supper's ready," she told him, leading him towards the kitchen. "Wash up."

Jake did, joining her at the table, where she had hung the gas lantern on the hook in the ceiling.

"Still won't eat it?" Jake asked, helping himself to the meat dish she had prepared.

"Not yet," she said. "Maybe some time."

"I need to get you store bought," he said, his face showing his concern. "You need the strength."

"I'll do with potatoes and vegetables for now," she told him with a smile. "I have funny tastes anyway. Baby does that."

"That's what Mom said — with the younger ones," he replied, his eyes distant with memory.

"You miss your family?" she asked, wondering. "Betty asked us over for Thanksgiving. Might have Elizabeth and John, too. Steve's family doesn't have anything going on this year."

"I do miss them," he said good-naturedly. "More than I thought I would. We'll get a chance to visit though. All in good time."

"Maybe around Christmas?" she suggested.

"I doubt it," Jake shook his head. "This is Montana. Too many miles to travel, I think."

"It is," she agreed, remembering her desires. "You sure about not moving back to Indiana? Your family would be closer then."

"No moving," he said, his face deep in thought. "God wants us here."

"Has Mr. Brunson said anything more?" she wondered, thinking Jake might have spoken with him when she wasn't around.

"He did stop in at the hardware," Jake said. "Looked at what we were doing and seemed quite interested, although I wasn't sure why."

"Maybe he likes log furniture."

"Could be." Jake pushed back from the table. "Asked all kinds of questions about the business end of it, and talked with Mr. Howard afterwards. Don't know about what all — I think the sales end of things."

"Maybe he could sell more," Hannah said. "He is from back east."

"I thought of that, too. Then his family...I don't know," Jake shook his head. "It'll all work out. He'd have to work with Mr. Howard, of course."

"Why couldn't you make furniture on your own?"

"Money. Up-front money. It takes a lot, and I don't have it." Jake didn't seem too disappointed, just reciting facts. "I'm happy with how things are now. Let's pray."

They bowed their heads together silently, giving thanks for the meal eaten. Hannah also gave thanks for Jake's work and for Betty, for family close by. She thought of giving thanks for the baby but decided to just be thankful Jake and Betty were expecting the best. For her part, she was glad she wasn't too depressed. That could come easily enough, she knew.

"You want help with the dishes?" Jake asked, but Hannah could see his mind was somewhere else.

"I can do them," she told him.

"I'll help clear the table," he said with a smile, and she let him.

Jake left her the gas lantern after he was done, lighting a kerosene lamp for himself, setting it beside him in the living room. Hannah knew Jake was trying to save money, leaving her the best light. It warmed her heart and brought tears to her eyes.

When she was done with the dishes, Hannah brought the gas lantern with her, its waves of light bringing Jake's eyes up to meet her face. He was reading from the Bible.

She hung the lantern on the hook and joined him. When she picked up the Family Life, he went back to his Bible reading.

Her thoughts, though, were not on the page in front of her. The black words refused to stand out from the paper surrounding them, swimming together. She felt instead the solid push of life around her.

Where was it going? That was the question. Each day seemed to push Jake and her further along, whether they wanted to go or not. Was this how it was for everyone?

Her eyes sought Jake's face. His concentration was total, his lips moving as he read. Was he soon to be a father? He was already a preacher and she a preacher's wife, all before their first child was even born.

Outside the window was the deep night. Hannah could almost feel the chill of the air against the logs. Jake must have noticed too, because he stirred himself from his reading.

"Better add some wood to the furnace," he said, getting up.

Hannah watched him as he left for the utility room and their small furnace that heated the parts of the house unreached by the kitchen stove. He looked aged already, or maybe it was just the night that made her think so.

She had thought the same thing last Sunday, watching him preach after the ministers came back downstairs. Jake had the first sermon again, which was normal for a young preacher, she supposed. Bishop Nisley might want to prove his minister well before he let him have the main sermon, an hour-long affair.

Hannah had watched Jake's face as he preached, at least while he was looking elsewhere. When his eyes came in her direction, she dropped hers to the floor. Here at home she didn't feel the need, but at Sunday morning church she felt as if she had no business being part of his holy thoughts.

Beside her, young Sylvia Stoll seemed to have no such

problem, meeting Jake's eyes when they came in her direction. Hannah felt dirty for even thinking it, but she couldn't help herself. What reason did Sylvia have for keeping her eyes raised when Jake looked in their direction?

Hannah asked herself if she would drop her eyes if Sylvia's husband, Ben, were preaching. That was hard to imagine, but Hannah supposed she wouldn't. Yet the conclusion made her feel no better; Ben wouldn't be preaching this well.

Jake yawned when he came back, taking his seat on the couch again.

"I heard some news today," he said, not looking at her.

"Yes?" She waited.

"Some meetings over in Kalispell. Tent meetings."

"Like what?" She turned to face him.

"Revival meetings. Some Mennonite group."

"And?" she left the question hang. Surely Jake was simply passing on information.

"A fellow came into the hardware passing out flyers. Mr. Howard let him leave some on the counter."

"You looked at them?" Hannah's eyes were wide in the flickering light of the gas lantern.

Jake chuckled, "I couldn't help it. They looked interesting. I've never been to tent meetings."

"No," Hannah said, "surely not. You wouldn't."

Jake laughed this time, shaking his head.

Not certain what Jake meant, Hannah sat up straighter. Did he mean no, or was he laughing at her questions? Hannah waited.

"I could ask Bishop Nisley whether we can go," he said, using a perfectly calm tone of voice.

"You wouldn't." Hannah grabbed his arm. "Don't even think of it. Everyone would find out, even asking. They would know you asked."

Jake laughed again. "I'm just teasing."

"Don't tease," she told him, not telling him all the fears behind the command.

"I'm sorry," he said, looking so. "I didn't mean it. It just looked interesting."

Not sure what to think she studied his face.

"I was teasing" he finally said, chuckling. "Really."

"Okay," she relented, drawing him towards her. "Don't scare me like that."

"Ben and Sylvia went," he said, dropping the words like a bomb.

"How do you know that?" she asked, sitting upright, frightened again.

"I'm a minister," he said simply, as if that were the most obvious thing in the world. "I'm told things."

"Surely people aren't tattling to you already." She felt a new fear run through her. "I don't want to be involved with that."

Visions of her growing up years flashed through her mind. Dennis, a distant cousin on Kathy's side, had always run to the preachers with every breach of rules he witnessed. Her parents had never liked such tattling, relative or not. Their dislike spread even further, though, reaching the preachers who would listen to such people.

"It's not like that," Jake said, seeming to understand her question. "John mentioned it last Sunday."

So Jake had known for nearly a week already? He had not shared it with her. Hannah swallowed hard, knowing this was how it might well go, but still feeling the shock of it.

"I hope they aren't serious," she managed. "I'd hate to lose Sylvia and Ben."

"Me too," Jake said, reaching for his Bible again. "Bishop hopes a talk will solve the problem. He's going himself, I think."

That Bishop Nisley would go, instead of sending one of his ministers, showed Hannah the importance of the conversation as well as the bishop's concern for his members.

"I hope it works," she said.

Jake nodded, busy reading.

Hannah sat still, frozen in place by a horrible thought that crossed her mind. If Ben and Sylvia left the Amish and went liberal, her concern over Sylvia's eyes meeting Jake's would go away. A deep embarrassment filled her. What if Jake knew what she was thinking? She would never tell him, that was for sure. Once again she felt the disruption of life's unexpected twists and turns.

"I'm going to bed," she said softly.

"I'll be there in a little bit," Jake smiled, his eyes gentle in the lantern's light.

CHAPTER THIRTY-ONE

BETTY EXTENDED THE dining room table from wall to wall for her Thanksgiving feast. Bishop Nisley and Elizabeth acted like old times, so that Hannah felt young again. In what now seemed a distant past, she and Jake had sat here, unmarried, eyeing each other across the table.

John and Elizabeth had approved then, and certainly seemed to approve now. Perhaps the bishop's concern about Jake was waning. Betty and Steve talked like family, and Hannah joined in. Jake seemed to enjoy himself even with no immediate family present.

A few days later Mr. Brunson stopped by and talked with Jake without getting out of his pickup. The court appearance had gone as expected, with a heavy fine. Jake came back in but made no mention of a son appearing at Mr. Brunson's place, and Hannah didn't ask. She didn't have the heart. There might be no son willing to make contact.

The next morning, Saturday, Jake was working in the barn when it happened. Hannah knew what was happening when it started, even though she had never experienced it before. She was losing the baby.

She started to call Jake but decided against it. Instead, she waited and told him when it was over. There was no hiding her tear-stained face. Jake insisted she see the doctor at once and went to hitch up Mossy.

Hannah wisely told him, when Jake had Mossy ready to go, that they needed to call ahead since it was Saturday.

This resulted in a stop at Betty's while Jake went to phone at the neighbor's.

Jake returned, after what seemed a long time, with the news Dr. Lisa would see Hannah in the office as soon as they could get there. It had taken a call to an emergency number and then the wait till Dr. Lisa returned the call.

After the examination, Dr. Lisa had little to say that Hannah didn't already know.

"You lost the baby," she said gently. "Don't take it too hard, okay? Nature has its way about these things."

"So I passed on the infection?" Hannah wanted to know.

"Likely. It's just a guess. It could have been for other reasons."

Hannah, though, felt sure that was the reason. It was her own fault.

"You shouldn't blame yourself," Dr. Lisa told her, seeing the look on her face. "These things are still in the hand of God. He works out what is best."

"That's what Jake says," Hannah told her. "I wish it hadn't happened, though. This could have been Jake's boy."

Dr. Lisa shook her head. "Let me get you a prescription. Pick it up at the drug store. If anything unusual comes up let me know. I think you should be okay."

Hannah thanked Dr. Lisa and left the office after paying, feeling guilty over the amount of Jake's money she had to spend. On the other hand, she figured it was a small amount to pay the doctor for an emergency call.

"You okay?" Jake asked her when she climbed into the buggy.

She nodded. "We need to pick this up. Nothing serious, I guess. It's just a precaution, I think."

"We're getting it anyway," Jake said, correctly interpreting her inclination to pass up the purchase.

They stopped briefly at Betty's place for Hannah to fill in the details. "Everything should be okay," Hannah whispered, in case any of the children were near enough to hear.

"The baby? For sure?" Betty wanted to know.

Hannah nodded.

When they got home, Jake stopped to check the mailbox. There was little except for what looked like a bill, and then Jake offered her a letter.

"Your mother," he said. "Nice it came today."

"Mothers know sometimes," she said.

"Maybe," Jake kind of grunted.

While Jake unhitched, Hannah sat down on the couch to read her letter.

Dear Hannah,

I know I just wrote last week, but I felt like writing today again. Seems like time is going past so fast. I think of you often. How are you and the coming baby doing? We pray the child will be spared any ill effects of the infection.

Hannah stopped reading as the tears stung. Her mother had no way of knowing, of course.

Tell Jake hi for us. Indiana is still open to people moving in, but we understand. Aunt Martha was here today. I have a quilt in the frame. It's for the school Christmas sale. I've let the women know, and seems like someone stops in most every day. Last week Mary Chupp stayed almost all day. It was good catching up on the news, as they live in the other district. Our two districts have the schoolhouse together. That has changed since you attended. I think there were four districts together then.

A bunch of couples have been called out in church recently. Dave and Esther Yoder last Sunday. Seems like more young people get married all the time, but then why should we complain. It's a sign of a growing and prosperous church.

We hope this finds you well, and in good health. May God keep both you and Jake. I think your dad wants coffee made. He's banging around in the kitchen.

Your mother

Hannah folded the letter, feeling comforted in a way. Even across the miles, her mother's love had reached her.

"She said to tell you hi," Hannah told Jake, who had just come in the door. "You really ought to write your mother."

"I think I will," Jake said, not needing much persuading.

Hannah went to fix supper, wondering what they were to eat. She found some leftovers and warmed them in the oven after starting the fire. With the cold weather, Hannah now set most of her refrigerator things outside on a shelf. Jake had nailed one up on the wall, high enough to be out of reach of animals. The squirrels could reach the items, she figured, but wouldn't be out much in the winter.

When she called for supper, Jake looked carefully over what she had prepared.

"No more of the deer meat," he stated.

"Really?" Hannah said, surprised by this sudden turn of events.

"I'll buy hamburger for the rest of the winter," he said firmly. "It's the principle of the thing."

"But...," she protested, thinking of the cost.

Jake only shook his head, sitting down.

"Betty said she would take it," Hannah told him, remembering. "She didn't want us to throw it away."

"We're not eating any more wild meat until we're old," Jake said. "I'll take the meat over tonight yet."

"I can do it Monday," she told him.

"Okay," he relented. "Be sure and do it though."

Hannah felt like saying thank you, but didn't. Jake might not understand. The load of her guilt felt much lightened — Jake must not think this totally her fault. He had said old, which must mean till she was done bearing children.

Feelings of sorrow and joy ran together in her heart. Jake must think her able to bear more children, or he wouldn't have made such a comment.

"It wasn't your fault," he said, not looking at her. "I shot the deer, trying to save money. We shouldn't blame each other or anyone. God still is in charge, and He knows what He's doing."

Hannah nodded, thankful for Jake's understanding.

"God will give us children as he wishes," Jake continued. "I think many more. I know I want children."

Hannah said nothing, not disagreeing, but Jake had thought this child would be spared, too.

"God will keep us," Jake said, still confident.

"It's been pretty hard already," she said. "Hard for me."

"Probably harder than I know." Jake reached over to squeeze her hand.

"I suppose so." She paused, but then just blurted it out. "You're a minister now. I don't know how to be a minister's wife. I want to move back to Indiana, and we can't, because you're a minister. Everything is changing so fast — for both of us. Like every day. I...I can't keep up. Now this."

"You make things much easier for me," Jake whispered. "You don't know by how much."

"It's hard for you?" she asked him in surprise.

"Yes," Jake nodded. "I never asked for this. Never dreamed of preaching. Never even thought of it. Even that morning I never thought of it. It wasn't until I heard the bishop say my name, and even then it seemed impossible. Do you think God would work like that? I know our faith says he does, and that is how the old people believe things work. Yet why choose me?"

Jake shook his head. "I prayed hard and asked God to help me. I asked for help from His spirit. Yet, I didn't know how it would ever go. Getting up there the first time — you don't know how afraid I was. Now John says I preach too good. I don't know what too good is. I don't know what preaching is. How would I know when it's too good?"

Hannah was watching Jake's face, surprised by the flow of words, her fingers tightening on his hand.

"It felt awful to lose my job, like part of me had left and gone away. How was I supposed to supply for you, and the baby coming? I tried to save money and bring in cheaper meat. Then I bring in this." Jake's eyes looked weary and torn.

Hannah got up and stood beside Jake. "You must not think so," she told him.

"But I have you." His face lit up at the words. "You don't know what that means to me."

"No I don't," Hannah whispered, her hand touching his head. "You don't know all the things I've been thinking already."

"It's okay," he told her. "It doesn't matter. God will help us. I know He will. He already has."

"Yes," she agreed, feeling a little of his faith, drawing on his strength.

"I'd better write that letter," Jake said, startling her. "You think I still can?"

"You'll have to let me read it," she told him.

"No," he made a face.

"Yes," she said smiling. "I do the dishes. You write. Then I read."

Jake grunted, acting putout, but he did go into the living room. After Hannah was done in the kitchen, she found him at the desk still writing.

"How's it going?" she asked.

"Slowly." He held his hands over the paper.

Without saying anything, she pulled it out from under him, reading out loud.

"Dear Dad and Mom,

"Greetings from your son in Jesus' name. If this is a terrible letter you can blame it on Hannah. She made me do it.

"I hope this finds you well. We have had a great sorrow

today. Hannah lost the child she was carrying through an infection, we think. We still have each other, though, and God, so we have much to be thankful for."

"That's all I need to read," Hannah told him, giving him a kiss on top of his head.

"Give it back then," Jake said. "I'm not done writing."

She did, noticing his ears were a little red around the edges.

"You should write more often," Hannah told him. "Your mom will like it. They might even come and visit us."

"Writing and visiting have nothing to do with each other," Jake said, taking the pen again. "Not unless you're telling them you're coming to visit. Then it still has little to do with it. It's just bearing the message."

"Are you preaching to me?" Hannah asked him.

"Maybe," he said.

"Then I agree with Bishop Nisley. You shouldn't do such a good job of it."

"That isn't funny," Jake said when she burst out laughing, but Hannah saw the smile on his face even before he joined her.

CHAPTER THIRTY-TWO

THE DAYS WENT by, dull and uneventful now, for which Hannah was grateful. She needed the quiet, and even the weather cooperated.

Then a few inches of snow fell, and the night following more came down. From what Hannah could see, it lay a foot deep in some places. Jake laughed when she suggested he stay home. He told her the main road was open, and besides, Mr. Howard needed him at the furniture shop, as sales were climbing. This was Montana after all, and snow was expected. He hitched Mossy to the buggy and left, the thin tires squeaking in the snow.

The past Sunday afternoon, driving home from church, Jake had given her news that now required her to clean up the cabin. Why the meeting had to be held here she didn't know — perhaps because of who was involved.

Jake had just told her what Bishop Nisley had said, and that was that. At seven tonight, Mose Chupp and the bishop were coming to their place to talk with Ben and Sylvia Stoll. The wives were coming along, since it wasn't a formal ministers' meeting. She wouldn't feel uncomfortable, Jake had said. Whether she would or wouldn't had little to do with the wives coming along, Hannah felt certain, but didn't mention that to Jake.

Jake later informed Hannah that according to Bishop Nisley's information, Ben and Sylvia had gone not just to one meeting in Kalispell but to all of them. How was this done? Hannah wondered out loud. Jake said they stayed with some friends and so didn't have to drive back and forth every night.

Jake came home a little early so they could be finished with supper in time. Hannah grew more tense as the time approached and told Jake to leave the kitchen work to her, even though he had offered to help. The first buggy came in the driveway as she was drying the dishes.

Jake stepped out on the porch to welcome Minister Chupp and his wife while Hannah waited inside. She could hear Jake say good evening, then the sound of shuffling feet. Opening the door, she smiled a greeting while Jake stayed on the porch to wait for the others.

"I'll take your coats," Hannah told Clara and Mose, motioning for them to take seats on the couch. She had chairs set up around the living room for the others.

"How are you making out in your cabin?" Clara asked, looking around. Mose just smiled at her, nodded his head, and took his seat.

"Okay," Hannah told Clara. "I like it. Different, I guess."

"I suppose so," Clara said, sitting down. "We've been wanting to visit. This is the first chance we've had."

"I guess we've never had church here," Hannah chuckled, referring to the turn each Amish family takes in hosting the church services. "When that happens, it's got to be summer and in the barn. The house is way too small."

"Nothing wrong with that," Clara assured her. "I'm sure it can be arranged."

The thought left Hannah's head spinning.

"I'm sure they'll get around to it," Clara went on. "It's not summer yet."

Mose smiled and nodded again.

"I hope it isn't soon. I have to get ready," Hannah said. "Why haven't I thought of this before?"

"You haven't been married long," Clara chuckled. "Just one of the responsibilities of married life."

"Yep," Mose got his agreement in, nodding his head again.

The cabin door opened behind them to admit Ben and Sylvia. Hannah saw John and Elizabeth's buggy coming in as she turned around.

"Good evening," she said, putting on her best smile. Inside she wished she had never thought about Sylvia looking at Jake in church, but it wasn't intentional. The thoughts had just come.

"Good evening," Sylvia and Ben said together, their faces sober.

"I'll take your coats," Hannah told them. Surely Ben and Sylvia weren't leaving for a more liberal church, she thought as she took the coats to the bedroom. Hannah hoped sincerely they weren't.

Jake already had Elizabeth and John inside when Hannah came back from the bedroom. She greeted them with a good evening and took their coats as well. When she came back the third time, the conversation of the evening began, Bishop Nisley wasting no time getting to the point.

"I hope Ben and Sylvia understand the reason for this meeting. We mean only good — all for Ben and Sylvia's good. We are here to help and to inquire out of concern. I hope no hard feelings come out of this."

Jake and Mose nodded their heads. Hannah wondered how in the world she and Jake were even at this meeting but knew she must get used to sudden and interruptive events.

"It has reached our ears," John continued, "that you attended meetings. Revival meetings, I think they are called by our Mennonite friends. This is of concern to us."

"We meant no harm," Ben said. "We were invited by relatives in Kalispell. They set up a tent there, these Mennonites. I guess it sounded interesting."

"Revival meetings?" John asked them.

"Yes," Ben said.

"What do they mean by revival meetings? What is being

revived?" John asked. "Do they feel their spiritual lives are dead? Have they no more commands of our Lord to fulfill? Which of God's words no longer requires obedience?"

"Don't be too hard on them," Elizabeth said, reaching over, touching his arm. "I'm sure they meant no harm."

The bishop cleared his throat. "Perhaps, but this could lead to great error."

"We felt there was a lack in our spiritual lives," Sylvia spoke up. "I was really blessed by the preaching."

"I see," John said, settling back into the couch.

Hannah was sure the bishop was thinking something, but he didn't say it.

"Surely you understand the need for obedience," Mose spoke up. "Have you been keeping the commandments of God?"

Ben shrugged, "We try."

"We are afraid," Sylvia said.

"That's not unusual," John said. "Many of us fear. Sometimes the fear of the Lord is a good thing."

"It's not that," Ben said, hanging his head, seemingly unwilling to continue.

"See," Sylvia said. "Maybe I wasn't born again. Before...I mean. Now I think I am. We went to...up when the preacher had the altar call. We wanted to be right with God."

Ben nodded, "He really preached about repentance and getting rid of sin."

"The preacher?" Mose asked.

Ben nodded again.

"You were practicing sin?" John asked, his brow wrinkled.

"We just felt it," Sylvia spoke up. "Inside us. This preacher spoke of the blood of Jesus washing us."

"There's nothing wrong with that," John agreed. "This sin? You were sinning?"

Ben managed a grin. "Not really. I mean, I did break a few of the church rules at times. Maybe small ones. That's all."

"It was we who were the sinners," Sylvia added.

"We are," John agreed. "All of us. So I still don't understand."

Hannah glanced at Jake, but he had his eyes on the floor. Obviously this was bishop work. She again wondered why in the world they were even here.

"I guess we felt something. For the first time. In here." Ben lay his hand on his chest. "We wanted an experience with God."

"I see," John said. "An experience."

"Yes," Sylvia nodded her head vigorously. "We felt washed afterwards. We confessed our sins with the preacher."

"You confessed your sins?" Mose asked. "Which ones?"

"Things we had done — as children, the usual, I guess," Sylvia said. "Ben didn't have as many. I confessed the lie I told my mother — I never told anyone about it before."

"That is why we have pre-communion church," John said. "It's time then for confessions."

"Not for those things," Sylvia said. "At least I never thought of it so. Just church things."

"It just felt different," Ben added.

"I can understand that. Some confessions are to be private," John said. "Have you told your mother this?"

Sylvia shook her head. "I felt cleansed at the meeting."

"You probably should," Mose spoke up. "That would be between your mother and you."

"I suppose so," Sylvia said, seeming deep in thought.

"The other things, too," John added. "Whatever you told this preacher, if they involve other people, they should be told."

Ben nodded his head. Sylvia still seemed to be thinking.

"See, we are not priests," John said. "We don't stand between God and man. We don't hear others' sins. We confess our sins to God. If we do sin against the church, we confess to the church. If we sin against others we confess to them. The confessing then is to restore fellowship. It is not to forgive our sins. Only God can do that."

"His blood," Ben said. "They spoke of His blood."

"That is how it is done," John agreed. "The blood of Jesus. They are right about that. *Nur durch das Blut von Christus.*"

"So…maybe no harm has been done," Mose said, seeming to relax in his seat.

"Maybe," John allowed.

Ben cleared his throat, his eyes on the floor. "We would like to leave."

"Leave?" John asked, his voice stunned.

"Join the group in Kalispell," Ben said. "We feel a oneness with them. They are starting a new group with those who went to the altar."

"You're sure about this?" John asked. "I'm sorry to hear it. Isn't this sudden like?"

"Maybe," Ben allowed, his eyes still on the floor.

"We hope this will cause no trouble with the church," Sylvia said. "God is really drawing our hearts."

"I see," John said, his face a question. "This drawing? It is out into the world then?"

"Not the world," Sylvia said quickly. "To the church of God. To other believers."

"I'm sorry you feel this way," John said.

"You surely don't think — think we aren't the church of God?" Mose asked, the question lingering in his voice.

"No," Ben shook his head vigorously. "It just isn't necessary to live like this."

"Like this?" Mose asked.

"Cars and such," Ben said. "The preacher said so. We can have God without living like this. It might even be holding us back."

"From growing spiritually," Sylvia added.

"Yes," Ben said. "Spiritually."

"You realize what's out there?" John asked. "In the world — the temptations, the evils, the trials that happen to one's faith. It's different from what you're used to."

"I suppose," Ben said. "The preacher said the grace of God would be sufficient."

"Yes," John nodded his head. "God might even have grace for ignorance, but I doubt you'll be spared everything."

"John," Elizabeth laid her hand on his arm again. "They're young."

"There is no reason to spare them the truth," John said. "You realize this will need to be told to the church."

"You…you won't be excommunicating us?" Ben's voice trembled.

"Will this be a Mennonite church you're going to?" John asked.

"Yes," Ben said. "I think so."

"I will see what the church says. The other ministers, too. If you don't get a car until you join…this new church — if it is a Mennonite church? — then keep yourselves in the *ordnung* till then. I know it may seem foolish to you, since you are leaving anyway. You'll need all the help you can get, though. A little keeping of the rules won't hurt and might even help you. We are not the keeper of men's souls. We just watch the best we know how. Our faith has always been a voluntary one, a gathering of like hearts. If you wish to leave, I don't stand in your way."

Ben looked relieved, Hannah thought.

"If it's a wacky church, that's another matter," the bishop added. "There are some out there."

"It won't be," Sylvia said. "The preacher is a very spiritual man."

"I hope so," John said. Hannah noticed Elizabeth laid her hand on his arm again.

The bishop then dismissed the meeting, saying more would be discussed among the ministry the next preaching Sunday. Perhaps Ben and Sylvia would be willing to give this more thought? They both nodded their heads.

After everyone had left, Jake stood watching the buggy lights grow distant.

"I'm sorry to see them go," he said.

"I am too," Hannah said, surprised how much she really meant it.

CHAPTER THIRTY-THREE

HANNAH SAT IN her usual place on the hard bench, but Sylvia Stoll was not beside her. Instead the line of young unmarried girls started. Apparently Sylvia and Ben had already left the Amish church, or they were absent for sickness. Hannah guessed the former, based on how the meeting concluded the other night.

The wind had blown all night, and on the way to church a cold blast came from over the Idaho mountains. Betty whispered, when Hannah greeted her in the kitchen, that it was another sure sign of a hard winter. Outside the living room window of Amos Raber's place, where church was being held, the branches on the trees were still whipping back and forth.

Hannah shivered on the bench, though the house was well heated. Amos kept his old furnace chugging along just fine, leaving every so often to add wood to the fire. The cause of her discomfort was not the temperature but the emptiness inside of her.

Hannah hadn't expected such strong feelings when she lost the baby. A void filled her, the life that should have been there gone. She felt like crying, weeping over a grave, but there was none.

Around her the singing rose and fell while the ministers were meeting upstairs. It shouldn't be long before they returned and began preaching. Jake would be preaching this morning, she supposed. It might even be his first time doing the main sermon. Strange, she thought, how preaching suddenly held such interest for her.

The song ended with one last exertion, the notes rising in a joyous outburst of sound. Around the room, silence descended instantly, as if no one wanted to be the first to move. Then came a cautious shuffle of feet, and someone fumbled for his handkerchief, loudly blowing his nose.

With the announcement of the next song number, the room filled with expectation, as if everyone simultaneously drew in breath for the start of the singing. The sound of shoes on the hardwood steps came first, though, followed by a collapse of the room's collective preparation. All around Hannah came the soft closing of songbooks. She shut her own book, laying it under her bench. Preaching hour had arrived.

Bishop Nisley delivered the first sermon, followed by the scripture reading. Since Christmas came in two weeks, Bishop mentioned the fact briefly. Jake, though, delivering the main sermon as Hannah expected, discussed the full story of Jesus' birth.

Standing close to the double living room windows, he said that Christmas was likely not the birthday of Jesus, yet it could be a time to reflect on God becoming a man. Starting with what Hannah assumed were Old Testament prophecies, Jake spoke of the promise of a child who would be the hope of mankind. In a world of sickness, sin, suffering, and war, God would give His answer in His own time, His solution to the world's troubles.

The baby, born of a virgin, would grow up to trod on the head of the serpent and be bitten in the heel for his troubles. He would be called Emanuel, the Everlasting Father, the Prince of Peace, and of His reign and kingdom there would be no end. He would be known as the Man of Sorrows, Jake said. He would weep over his people, who would reject him. He would be taken as a lamb to the slaughter, to be killed like a sheep who made no protest before its shearers. The world would fail to understand how God could save without an army, without a war of slaughter against his enemies, without reigning as a King from Jerusalem.

The religious leaders, Jake said, were expecting something God wasn't doing, something He never said He would do. Their years of Scripture study had led them away from God into their own understanding. The church leaders now thought God was like them — hard, unforgiving, enforcing a harsh code of justice.

Many had forgotten the beginning, when God walked in the garden with Adam and Eve, talking to them in the cool of the day. People of Jesus' day were no longer being told that God loved His people, that He created them out of that love, and that He could do no differently. His nature demanded it.

In the Old Testament, Jake said, God spoke of comforting His people. He commanded the prophets to cry out to Jerusalem, to proclaim the end of her warfare, her iniquities pardoned; one could receive double from the Lord for any wrongs committed.

Jake said God was no longer in the garden. Sin had defiled it. Man could work all he wanted, but the earth would never be heaven again. This was no longer our home. God's people were now to be pilgrims and strangers down here, never quite at home, preparing for their move to a better world where they would live forever.

The wonder of the child's birth, Jake said, was not that the earth had become heaven, but that heaven had come down here. God became man, not to live in one place or to be at home in one country, but to be at home in every man and woman's heart, preparing them for the move to God's new world. There would never be another Garden of Eden, just a garden in the heart of all who believe in Jesus.

God wanted to live fully through those who believed in Him. Wanted them to go into all the world, wherever sin was, living the life of God fully — the humble, unarmed, holy life that the child brought into the manger. Such a life inevitably would bring persecution and hatred from those who didn't understand.

Our forefathers, Jake said, never believed the earth could be made into heaven. They never sought to bring about another protected place, where no scorpions crawled or wolves tore up lambs, where people could eat from the tree of life whenever they wanted to. Instead, they went about their lives like sheep among wolves, because that was how God came into this world.

It was a great mystery, Jake said, what God was doing. He revealed his plans slowly, throughout the pages of Scripture. He started working with one man, Abraham, and one nation, Israel. This led many religious leaders to think that where God started He was going to stop. They thought this meant God loved only Jews, and worked only through war and battle.

But God was going somewhere, Jake said, starting to walk around a little himself, his hands clasped in front of him. Hannah watched Bishop Nisley's face, afraid of what she would see. Did Bishop think Jake was preaching too good again? Especially on this, his first main sermon?

Relieved by what she saw, Hannah relaxed. A faint smile played on Bishop's face. She was certain he even nodded his head once. Apparently Jake was not straying too far, or maybe he had proven himself in other ways and Bishop now trusted him.

Through His work with Israel, God was taking the best route to Christ, Jake said. God could do anything, could do whatever He wanted, but God had chosen the best. Along the way, He had allowed war, He had allowed David to have many wives, but when Christ came the fullness of God's will was revealed.

The baby in the manger showed what God truly intended for his people. It showed how they were to live in a world of sin and sorrow. If God could fulfill his promise of bringing Christ into the world, if He could move past wars to the unprotected manger, then God could also fulfill His promise now.

That promise, Jake said, was the day coming, a day when all tears would be wiped away, all sorrow and sin removed in a new heaven and a new earth. It would be just as wrong for God's people today to think that suffering and sickness could be removed from our present earth as it would have been for people in King David's day to think they could live without fighting wars.

God allowed imperfections because that was what was best. All things are in God's hands, and this was the best way to get where God was going — Heaven. We must not make the mistake religious people of Jesus' day did and think the presence of imperfections reflects on God's character.

Hannah wasn't certain, but she thought a tear hung on the edge of Jake's eye. It vanished, though, and there seemed to be no more. She did know that Jake's next words brought tears to her own eyes.

The loss of children, of those we love, even of those unborn, troubles us. It leaves an emptiness inside, and we wonder why God would allow such loss. We go to funerals and mourn our departed loved ones. We cannot even begin to understand the suffering and sin in the world.

Why, then, would God send us only a child in a manger as an answer to all of this? Why not wipe out sin? Why not destroy the devil? Why not stop all the killing in the streets of our big cities? Why not raise up a righteous government in Washington that can rule without sin? Would that not seem like a better answer to us?

It might, Jake answered his own question. Yet it would be just as wrong an answer as the one people wanted when God planned the birth of Christ. God chose the best path for His Son's coming into the world, and He is now choosing the best path for taking us into the next world.

We must not, Jake said, think that the presence of suffering makes God unloving and uncaring. That was the mistake the religious leaders of Christ's day made. They thought the stoning of those committing adultery made God a harsh judge, so they became harsh themselves. They thought the giving of commandments made God unmerciful, so they became unmerciful themselves.

Jake looked across the gathering of men and women, many watching him with upraised faces. We must live — Hannah could tell Jake was concluding his sermon — blameless and harmless in a sinful and suffering world, because that is the way God wants us to live. It is the best, because God does only what is best. We should not blame God because He doesn't explain everything to us.

Jake paused as if thinking, then must have decided that was all he wanted to say. He then asked for testimonies, naming Bishop first, then two more, choosing from the older men.

Hannah sat tense as each man said what he had to say. She was sure someone would say Jake had erred in his sermon. No one did, though, pronouncing it the Word of God and wishing God's blessing.

Jake rose again, announced prayer, and then closed the service after they all knelt. The younger children made a rush to leave the room, followed more slowly by the young people. Hannah rose to help prepare the noon meal in the kitchen.

CHAPTER THIRTY-FOUR

"SYLVIA AND BEN aren't here," Betty whispered to Hannah. "I know," Hannah whispered back. They were approaching the kitchen and would soon be within earshot of the other women.

"They're leaving," Betty said, horror in her voice. "To a liberal church."

"I was afraid of that," Hannah said in genuine distress.

"Are they being excommunicated?" Betty's voice was still a whisper.

Hannah knew this was dangerous territory, especially for a minister's wife. If she had information, she shouldn't be sharing it. "Bishop will decide that," she finally said, thankful the kitchen was fast approaching.

"I would think so," Betty said, and then they were there.

Small bowls of peanut butter were set out on the table, and Elizabeth was filling more from the larger mixing bowl.

"Hi," Elizabeth said with a smile when Hannah and Betty walked in.

Amos' wife, Mandy, was placing butter on plates. "You can help with these," she said in Hannah's direction, barely looking up, her face showing her concentration.

Hannah knew what that meant. She picked up two plates in each hand and headed back towards the living room. When she arrived, the men had already set up wooden tables, made out of the benches, and two women had rolled out vinyl covers.

Glancing behind her, Hannah saw Betty following with peanut butter bowls. Together they set out the items with even spaces between them. By the time they came to the end of the table, other women were already placing the forks and knives. The first round of food was ready to go five minutes later.

Hannah stood in the doorway of the kitchen as prayer was announced and the eating began. Jake, she saw, got to eat first. He was a minister now, she thought, and got to climb up the ladder of seniority.

The same would no doubt be true for her — eventually, she figured. At the moment the women weren't insisting, letting her keep her old routine. This suited Hannah just fine, as any rhythm from her old life was quite comforting.

She got to eat on the second round, and then helped with a few stragglers on the third round. It consisted of only one table, set up in the master bedroom. Elizabeth helped her serve, for a purpose Hannah felt certain. She didn't have long to wait for the answer.

"I hope you weren't too disturbed the other night," Elizabeth stated more than asked.

Hannah shook her head.

Elizabeth smiled. "I told John he shouldn't conduct church business in front of everyone. He just thought it might help having it at your place — make Ben and Sylvia more comfortable.

"I hope so," Hannah told her, meaning it.

"They didn't show up today." Elizabeth glanced around. "John will be disappointed."

"Jake too," Hannah said.

"John is hoping it won't spread," Elizabeth said, looking worried. "I think he's changed his mind about Jake."

"Oh." Hannah glanced around to see if anyone was listening. No other women were close, the few children at the table intent on eating their peanut butter sandwiches.

"Yes," Elizabeth nodded. "I think he's right, especially after today. John will be happy."

Hannah let her face show her question.

"Jake's kind of preaching might be just what is needed for our young couples. You heard what Sylvia and Ben said — about the spiritual part. This might help. John thinks God might be helping us out."

"Are there more people thinking of leaving?"

"John's afraid so. Seems a real movement going on in Kalispell. There's a lot of temptation."

"Here too?" Hannah raised her eyebrows.

"Not so much. John's just afraid more of it's coming our way."

"So Sylvia and Ben are gone?"

"We don't know for sure." Elizabeth looked worried. "I suppose they went to church over there — had someone drive them. It does sound like they're serious, I'm afraid."

"What can we do?" Hannah wasn't looking for an answer, just feeling the weight of her and Jake's youth.

"That's what I really wanted to talk about." Now Elizabeth glanced around, but the coast was still clear.

Hannah waited, wondering what more could possibly be coming.

"At the ministers' meeting this morning," Elisabeth said, "I think John told the other ministers. Jake really. Jake will tell you if John did. He wants Jake to talk with Will and Rebecca Troyer."

"Will and Rebecca?" A picture of the couple flashed into Hannah's mind. They were already married when she took care of Betty's riding stable. The prior summer, she thought. Hannah knew Will had moved in from a community in Bonner's Ferry, but Rebecca was local.

"They weren't here today. I'll let Jake tell you," Elizabeth said. "If John told him. Maybe they decided something else."

"Are they leaving?" Hannah couldn't help asking.

"It's something else. Kind of," Elizabeth said, not really explaining anything.

Betty came bustling up. "Oh, here you are. Have you enough help on the table?"

"I think so," Hannah told her.

"Oh," Betty glanced at Elizabeth. "Did I interrupt something?"

"Not really," Elizabeth smiled. "I was done."

"Oh," Betty said, and Hannah could see Betty was curious. The burden of holding confidences came weighing on her shoulders again. To Betty it might be a curiosity, but to her it was something she could have lived without.

"I'll go get the water," Elizabeth said, intending to refill the water glasses on the last table.

"Church things," Hannah told Betty when Elizabeth moved out of sight. More than that she was not planning to say.

"Oh," Betty said, and then left the subject there, much to Hannah's relief.

Elizabeth walked by with the water pitcher, smiling at both of them. *Apparently she trusts me*, Hannah thought, not sure she liked that feeling either. She would rather not be carrying secrets that needed trusting.

"Why don't you come by this week?" Betty asked. "On Thursday afternoon we're having the youth over. Games and such afterwards. We're making Christmas packages for a ministry in Libby. You could help me get ready. Jake could just stop by on his way home."

"Oh," Hannah felt an immediate interest. "I'd like that."

"You'll ask Jake then?"

"He shouldn't object," Hannah assured Betty. She liked the feeling of doing something that wasn't associated with Jake being a minister.

"The young people will enjoy it. I think a lot of them like Jake as a minister," Betty said, spoiling the moment.

Hannah tried not to show her feelings but must have failed.

"I want you over," Betty said quickly, the look on her face matching her words.

Hannah thought for a moment of doubting Betty, but then decided she was her aunt after all. Surely family ties were stronger than their new roles as minister and minister's wife.

"You'll come then?" Betty asked.

"If Jake doesn't object," Hannah told her.

"Good. Oh there's Steve," Betty said, looking out the living room window towards the barn.

"Jake's not far behind," Hannah replied, not seeing Jake at the moment but figuring he must be about ready to go home. True to her words, the next man to come out of the barn was Jake, leading his horse behind him.

Betty left to get her shawl from the table by the back door, where the women had thrown their wraps that morning. She found it about the time Hannah came up.

"Thought I'd never find it," Betty said, disappearing out the door.

Hannah found her shawl and bonnet on the second try, relying on memory. Betty was already in Steve's buggy when she came out, Mossy following right behind them. She wrapped the ends of her shawl up tight as she went down the sidewalk and climbed into the buggy.

"Chilly," Jake said, pulling his black suit coat tighter around himself and shaking the lines to get Mossy moving.

"You should have brought your winter coat," Hannah told him, thinking she would see that he wore it next Sunday.

Hannah felt strange as she glanced at Jake out of the corner of her eye. He looked the same, yet this was the person who said all those things this morning in his sermon. She struggled to connect the two, then gave up. They were simply too far apart. One stood way out there beyond her grasp, the other sat right beside her, talking just like the Jake she had always known.

"Bishop wants us to go talk with Will and Rebecca," Jake said, just like that.

"Elizabeth told me he might," Hannah replied.

"Oh? She did?" Jake sounded surprised.

"Only that he might."

"Did she say why?"

"No." Hannah looked at Jake. "I hope they aren't leaving."

"Like Sylvia and Ben?"

"Yes," Hannah nodded.

"It's something else," Jake said, shaking his head. "Kind of."

"Why are we going?" Hannah wanted to know, leaving the other question for later. "Why doesn't John go himself?"

"He thinks this might work better."

"Why do you have to do the work, so sudden like?" Hannah hoped she didn't sound bitter, but she wished Jake didn't have to do this.

"Bishop wants it," Jake said as explanation.

"I know why," Hannah told him. "Elizabeth told me."

Jake raised his eyebrows.

"Bishop likes you now and thinks you might do Will and Rebecca good. He changed his mind a little, Elizabeth said. People like your preaching, like this morning. You are being put to work. You like that?"

"Maybe that's what we're here for." Jake glanced at her, keeping the buggy reins tight for the turn into their road.

"Instead of Indiana?" Hannah wished she hadn't said it, but the words just came out.

"I suppose so. Don't you think so?" Jake asked.

"It's all so new," she told him.

"It's the work of the church," Jake said. "I didn't choose it."

"You enjoy it," she told him.

"Maybe," he allowed. "It makes it easier that way."

"It's not easier for me," she told him, a catch in her voice.

Hannah saw the look of concern flash in Jake's eyes. She

was expecting the preacher look, the one he had worn earlier in the day. She thought he might even say long things about duty and being a good minister's wife. When he did none of that, but brought his arm around her in the buggy, pulling her close, she squeezed back the tears.

"I'm sorry," he said. "I wish it wasn't so hard."

That brought a sob she couldn't hold back.

"You've been a wonderful wife," Jake said, which didn't help much either.

"I lost your child," she told him between sobs.

"No," he said. "Heaven gained him. It was for the best. God only allows what works for the best."

"It's still too awful," she told him, her head on his shoulder.

"For my thoughts are not your thoughts, nor are your ways my ways, says the Lord. As the heavens are high above the earth, so are my ways higher than your ways, and my thoughts than your thoughts," Jake said, and Hannah knew he was quoting from the Bible. Looking out at the Cabinet Mountains towering in the air, the wind pushing the trees on the slopes, she didn't care. The words and the sound of Jake's voice soothed her spirit.

Chapter Thirty-Five

Jake insisted on visiting Will and Rebecca that evening, even when Hannah mentioned they might be at the hymn singing.

"Hardly," Jake said. "It's important anyway. They weren't there today."

"So what is going on?" Hannah asked once they were on the way, figuring she had a right to know, since she was going along.

"Did you know Will wasn't originally from the Amish?"

"No," Hannah shook her head. "Never heard that. Then I didn't grow up around here."

"No one mentioned it either. Till today." Jake slapped the reins as Mossy hesitated.

"He seems Amish," Hannah said, puzzled. "His brother too."

"Their parents came from the Baptists. Joined a group in Bonners Ferry when Will and his brother were children — a Mennonite church, or a version of it. Will, though, wanted something even more conservative. His brother followed his lead, I guess."

Hannah waited.

"Seems Will thinks it was all a mistake. Wants to go back."

"To the Mennonites?" Hannah glanced at Jake.

"No...the Baptists."

"Baptists," Hannah gasped. "What about Rebecca?"

"That's the problem."

"They have two children."

"That's even more of a problem."

"Then why didn't Bishop go himself, Jake? This is too big for you."

"That's what I said," Jake nodded his head. "I'm just doing what I was told to do."

"Is Rebecca going with him?" Hannah grabbed Jake's arm, her fingers digging in.

Jake shook his head.

"Oh my," was all Hannah could think to say.

They drove in silence, each lost in thought. Hannah thought of Rebecca, remembering the faces of her two children and wondering at the choice that must now be heavy on her heart.

"It's so terrible," she finally broke the silence. "We are so young. This is just too much."

"I know," Jake said, his voice strained.

"What are you going to tell them, Jake? What can you tell them? What if you say the wrong thing? Rebecca could lose her husband. She can never have another one. You know that, Jake. I know she doesn't want to leave. I know Rebecca. Mennonite, maybe — never Baptist. Jake," she grabbed his arm again. "We have to go back. Bishop must go himself. He really must. You have to tell him. You can't do this. It's too dangerous, Jake. It really is."

"We can't," Jake said simply to her outburst. "The way may be hard. Yet we must walk it. It is not for me to decide."

"What about me?" she asked, looking at Jake desperately.

"You are stronger than you think," he said gently. "Much stronger."

"Really," she said, the thought moved her. "You think so?"

"I know so," Jake said, his voice low. "You're my wife."

Hannah looked skeptically at him. *Was Jake serious, or just convincing her to go along?*

"You are," he said, with a smile this time.

Taking a deep breath, Hannah calmed herself. "You're going to need a lot of wisdom."

"Maybe God will help them," Jake said.

"Maybe He will help us," she replied, surprising herself with the statement.

In the driveway of Will and Rebecca's home, Hannah caught sight of their two children disappearing into the house. She figured they must have been playing outside and seen the buggy coming.

"The children," she said, to no one in particular, as Jake pulled up to the hitching rack. "What will happen to them?"

After tying Mossy securely, Jake led the way towards the house. The place seemed wrapped in stillness, Hannah thought. Perhaps it expressed the sorrow of what the occupants must be feeling.

Jake knocked carefully, stepping back from the door to wait. For a long moment Hannah believed no one was coming. They were being ignored, she thought, rejected before their errand had even begun. Surely Bishop would understand if Jake failed for this reason. No one could fault him, since he was trying.

Will opened the door rather abruptly, but he was smiling. A little sad around the edges, Hannah thought. She searched for signs of Rebecca, finding no one in the parts of the house she could see.

"Good afternoon," Jake said. "Is it okay if we come in?"

"I guess," Will said, opening the door wider.

Hannah went in first, and Jake followed, taking off his hat and winter coat.

"You can put those on the chair," Will motioned towards the kitchen. "Rebecca will be right out. She's in the bedroom."

The two children—a boy, the older, and a girl, only

three or so — squirmed on the couch. Hannah went over to sit beside them, saying softly, "Hi."

Andrew only smiled, ducking his head, but Edith said "hi" very quietly, her lips barely moving.

"Oh, you surprised me," Rebecca's voice came from the bedroom door. "I was in my work clothing."

"That would have been perfectly okay," Jake said, from where he sat. "We don't want to disturb your evening."

"I'm so glad to see you," Rebecca said, offering to shake hands with Hannah, then Jake. Hannah was certain she saw tears threatening to come in Rebecca's eyes.

Will was in the process of bringing two chairs from the kitchen. He set one down, his hand indicating it was for Rebecca, as he took the other.

Rebecca sat down slowly. "I'm so sorry we couldn't be in church today. I missed it so."

Will nodded soberly.

"There will be other times," Jake said. He looked comfortable enough, Hannah thought, glad for that at least.

"I hope," Rebecca said, and the tears came now, running down her cheeks.

Will looked embarrassed, glancing at the children sitting beside Hannah.

"I'm sorry," Rebecca choked. "Maybe the children can play upstairs?"

"Do you want to?" Will asked them, rising. "Upstairs in the bedroom. With your toys?"

"We want to go outside," Andrew spoke up. "In the yard."

Will seemed uncertain, glancing out the living room window at the gathering darkness.

"It's okay," Rebecca said. "We can call them in when it gets too dark."

"Go then," Will said, watching as Andrew and Edith scampered for the front door.

"You have such nice children," Hannah half whispered.

"They have a good father," Rebecca said, and again tears sprang to her eyes.

"I suppose you have come to talk?" Will asked as the front door closed. "John sent you?"

Jake nodded.

"Are we being excommunicated?" Rebecca asked with alarm in her voice.

"Surely not," Will said. "The bishop isn't like that."

Rebecca looked unconvinced.

"You are not being excommunicated," Jake said firmly. "We are interested in helping. That's all."

"You know what the problem is?" Will glanced sharply at Jake.

"You want to return to the Baptists," Jake told him.

"Amish don't approve of that," Will said.

Jake nodded.

"You'd excommunicate me then," Will stated flatly.

"Don't say that," Rebecca said, alarm again in her voice. "That's terrible. To even think it is terrible."

"You would, wouldn't you?" Will didn't plan to drop the subject, Hannah could tell.

Jake seemed to be pondering, finally saying, "I suppose the church would. I'm not the bishop though."

"That's what I thought," Will said, satisfaction in his voice. "You think that's right? Just for joining the Baptists? That's where I came from."

"Your parents did. You didn't," Rebecca fairly wailed. "Don't even think such things. Please."

"See...." Will raised his eyebrows. "What do we do?"

"You don't have to go back," Jake said. "I always thought you were happy here."

"Maybe," Will grunted, squirming on his chair. "I guess I thought so, too. Maybe me and my brother overreacted though. That's what bothers me now. Sure there were things my parents saw wrong — problems with the Baptists. I just went too far the other way, I think."

"There are problems everywhere," Jake said, which

Hannah thought was the wrong thing to say if he wanted Will to stay Amish.

Will, though, seemed to like the answer.

"See," Rebecca said, "it wouldn't be any better there. Besides I'm not going."

Glancing at her, Will asked Jake, "You think Rebecca ought to submit to me? Isn't that what the Amish believe? Where husband goes, wife goes."

There was silence in the room. Jake cleared his throat. "I'm just a young fellow. How would I know the answer to that?"

Hannah almost sighed out loud, so great was her relief at Jake's answer.

"You do," Will told him. "I'd like to hear the answer."

"I don't think she should," Jake said, just like that, the suddenness of it jarring the room.

"That's a mouthful," Will chuckled. "You think John will back that up? Maybe it's just because you want Rebecca to stay Amish."

"Don't think so." Jake set his lips firmly. "I'd say so regardless. The answer would be the same coming the other way. If one objects, the move shouldn't be made."

"Even if you'd lose a member coming from the English?" Will asked, his eyes intense.

"Yes," Jake said firmly. "That's what I would say."

"So what about the submission thing?" Will wasn't done with his questions yet, although Hannah was glad to see him smiling. Rebecca wasn't making a sound, her face as white as a sheet.

"Submission is the woman pleasing her husband. It's not a woman changing her honestly held beliefs," Jake said. "If the woman has to change who she is, then it's not submission, it's perversion. God never asks for that."

"Then what am I supposed to do?" Will asked, his eyebrows raised.

"Love your wife," Jake said. "Your children. That's probably as good a work as you'll do being Baptist."

"I can do it being Baptist," Will said.

"You can do it better being Amish," Jake replied.

"I guess so," Will chuckled. "I guess my brother was right."

"Right?" Now it was Jake who had the question.

"He stopped by before you came," Rebecca said weakly.

"Said you can really preach. Today...." Will chuckled again.

"You shouldn't say things like that," Jake told him.

"I suppose not," Will allowed. "Well...I'll think about this. Don't look so white, dear." He gently rubbed Rebecca's shoulder.

"I can't help it," Rebecca replied, the tears running again.

"You've had supper yet?" Will asked.

Both Jake and Hannah shook their heads.

"Then you're staying," Will pronounced. "We haven't eaten either."

"I don't have anything," Rebecca said, wiping the tears from her face. "I wasn't expecting anyone."

"I'll help you," Hannah spoke up, not certain how she would, but willing.

"See," Will said. "You'll think of something."

Rebecca swallowed a few times but smiled when Hannah got up from the couch. Together the two women left for the kitchen, while Jake moved to sit where Hannah had been.

"A little more comfortable," Hannah heard him say.

"I'll see what the children are doing," Will replied.

"I'll come along then," Jake told him, getting up.

At the front door, a sharp cry of "Andrew, Edith" soon brought a patter of little feet onto the porch.

"Time to come inside," Will said, Jake standing just behind him.

"We were tired anyway," a little voice replied.

"Then come in here. Play in the living room," Will told

them, ushering the two inside. They crept past the kitchen doorway with Jake and Will following.

"They are so dear," Hannah said again.

"I heard you lost yours," Rebecca said softly. "I'm so sorry."

Hannah couldn't find her voice at the moment.

"Maybe God will bless you again," Rebecca said. "Like you are blessing others."

How she was blessing others, Hannah wasn't certain, but she nodded her head.

With the two working together, soup and salad were soon prepared. Rebecca remembered a cream pie in the refrigerator, half of it still left, and the two families settled in for supper.

The evening passed quickly enough. Even with the chatter of their voices, the house still seemed quiet, although peaceful now.

"I hope we did some good," Hannah told Jake on the way home.

"I hope so," Jake agreed. "Bishop will probably want to talk to them himself."

"It would be terrible if they left," Hannah said. "Rebecca so doesn't want to."

"I know," Jake said in his preacher voice, and Hannah was surprised it didn't bother her.

CHAPTER THIRTY-SIX

"WITH THE INTENSE activity on Sunday, Hannah forgot to mention the young people's gathering at Betty's until Thursday morning. Jake raised no objections, though. In fact, a little grin spread over his face — maybe, Hannah thought, it made him feel young to be invited to a youth gathering.

"You feeling any better?" she asked, wishing he hadn't been so sober-faced since Sunday. "You can't think about church troubles all the time."

"No," he agreed, "I can't. Wish I could talk to John before Sunday, though."

Not wanting to be involved in a weekday visit to the bishop, Hannah thought quickly. "Betty will pick me up after lunch. She suggested you just drop by on the way home. Why not swing past the bishop's then? You'd have plenty of time before the gathering starts."

"I'd still be there early?" Jake asked, thinking out loud.

"Maybe you can help get ready, with the Christmas packages. Maybe just be there," she smiled at him, trying to draw him out from his church world.

Her words seemed to help, as Jake left for work with a smile.

Betty picked her up around one, and the two had everything ready in plenty of time. By seven-thirty the gathering was in full swing, buggies parked all over the yard and horses packed tightly in the barn. These were not all the

275

same youth from a few years ago, but Hannah easily lost herself in the spirit of the night. It seemed as if time rolled away and she was truly young again. For a moment, she no longer was a mother who had lost her baby, or a preacher's wife, or a woman with a cabin to keep.

With a jolt, she suddenly realized Jake hadn't arrived. She landed back in the real world with a thud.

"Jake's still not here," she whispered to Betty.

Betty nodded.

"Do you think something happened to him?"

"Wasn't he stopping in at the bishop's?" Betty walked out to the kitchen with Hannah following.

"Yes."

"That could take some time."

"This much?"

Betty made a face. "Church things? Of course."

Hannah could only nod in agreement. It could well be church things, pressing church things. Things more important than Jake being here, apparently.

"I'm going outside for a minute," Hannah said, going to get her coat.

Betty nodded in sympathy and returned to the living room.

Leaving the ringing of young people's voices, Hannah stepped out the kitchen door.

Where was Jake? The chill night air enveloped her immediately. With the sun down it didn't take long for the temperature to drop in these mountains. Overhead a brilliant swath of stars stretched almost from horizon to horizon, slightly offset to the south. Over her shoulder, just clearing the ridge of the house, the moon hung with one bright star to its upper right.

Hannah gazed at the star, the line of light seeming to come from the depths of immeasurable space, piercing right into her soul. She shivered with the feeling.

Surely Jake was just talking long with bishop? Stepping out into the yard, she listened for horse's hooves on the pavement. Jake should be coming from the south. Hearing nothing, she walked out to the road to listen. The only sound was the great stillness of the sky above her. Even the voices from the house had faded away.

This was her life, she thought, the loneliness of it almost overwhelming her. Jake was being taken away from her. This was how it would always be — church work, demanding ever more of their time, Jake's time, until none was left.

The chill penetrated her coat, even as her thoughts pierced her heart. Pulling her arms tightly around herself helped keep out the cold air, but the thoughts came in anyway. Only the sound of hoof beats on the pavement would comfort her at the moment, but no sound came.

Walking back towards the house, she struck on a worse thought. What if something had happened to Jake? An accident? So startling was her fear that she walked back out to the road to listen again, shivering in the cold.

There was no sound of sirens in the distance, but then, she told herself, there might not be. The accident could have happened anywhere, somewhere far from here. Maybe just outside Libby, before Jake had even gotten out of town.

Jake could have been taken to the hospital. How would she be notified? Jake carried no ID with him. He would just be a nameless Amish person lost in some numbered room at the hospital.

That was if he made it to the hospital? A worse fear ran through her. *Had not Bishop Amos died in a wreck just after ordaining Jake? Was this something that could be passed on?* At the moment, anything seemed possible.

Her face must have shown her distress when Hannah went back inside, shivering from the cold.

"Nothing?" Betty both asked and answered the question. "They're probably just talking long."

Hannah nodded numbly, forcing herself to move to the living room. It wouldn't help to stay in the kitchen, away from the others, and draw attention to herself. Pasting on a smile, she joined the group.

The ministry in Libby, *Helping Hands*, was preparing Christmas packages to distribute to the area's needy children. Who those were, the Amish were not told, but they had helped prepare packages for the past two years. Items from the *Goodwill* in Libby and its sister store in Kalispell supplied the selection of clothing and toys.

Hannah offered to take her turn at one of the six ironing boards set up to press the clothing before being placed in the packages.

"Over here," Bishop John's oldest daughter said cheerfully. "My arm's about ready to drop off."

Hannah smiled, because it wasn't Emily's fault she had a queasy feeling at this reminder of Bishop Nisley and church work. *Then perhaps something worse was keeping Jake.*

The flood of emotions almost overwhelmed her composure. Hannah gripped the handle of the iron, leaning against it for support. Its angry sizzle at being pressed into the cloth caused her to jerk the iron upwards.

"Oh," she said at Emily's puzzled look. "I'm not always that clumsy."

"The iron gets a little hot. Quickly," Emily said in a helpful tone of voice.

Hannah wondered if Emily would be this thoughtful if Hannah wasn't the young minister's wife.

Sliding the iron across the dress, her hand did what she wanted it to, and Emily left, finding a seat beside Enos Chupp, who was folding clothes before placing them in the packages.

Enos was Mose Chupp's second boy and a little older than Emily, Hannah guessed. Not that long ago, she would have known every boy's age, pretty close to the month, but how things had changed, she lamented.

Emily smiled shyly, Hannah noticed, her hands slowly folding clothing, her eyes seeking Enos' face and then dropping quickly to the floor. Enos didn't seem to be rejecting the attention, his lips moving easily as the two engaged in conversation.

Oh to be young again, Hannah thought, turning her mind back to her ironing before she burned something else. *Love and where it leads. I ought to know,* she told herself.

Betty served refreshments after the packages were done. The young people took their plates into the living room, the hum of conversation filling the room. Somehow Hannah made it through the evening, and still there was no Jake.

"Jake still hasn't come," Betty whispered, noticing Hannah's drawn face. "Maybe Steve should go look for him."

"No," Hannah shook her head, simply not letting her mind go there. Whatever was keeping Jake, a long conversation with Bishop Nisley was easier to handle than the other option.

"But what if?" Betty asked, apparently having no qualms about going into terrible territory. "Surely they would have let you know."

"He's just talking long." Hannah pressed her lips together firmly, struggling to control her fears.

"You have more courage than I do," Betty stated admiringly. "It's getting pretty late."

"I know," Hannah said, dreading the coming moments when the young people would leave and still there would be no Jake.

That's just what happened some thirty minutes later, as the boys began drifting out to the barn, hitching their horses to the buggies. The horses snorted white steam and jerked their heads into the air as buggies picked up sisters or cousins and took off into the night.

Hannah sat on a chair at the kitchen table to calm herself. When the last young person had left, she knew she had to face the worst. Someone would have to go looking for Jake, and she knew what he would be looking to find.

She would not be going along — Betty would see to that. Steve would be sent on his own, and the tense, drawn-out waiting would begin. Already her knuckles were white under the kitchen table. *Was this to be her path, chosen by the Almighty? Her unborn lost, her youth lost to church ministry, and now a husband lost in the night hours?* She pushed the unthinkable away, gathering herself together.

The noise of the last buggy wheels crunching in the snow outside must have been what kept Hannah from hearing Jake drive in. He tied Mossy to the hitching post and said "hi" to the retreating youth.

He feared what awaited him inside and said as much to Steve, who had been helping the last of the boys hitch up.

"I really am late," he said, his breath coming in white streams.

"Hannah's been doing real well. Betty kept her entertained," Steve said cheerfully. "You missed out on a good youth gathering. We have quite a nice group here."

"Always did," Jake agreed. "We were with the group not that long ago."

"Still young?" Steve grinned.

"I don't know about that." Jake waited while Steve opened the kitchen door.

The suddenness of his appearance brought Hannah to her feet.

"I'm so sorry," Jake said, looking profusely so as he walked over to her. "I would have let you know, but there was no way to. It just took so long."

Hannah couldn't find words, knowing her face showed her distress.

"Bishop keep you?" Betty asked from the living room door.

Jake ignored Betty as he sat down, taking Hannah's hand and drawing her down to the chair. He said nothing, his eyes doing the talking, full of emotion and regret over the pain his actions had caused. Hannah resisted being drawn in, but then let go as the tears came.

"I didn't know what kept you," she told him.

Jake squeezed her hand, his eyes saying *You are a wonderful woman.* To Betty he asked, "Any food left?"

"Just like a man," Betty said. "Comes in late. Thinks of nothing but food. Food and his stomach."

"There's plenty left," Steve said with a chuckle. "Help yourself."

Jake did, and Hannah, finding her own appetite return, fixed herself a plate. Betty fussed over them, as if they both needed attention, which Hannah figured they probably did. The hard-working young minister and his distraught wife — who would have thought it?

With her head on Jake's shoulder on the way home, they drove in silence. It was better that way, Hannah thought. Apparently neither Jake nor she could change what they were becoming.

"Bishop said Will and Rebecca are staying," Jake said sleepily after they were in bed.

"Really!" Hannah sat upright at this good news. "You should have told me earlier."

When Jake said nothing for a long moment, she looked at him in the near-darkness of the room, finally figuring out he had gone to sleep.

Chapter Thirty-Seven

THE FRIDAY BEFORE Christmas, the first serious snowstorm blew in from Idaho. Before lunch the snow started and increased all afternoon. By the time Jake came home from work, conditions had worsened considerably.

Hannah watched him unhitch by the barn, snow flying past the buggy and swirling around the barn door. Jake pulled on Mossy's reins, trying to get him to move inside more quickly. Apparently the horse, after his drive from town, was too tired to care.

Jake shook off his coat and hat on the front porch before coming inside, grinning broadly. Not sure if he was enjoying the weather or had some other cause for merriment, Hannah looked at him, puzzled.

"Quite some storm," Jake said in response to her look. "I have this."

"What?" she asked.

"A bonus check." Jake drew a piece of paper from his coat pocket and waved it. "A big check. Mr. Howard sold all the furniture we've made so far. Christmas sales, I think. It was a little hard on him, but he kept his promise. Paid me my share of the profits." Jake grinned even broader now that his face was warming indoors.

"That's good." Hannah let the feelings of relief flow over her, a little ashamed that money meant so much to her — but in their situation that was just the way it was.

"Two mortgage payments," Jake pronounced. "Two. That will put us past January."

"We might need it," Hannah told him, her mind on the snow outside. She could just see them snowed in for weeks on end and Jake unable to work.

"I think the worst is over, money wise," Jake said, still grinning. "The furniture shop seems a winner."

"Supper's ready," Hannah informed him.

"I brought you something," Jake said, his face sober now. "I thought it was time."

"What?" she asked, puzzled.

"It's still out in the buggy. I wanted to tell you first."

Hannah waited, letting Jake take his time. Surely this was not more bad news.

"Meat," Jake said. "Hamburger from the store. I want some for supper."

"Can we afford it?" was the first thing out of her mouth.

"With this," he said, his grin returning, lifting up the check again. "I'll cash it Monday. We'll have left...what doesn't go to the bank for payments."

"Meat," she said, having forgotten how much she missed it since taking the deer meat over to Betty's. "You thought of it?"

"First thing," Jake said. "I know you've been missing it."

"I wasn't complaining." She gave him a look.

"I know. You're too good a wife," he grinned again.

"And you have a silver tongue," she told him.

"I thought maybe golden?" he teased.

"Silver is good enough. You go bring in the meat. I need to start frying if you want some for supper."

"Be right back," Jake announced, reaching for his coat again. As he opened the front door, the snow and wind blasted into the cabin.

"It's getting worse," she said in alarm.

"We are snug as bugs in a rug," Jake said, as he disappeared out the door, the latch firmly clinking in place behind him.

Hannah got the fire going again. When Jake came in she unthawed the hamburger over the stove, and soon added the rich aroma of freshly fried hamburger to their supper table. They sat down to eat. After prayer, Jake squeezed ketchup liberally onto his plate, and dipped each piece of meat before bringing it to his mouth.

Watching him, Hannah found her own pleasure growing. Was this not how things were supposed to be? Life with your husband, gathered around the dinner table, snow flying outside? Closed in, together? For the moment all the outside problems seemed far away. Jake didn't even look like a preacher, almost smacking his lips over his supper.

The snow was still falling when they went to bed, drifts up to the top of the front porch, but Hannah didn't care. Jake's check had taken care of that. Let it snow. Let it do its worst. They were safe inside.

In the morning it was still snowing and didn't slow much all day. Jake stayed inside, not seeming to mind, reading his German lesson book. For Hannah, that was an unpleasant reminder of the outside world, but she decided not to let it bother her. Her delight with the snow grew.

By evening, the outside world seemed completely shut down, and still the snow fell. Jake raised the question that had been on Hannah's mind earlier.

"You think there will be church tomorrow?"

"Don't know," she told him, walking to the front window and looking out. It was hard for her to imagine how even a buggy could get through the drifts piled in the yard, let alone on the road.

"I wonder how we will know?" Jake thought out loud.

"Do people stay home from church here?" Hannah wondered. Rarely in Indiana did such a thing happen. The roads usually were plowed before one had time to think of staying home. This was strange country, though, she reminded herself.

"Depends. I guess." Jake seemed to be debating something. "I'm going over to Steve and Betty's to find out," he announced.

"You're not," she told him firmly. "It's too late already. You could get stuck in those drifts, and with night coming."

"I guess so," he bent to her logic. "We just have to try in the morning."

Thinking the problem had been solved, Hannah got up to prepare supper.

"I'm going to Mr. Brunson," Jake announced suddenly a few minutes later.

"Tonight?" she asked from the kitchen.

"He might be having trouble," Jake said. "Someone should check up on him."

"You just have the itch to get out of the house."

"I suppose so," Jake grinned, but Hannah could tell it was more than that. She really had no objections, feeling concern for Mr. Brunson herself.

"Don't get stuck," she said as Jake went to bundle up. "I'll have supper ready by the time you get back."

The sight of Jake struggling through the snow troubled her, but Hannah comforted herself with the knowledge of his strength. It would take a lot to stop him or even slow him down. He took huge strides, tracking back and forth to avoid the worse drifts, but making good time up the slope.

When he got back, he looked happier than when he left. Apparently the time out of the cabin in the elements had done him good.

"No problems," Jake announced. "The old man seems well settled in. Has plenty of wood, he said. Stocked with food. Doesn't need to get out till spring, if necessary," Jake chuckled.

"What about his son?" Hannah asked, remembering Mr. Brunson's story.

"Didn't say anything. We'd have seen if someone had come. Hasn't been a car back there in weeks. I'm going out to the end of the driveway for the mail."

"For the mail?" Hannah asked in astonishment. "No mailman went today. Supper's almost ready."

"They probably plowed the main road. We have all night for supper. Not much daylight left."

"You'll get stuck. Really you will."

"I want to see about tomorrow — see if it's as bad as it was up to Mr. Brunson's. Maybe the roads aren't plowed."

"The mailman hasn't gone. You're just wasting your time."

"Plenty to waste," he informed her, already partway out the cabin door.

This time Hannah didn't watch him go. If he could make it up the mountain, he surely could make it down to the main road. As darkness fell and no Jake came back, she did begin to worry a little.

Visions of Jake stuck in a snow bank flashed through her mind, but with her unfounded fears last week, Hannah was not about to go down that road again. If this had been church work, she figured, there might be cause for concern, but this was just a walk out to the end of the road.

With supper ready and spread on the table, she went to look out the window for any signs of Jake. Surely he ought to be back by now. His tracks were still visible in the snow, blown shut a little, but there. Missing were the returning tracks.

Sighing, she went back to the kitchen and tried to occupy herself, but that didn't work for long either. The supper was getting cold. That pressed on her but was soon forgotten in her increasing concern over Jake's possible condition. What really could happen on a walk to the end of the road?

Sticking her face out the cabin door, Hannah was startled by the chill in the air. Apparently the temperature was falling rapidly. Her emotions swung from irritation with Jake for once again needlessly scaring her, to genuine fright that something might have happened.

Finally she knew she had to do something. There was no phone to call out with, and thoughts of going up to Mr.

Brunson for help were rejected. The walk up there would be as arduous as the one out to the road and might accomplish nothing anyway. Mr. Brunson was old and could hardly be expected to traipse through snowdrifts this size.

There was only one thing to do, and that was go herself. Resolved, Hannah bundled up in her thickest coat and put on a pair of Jake's pants under her dress. She wrapped two scarves around her neck, but the wind still cut through them when she opened the cabin door. That was when it occurred to her she needed light and perhaps a blanket for when she found Jake.

She knew she would find him, the knowledge firm and certain, as if put there without a lot of emotion attached. Getting Jake's torch out from under the bed, she draped a blanket over her arm and set off.

The first snowdrift was worse than expected, and she almost floundered, tempted to turn back. She imagined seeing Jake pass her in the dark, beating her home and laughing when she got there.

This was not possible, she told herself, shaking her head. Jake would see the light if he walked past her. There had been no Jake at home when she left, so he had to be out here somewhere.

"Jake," she yelled, the wind catching her words.

Pressing on, following Jake's tracks, she skirted a snow bank. With the depth of snow here she sank in above her boots, even when staying with his tracks, and had to make a wider detour.

"Jake," she tried again but soon gave up, needing all her energy for travel.

It seemed forever, her eyes glued to the tracks in the snow, before the main road came into sight. It appeared plowed with some snow drifted back.

"Jake," she hollered, with what strength she had left.

"Here," the distinct voice came back, joy in the sound, she was certain. Surely Jake wasn't playing games with her. This had gone well beyond anything called fun.

"Where?" she yelled back, finding energy coming into her body.

"Over here. Beside the post," the answer came back.

Hannah walked the next drift and there he was, seated on the ground, the snow scraped away from where he was sitting.

"What's wrong?" she asked, still skeptical.

"Twisted my ankle." Jake rubbed his leg. "Got this far back. Slow going though. I knew you'd come. There is a letter from your mom," he teased, pulling it out of his pocket, his voice cheerful.

"You really are hurt?" She looked at him, the wind whipping around her, wondering why she was having an argument with Jake in this weather.

"I wouldn't make you come out. Not just for fun, in this snow." Jake sounded serious enough.

"How'd you know I'd come?"

"You're a good wife," he said. "Now to get me home. Clumsy fellow I am."

"I can't carry you," she said, stating the obvious.

"You can't get Mr. Brunson either," Jake said, reaching the same conclusion Hannah had arrived at earlier.

"Then what?" Her teeth began to chatter from standing there.

"First I'll take the blanket." Jake held out his hand. "Thanks." He wrapped it tightly around himself.

"I only brought one," she told him, wishing it had been two.

"It's enough," he said. "Go back to the barn and harness Mossy. Tie one of the traces on the little sled. There's rope on the wall. I'll get both traces on when you come back. Ride the horse, though — don't walk back."

"You'll be okay?"

"Yes," Jake nodded, shifting his weight on the ground. "I'll wait here."

CHAPTER THIRTY-EIGHT

HANNAH STRUGGLED BACK in the snow, pushing too hard and having to stop, her breath coming in gasps. This was not going to do, she decided. Jake would not be helped if she injured herself. Bending over, she tried to get some shelter behind a snow bank while she rested. The effect from the bank was minimal, and she moved on as quickly as she could.

At the barn, Mossy looked up as she barged in, the warmth of the building feeling like balm to her cheeks. Getting the horse out of his stall, she threw on the harness, found the sled, and tied on the rope.

The whole contraption seemed gangling, almost getting tangled up as she led Mossy outside. He objected to going, shaking his head in protest. She talked quietly to him, telling him Jake needed them, that he had to be a good horse and behave.

Whether or not he understood, her voice still calmed him down. He even stood still while she clambered up the harness by standing on a leather strap. She shook the lines draped across Mossy's neck to get the horse going. It seemed to have the same effect as if Mossy were pulling a buggy instead of the little sled bouncing along in the snow.

The trip went considerably faster than it had on foot. Jake hollered when she got closer, apparently trying to help her locate him. Reaching the spot, she started to get down when she thought better of it. Jake could tie the other tug on when she got close enough to him. He had no objections to her plan, and she maneuvered Mossy into place.

Hopping around on one leg, Jake soon had the sled tied up and told her to take off. Glancing back, she saw him hanging on as the sled went up and down on the snow, sinking at times almost to the floor boards. Jake, though, never let go.

Pulling up to the front porch as close as the horse could go, Hannah ignored Jake's protests. He wanted to help her unhitch, then hop in from the barn, he said.

"Thanks, big man," she told him, through frozen lips, from on top of Mossy. "But tonight you listen. Get inside."

"Okay," he grumbled, hopping off the sled, releasing the tugs first before going in, still muttering to himself.

When she came back from putting Mossy in the barn, Jake had his leg up on the chair, the sock off and the swollen redness visible.

"Is it broken?" she asked.

"Don't think so," he told her, wincing with the pain.

"Some pain pills," she said, heading for the bathroom cabinet. She came back with three and a glass of water. Jake willingly gulped them down.

"You should see a doctor," she told him.

"On a night like this?"

"That's why it happened."

"I know," he groaned. "It's also why I'm not seeing a doctor. It's just sprained."

"How do you know that?"

"I just do. Besides, we can't get out anyway."

That Jake was right was obvious, so she offered to bring him food. Cold now, she knew, but still food. He accepted, wincing when she set the plate on his lap.

"Your letter," he groaned, pulling the now wet envelope out of his pocket.

"I'll look at it later," she waved it off.

"I'm okay. Read it now," Jake said as he handed it to her.

Hannah was interested, she had to admit, and Jake was busy while he ate. Sitting on the couch, she opened the letter carefully. Its contents, written words on white paper, clashed with her evening, bringing news from a land different from hers.

"Read it out loud," Jake said, seeming interested. "It's got to be boring after this evening," he chuckled.

Figuring he was just trying to make the best of the situation, Hannah ignored the comment, but did begin to read aloud.

"Dear loved ones,

"I hope this finds you all well. Our first snow came last week, just a light dusting, but we loved it. Dad seems well recovered from the accident, for which we are thankful. Christmas will be at Aunt Esther's. A big affair. It would be nice to have both of you here, but we understand."

"It's boring," Jake said groaning.

"You need something?" Hannah stopped reading, glancing up.

"For this pain medication to take hold."

"It takes a while," Hannah told him, thinking she must sound just like a mother. Now wasn't that something new? Mothering Jake, but he needed mothering, she thought with distress.

"Finish your letter," Jake said wearily. "In quiet, though. My mother only wrote once."

"Oh," Hannah said, surprised. "You only wrote her once. Maybe you should write more?"

"Maybe I should? My leg hurts too much now."

"Not now. I didn't mean that. Later."

"Looks like I'll be here for a while," Jake muttered, glaring at his leg. "How clumsy can one be."

"You didn't have to go," Hannah reminded him. "Just be thankful we could get you back to the house on a night like this."

Jake just groaned some more, holding his leg.

"You want to go to bed?"

"Not till this pain lets up."

As it turned out, "let up" happened sometime after midnight, with Hannah sitting with Jake till then. Gingerly they made their way into the bedroom, Jake insisting on using a broom stick since they had no crutches in the house.

In the morning the snow had stopped, the sun coming up in a blaze of glory. Hannah let Jake sleep late. He couldn't go to church with his swollen foot, even if there had been no drifts on their road.

Hannah expected a snowplow to come up from the main road anytime, but none showed by the time Jake got up. He looked so rumpled and sleepy-eyed Hannah laughed out loud.

"You don't look like a preacher now," she teased him.

"I suppose not. You think anyone will come looking for us?"

"They think we're snowbound," Hannah said, laughing again. The feeling was delicious. Just her and Jake, and no place to go. "Probably wasn't any church anyway."

Jake snorted, "Around here snow doesn't stop. They probably had church."

Hannah figured he was right and told him, "They can have church without you."

A cloud crossed Jake's face, but then he made an effort to cheer up. He got out his letter pad and began a letter to his mother. Hannah playfully tried to read it over his shoulder, but he kept covering it up every time she got close.

"I'll mail it tomorrow," he told her. "When we go in to have this foot looked at."

"Tomorrow is Christmas," she told him.

"I guess it is." Jake shook his head, trying to clear it.

"You sure you didn't hurt your head last night?"

"Don't think so. Everything just feels strange."

That it did, Hannah agreed. Even the snowplow that went up the gravel road after lunch looked wild, the snow flying up like a white fountain.

Mr. Brunson's truck came down, following the snowplow back, so he must have been anxious to get out, Hannah figured. The truck slowed down at their driveway, seeming to hesitate. Going out on the porch, Hannah let Mr. Brunson know they were home in case he wanted something.

"You folks okay?" Mr. Brunson hollered without getting out of his truck.

"Jake hurt his foot last night," Hannah hollered back.

That produced an "Oh" from Mr. Brunson. He drove on into the driveway, parked his truck and came up to the porch.

Hannah had gone inside since she didn't have her coat on. She opened the door again and motioned for him to come in.

"Hi," Jake said from his seat on the couch, his foot propped up on a chair.

"So what have you done, young man?" Mr. Brunson demanded, but Hannah could tell he was worried.

"Went to the mailbox. Careless, I guess," Jake made a face.

"You've seen a doctor?" Mr. Brunson wanted to know.

Jake shook his head. "How could we? It's the weekend."

"They do see on emergency basis," Mr. Brunson told him. "Let's take a look."

"I guess the roads are open now," Jake said, pulling up his pant leg to reveal his swollen ankle. Hannah could tell by his glance out the window that Jake didn't want to see any emergency doctor. She guessed he was thinking what that might cost.

"Wiggle the toes," Mr. Brunson said.

Jake wiggled as much as he could.

"Turn the foot." Mr. Brunson did some squeezing at the same time.

"So what do you think?" Jake asked, looking for a positive answer, Hannah knew.

"Probably not broken," Mr. Brunson said. "I'm not a doctor though. You should have it x-rayed."

"After Christmas," Jake said, as if he was going to do that regardless.

"Sure you don't want me to take you in? I'm going that way."

Jake shook his head. "It's not broken."

Mr. Brunson shrugged. "Suit yourself. Tuesday's a long way off."

"We'll make it," Jake assured him, cheerfully enough, but Hannah could tell he was putting on a brave face.

With Mr. Brunson no more than out the door, her feelings were confirmed. Jake sighed deeply, his shoulders stooping as if a great weight had settled on them.

"I hope I get better soon," he said. "I can't be laid up long. Mr. Howard had quite a few orders lined up."

"You'll get better fast," Hannah said, putting her arm around him, hoping she was right. All that afternoon she thought of what she could do to cheer Jake up but couldn't settle on anything. Popcorn didn't really suit, and she had no apple cider. She wished someone would visit, but no one knew about Jake's injury, supposing they were simply snowed in, she figured.

Jake finished his letter, sealing it with a sigh. His leg hurt, he said, and he wanted pain medication more often than she would give it to him.

"Every four hours," she told him firmly. "No more than that."

Christmas day came and passed in much the same way. Hannah did think to make snow cream with the abundant snow. Jake had to grin while he sampled it. Betty was having Steve's family over for breakfast, Hannah knew, so she was tied up. With no other family in Montana, there was nowhere to go even if Jake could have traveled. She finally suggested they play some games, but Jake didn't want to.

Instead he wanted to sing a song and read the Christmas story. She agreed readily, sitting beside him on the couch. The singing was lousy, she thought, with just the two of them, but Jake did read the first two chapters of Luke with great tenderness.

"Those were some times," he said, laying down the Bible. "Angels...I wonder why we don't see much of angels anymore?"

"Maybe we have to live out on the hills," Hannah said, an image of the shepherds tending their flocks going through her mind.

"That must have been a glorious sight," Jake said, awe in his voice. "A sky full of angels. What must that have been like? Such singing."

"Better than you and me," Hannah chuckled.

Jake laughed, "I suppose so."

"What must it have been like to be with child without a husband?" Hannah asked, shivering at the thought. "You think anyone believed her?"

"Some did," Jake said. "Like Elizabeth."

"Mary talked to an angel. Just like that. Face to face." Hannah drew closer to Jake on the couch.

"He shall be called great," Jake quoted, "and shall be called the Son of the Highest."

Outside the wind blew on the drifts, swirling snow around.

"Those were the days," Jake said, as Hannah nestled even closer to him, not getting up for a long time.

They ate their supper early. Jake said he felt much better and wanted to retire. Hannah stayed up for another hour or so, rereading her mother's letter and then the two chapters from the Bible Jake had read. In the peace and sleepiness that followed, she joined Jake in bed.

CHAPTER THIRTY-NINE

JAKE INSISTED ON getting up early. They needed time, he said, to stop in at Betty's place. He seemed to think they must make contact with someone since they hadn't been to church on Sunday. Hannah got Mossy ready, pushing the buggy out into the lane, the snow coming up to a quarter of the wheels in places. Jake hobbled out with his broom stick, stuck it in the back under the seat, and climbed in. She had him hold the lines as she went back inside for an extra blanket.

The snow still lay heavy on the ground, but the sky shone clear blue. Jake took care not to bump his foot against the buggy dash as they drove, holding it with one arm when they turned onto the main road.

Betty came racing out the kitchen door when they pulled up. "Where were you two!" she exclaimed, before Hannah barely got the buggy door open. "I had to stay around the house all day yesterday. Steve's relatives just stayed much later than planned."

"We made it," Hannah said grimly.

"Were you snowed in?" Betty asked. "That's what everyone thought Sunday."

"Kind of," Hannah grinned. "Jake sprained his ankle Saturday night. That's where we're going now — to the doctor."

"Sprained it?" Betty was all concern. "Is it broken? How do you know it's sprained?"

"So you did have church?" Jake asked. "There's no way I could have gotten out until the plow opened our road."

"That's what we figured," Betty said. "The foot, though. How bad is it?"

"Mr. Brunson looked at it," Hannah said. "He thought it probably wasn't broken."

"What does Mr. Brunson know," Betty said. "The foot needs to be seen by a doctor."

"That's true," Hannah agreed. "We're going to the doctor now. Dr. Lisa will probably see him. Think we should call in ahead of time?"

"I'd just go in," Betty said. "She's informal sometimes. You might have to wait a little."

"That's what I thought," Jake said. "We'd better be going then."

"You think you'll be okay?" Betty was still concerned. "Need any help?"

"She'll take care of me. Even if it's broken. Which it isn't," Jake assured her.

"So like a man," Betty huffed. "I suppose you'll be taking care of yourself. Regardless."

"Something like that," Jake grinned. "Hannah will let you know if we fall off the cliff."

"You'd better be careful there. Pride before a tumble," Betty said, stepping back as Jake took off.

"I already had my tumble," Jake muttered. "I just have to get better now. I need to get back to work too."

"Mr. Howard will understand," Hannah told him.

"We have to stop in right after the doctor," Jake said as if reminding himself.

They drove into Libby, Jake urging Mossy on, keeping to the ditch side when traffic backed up behind him on Highway 2. Hannah tied the horse at Dr. Lisa's office, while Jake hopped toward the door without his broom. She caught up with him in time to hold the door open.

Inside, Jake told the receptionist what he wanted and was soon taken back for an x-ray. When he came back, he told Hannah the doctor hadn't seen him, and that he was supposed to wait.

A short time later a smiling Dr. Lisa told Jake the ankle was only sprained. He was supposed to keep it wrapped and should take a pair of crutches home with him. He would be good to go in a week or so.

"You doing okay?" Dr. Lisa asked Hannah when she was done giving instructions to Jake.

Hannah nodded.

"That's a good girl. Take care." Then she was gone.

Hannah stayed in the buggy while Jake went inside the hardware with his new crutches. He looked rather capable on them, she thought. He was doing quite well for himself in more ways than one.

When a good twenty minutes passed and Jake failed to come out, Hannah was almost ready to tie the horse and go see what was keeping him. Surely Mr. Howard wasn't persuading him to do any work today. That could be quite disastrous for his ankle, lengthening the healing time.

Jake's crutch appeared about then, coming out first as the door of the hardware opened, followed by the rest of him, and then the other crutch. He swung smoothly across the parking lot and used his good foot to hop on the buggy step. Hannah handed him the reins, and they were off.

On the edge of town she glanced at his face, noticing its drawn expression.

"The ankle hurt?" she asked him.

"Mr. Howard let me go," he said simply.

"Fired?" A feeling of alarm surged through her.

Jake just nodded, keeping his eyes on the road.

"Why?" she demanded. "I thought you were doing so well."

"Too well, I guess," Jake said grimly. "His nephew is taking over the furniture making."

"How can he do that?"

"There's no reason why he can't. I worked for him."

"It was you who made the furniture."

"Mr. Howard says anyone can make furniture." Jake's face was glum. "I don't think so. That's just what he said."

"So what are you going to do?"

"Don't know." Jake shook the reins as if to emphasize some point. What, Hannah wasn't sure.

When they got home, Jake hopped in the door while Hannah took the horse to the barn and tried to think of something for lunch, her mind spinning. Jake was in the kitchen when she came in, his crutches under his arm.

"What are you doing?" she asked him.

"Maybe I can do something in the kitchen," he said, his voice breaking.

She took him by the arm into the living room, making him sit on the couch.

"We'll make it. Somehow," she told him, running her hand through his hair.

"I suppose so," he said, his eyes dull. "Doesn't look like I'm doing too well."

"You'll think of something," she told him, struck by what she wasn't saying. *We have to move back to Indiana.* This would have been the time for it. Yet for some reason it was the furthest thing from her mind.

Her thoughts were interrupted by Jake's kiss on her cheek. "You're too good for me," he said, his voice catching again.

"No," she said, blushing, allowing herself to be pulled into Jake's embrace.

They held each other for a long moment, looking out the cabin window at the snow, the barn standing out against the blue sky.

"I'll get some sandwiches," she finally said, getting up.

❧

The snow didn't melt that week, the temperature rarely rising above freezing, and another storm moved in on Sat-

urday. Thankfully, the snowplow came up their road sometime after midnight, allowing them to attend church. Jake
didn't have to preach, for which Hannah was glad. His
troubled face all week had spoken of enough stress.

During the day, Jake read to pass the time, saying little
of future plans. Hannah supposed he had none at the
moment, even with her hopeful words. They might well be
at an impasse, at least until spring, when Jake could obtain
another job. How that was going to work she wasn't sure. At
least the mortgage was paid for January, and they wouldn't
starve with what food she had around.

Tomato soup, she thought. *That is going to get awfully old.*

Hannah soon found out she was wrong about Jake
having no plan. He started exercising his ankle the following week, testing it carefully before placing weight on it.
That was apparently plan number one — getting better.

Three days later, he limped out to the barn. When he
stayed out for a good hour, she thought perhaps he had rein-
jured his ankle and went to check. She found him studying
the back side of the lean to, scratching figures with paper
and pencil.

"I'm turning this into a shop," he announced when she
walked in. That was apparently plan number two.

"Money? It takes money," she told him.

He nodded. "A little. Selling is the big thing. Tools I can
borrow from John and Steve until I sell."

"You're not serious?"

When he turned, she knew by the set of his jaw that he
was.

What followed was a makeshift room, just stud walls
with some black board nailed up, a stove, and tools bor-
rowed from Steve. Jake's only investment was in the wood
and parts he needed.

Hannah started taking him lunch in the shop room, as
Jake took to calling it. His breakfast and supper he ate in
the house. Mr. Brunson stopped by for something, Hannah
never found out what, spoke with Jake in the shop room,

and just shook his head. He didn't shake it quite as hard the following week.

Betty said, on one Sunday morning with snow coming down once again, that this was the hardest winter she had been through yet. Then towards the end of January another blizzard blew in, this time from Canada, and the Christmas snow hadn't even begun to melt.

Jake worked like a man on a mission, mostly by hand, since he had no power tools to speak of. He told Hannah if Jesus could work with hand tools he could too. Hannah told him to quit when the blisters came — they could make it on tomato soup and potatoes until spring.

When he refused, she drove Mossy down to Betty's place to ask for salve. When Betty started asking questions, the tears came, followed by the spilling of the whole story.

"There's nothing you can do," Betty told her. "You have to help him."

"He works from dawn to dusk." Hannah wiped her tears with the back of her hand.

"A man must work," Betty assured her. "What's he making?"

"I haven't seen it," Hannah admitted.

"Then go look," Betty told her, her arm around her shoulder. "Just remember you have a good man. Don't ever forget that."

Hannah took the salve and bandages out to Jake when she got home. He quit willingly enough so she could wrap his hands.

"It's really nothing," he said with a grin. "You shouldn't make such a fuss."

"I'm not," she told him, thinking of Betty's instructions. "What are you making?" she asked. A glance around showed only pieces of wood and small logs lying on the floor.

Jake grinned, pulling from behind the table a small rocker, still unvarnished but done.

"My third try," Jake said. "This one is good enough. Can I varnish it indoors?"

Hannah didn't have to think twice on that question, nodding her head silently. She considered it a small matter after the obvious intense work Jake had already put in.

She took the rocker with her, carefully carrying it across the snow-covered yard, lest she slip and damage Jake's hard work. In the house, she spread sheets of the Budget out on the floor and waited for Jake's instructions on how to proceed. He told her that night, and she applied the first coat in the morning, right after breakfast.

They worked out a system for finishing the pieces, even a larger item, a log desk, which took the help of both Mr. Brunson and Hannah to move into the house. With three coats of varnish, it fairly glowed in the light of the gas lantern at night.

"Good job," Jake said approvingly.

"Now to sell it," Hannah said.

"I know," Jake said. "We'll think of something."

Hannah nodded, because she figured Jake would — it was the how she didn't know. That was a scary thought, but she pushed it away.

CHAPTER FORTY

WITH THE FEBRUARY mortgage payment approaching, Hannah sat in silent amazement, watching Jake preach on a Sunday morning. *How was he doing it?* She knew what had been on his mind last night. She had seen the look of stress on his face. She had been in the bed when he tossed and turned. All that was gone now.

Jake was quoting what sounded like scriptures, saying the words slowly and reverently, going on and on. When he had memorized them, Hannah had no idea. His eyes swept the congregation, his chin firm, his beard already down to the second button on his shirt.

Hannah didn't quite know what to do with the deep and various emotions she felt. Sorrow still lingered around the edges, but in the center grew something ever larger, a feeling she didn't quite know what to call, a swelling of admiration and awe for this man.

To show her emotion in church was completely out of the question; she simply beheld in her heart the wonder of what Jake had become. That they might be turned out of their cabin in February seemed insignificant at the moment. Though fear and uncertainty would surely return, for now it seemed enough to know that Jake was hers and would be with her whatever happened.

Jake concluded his sermon, asked for testimonies, and then closed. He did that too, she thought, almost without effort. Afterward she saw Bishop Nisley speaking with him where they sat on the bench. From Jake's expression she was sure it had nothing to do with his sermon.

"He wants to know how we're doing," Jake told Hannah on the way home. "Money wise. Since I have no job."

She waited, turning to look at him.

"I told him I was building furniture on my own, with Steve's tools."

"And?" Hannah asked.

"He said he was glad to hear that, and if I needed help to let him know."

"You tell him you aren't selling anything?"

"No," Jake shook his head. "It's not the time yet. We have to try first. Maybe in town on Monday?"

"Where? You have a place to set up?"

"Maybe Mac's Market?"

"There?" Hannah envisioned them standing inside some corner of the market, embarrassingly trying to sell log furniture to people who simply rushed on by.

"It's not really in season," Jake said, pulled on the reins to turn Mossy into their road. "We have to try though."

Hannah shuddered, the emotions from the morning service disappearing quickly. "I suppose so," she managed.

"I'll do it," Jake smiled grimly, picking up on her reaction. "I'm not expecting you to."

"What about working?" Hannah asked, not sure she should stay home while Jake went to sell.

"There's no sense making more, not if we can't sell."

The words hung in the air, an awful finality about them. Hannah remembered the hours Jake had put into this effort, the cold he had endured working in the barn. *Was this then to be the end? The risk, but all for nothing?*

Behind them came the sound of an approaching automobile, and Jake pulled over to let it pass. It went around them slowly, a dark blue jeep. Hannah got a good look at the driver, a young man in his late twenties or so. He seemed to be unsure of himself, keeping to a slow pace even when he was around their buggy.

"Not someone we know," Jake commented.

"Maybe Mr. Brunson?"

"He doesn't get visitors. I've never seen any."

The thought went through Hannah's mind like fire. "It's his son," she said, grabbing Jake's arm.

"Surely not," Jake said.

"Wouldn't that be something?" Hannah breathed in deeply. "What if it is?" She could see it as clear as day — the man getting out of his car, Mr. Brunson coming to his door, the astonished look on his face, the change to complete joy. Then the rush of the two men towards each other, the embrace, the tears, and the joy that would surely follow after their long separation.

"You are dreaming again," Jake said with a smile.

Hannah had to chuckle, because it was true. "It's still a sweet dream," she told him.

"It's just a hunter," Jake decided. "Scouting for next season."

"I like my version better," Hannah said as Jake turned Mossy into their driveway.

"Mr. Brunson hasn't even talked about his family. Not lately."

"Why doesn't he just go visit?" Hannah wondered, leaving behind her dream from the moment before.

"You know what he said. Not welcome maybe? After all these years?"

"It's his son," Hannah said firmly, getting off as Jake brought the buggy to a stop. She waited while he took Mossy to the barn, then walked with him towards the cabin.

"I think I should get something extra for supper. Something special," she told Jake, certain again that Mr. Brunson's son had come.

"What for?" Jake asked, perplexed. "Betty say she was coming over?"

"Mr. Brunson might bring his son down. I'd like them to stay for supper."

Jake raised his eyebrows but didn't comment.

"I might even make the cherry pie."

"On a Sunday?"

"It's a special time." Hannah glanced up, hoping Jake didn't disapprove.

"I guess we'll just have cherry pie then. Haven't had it in a while."

"They will come," Hannah said, but Jake just smiled.

With the afternoon half gone, they sat in the living room of the cabin, each deep in thought. Hannah thought of Mr. Brunson; she assumed, from the look on his face, Jake thought of the sales he needed to make the next day. Gone were his preaching expressions from only hours ago, the lines on his face once again taking over.

It looked to be a long evening, as Hannah soon gave up her idea of making a cherry pie, thinking that Sunday should be kept as a day of rest. At around four she thought of suggesting they go somewhere — perhaps a visit to Betty or the young folks' hymn singing that evening. Before she could ask Jake, Mr. Brunson's pickup pulled in the driveway, with the young man from the jeep in the passenger's seat.

"Mr. Brunson," Jake said, getting up.

"And look who's with him," Hannah said, wishing she had made the cherry pie, but it was too late now.

Jake opened the cabin door and waited. Hannah couldn't resist and stood behind him, looking over his shoulder. Mr. Brunson came up the walk with the young man close behind. Hannah felt certain she saw joy all over Mr. Brunson's face, but maybe she just wanted to see it, she told herself.

When Mr. Brunson got closer and looked up, she knew she wasn't dreaming. There were tears in his eyes.

"My son, Eldon," he said. "This is Jake and Hannah. I just had to stop in and let you know."

Mr. Brunson looked briefly at Hannah, his eyes shining as she had never seen them.

"Glad to meet you," Eldon said, stepping forward and

offering to shake hands. "Dad said you look after him real good."

"No," Jake chuckled. "More like him taking care of us."

"Don't let him shoot any more bears," Eldon said with a laugh. "One was all we needed."

"So you did notice?" Jake asked.

Eldon glanced at Mr. Brunson. "Dad said he told you. We did notice — it was the first clue we had in all these years. I've been looking hard. Lost two of my family — no sense in losing my dad."

"Guess I just let my grief get the best of me," Mr. Brunson said, making no attempt to hide his tears.

"I would have told him all that," Eldon said. "It wasn't his fault. No one ever said it was. He just disappeared on us. I never hated him."

"I guess the years up here kind of healed the hurt," Mr. Brunson said.

"You moving back then?" Jake wanted to know.

"Don't think so. I like it too much now," Mr. Brunson told him. "I'll visit probably — often, I guess. Eldon drives back to Missoula tonight and flies out in the morning."

"Won't you come in?" Jake asked, as if he suddenly remembered Hannah's prediction. "Hannah was going to make a cherry pie. When we saw the jeep pass us on the way home from church, she was sure it was your son."

"We have to be on our way," Eldon told Jake, glancing at his watch.

"She's a sharp girl," Mr. Brunson chuckled. "No cherry pie then?"

"No," Hannah told him. "No cherry pie. I decided it was a Sunday."

"That it is," Mr. Brunson said. "This did happen on a Sunday. The Lord's Day. Look at me — Eldon has actually come. Anything can happen."

"Yes it can," Jake said. Hannah could tell he was trying to encourage himself for his trip to the market tomorrow.

"One more thing," Mr. Brunson began talking fast. "I

JERRY EICHER

know it's kind of sudden. Eldon's going back this afternoon, and I'd like to send a piece of your furniture along with him. There are all kinds of sales opportunities back east for that kind of thing."

Eldon nodded.

Mr. Brunson continued, "I know I haven't told you anything yet. I've just been thinking. Eldon's coming put the last piece in place. Perhaps this spring I could help you out with a better place to work. Maybe in town. Get you set up right and produce a lot of this stuff. You do real good work."

"That is if it sells back home," Eldon said.

"It will," Mr. Brunson said. "Get us a piece, Jake. Eldon can take it back with him to the airport. Ship it from there. You like that idea, don't you?"

"Like it?" Jake asked, but his face gave the best answer. Relief and joy were written all over it.

"We really have to be going," Eldon said.

"The piece — maybe the small rocker," Mr. Brunson suggested. Jake went and got it, and the two men left.

"You think he can sell for you?" Hannah asked.

"Seems too good to be true."

"You would deserve it. You really would."

"God doesn't decide things like that."

"Maybe He will this time," she smiled. "Isn't it wonderful about Eldon? Now he knows where his father is."

"That it is," Jake agreed. "You want to go somewhere tonight?"

"Isn't it too late?" Hannah glanced out the window.

"Not if we hurry."

"I'd love to tell Betty the news."

"Then let's go," Jake grinned, grabbing his coat. Hannah followed him a few minutes later, in time to lift the buggy shafts.

Betty welcomed them in, and Steve hollered from the living room, "The starving and the poor are welcome. We have food."

"Steve," Betty said. "That's not nice."

Jake just grinned. "The clouds could be breaking. Who knows."

"Mr. Brunson may be able to sell Jake's furniture," Hannah said. She decided to save the news about Mr. Brunson's son for Betty's ears.

"How's that?" Steve asked.

"He's got a good contact in the east. His son came to visit. Might actually work out," Jake told him.

"That's good news!" Betty exclaimed. "This had me worried."

"It is good news," Steve agreed.

"God is helping out. I guess," Jake said. "We appreciate it."

Hannah just nodded.

Betty left a moment later for the kitchen. Hannah followed and helped her prepare a fruit plate. In the middle of slicing apples, she told Betty about Eldon and Mr. Brunson's happy reunion.

"That is so wonderful," Betty said when Hannah was done, her eyes edged with tears. "He could have ended up old and never back with his son."

"I'm glad he didn't." Hannah finished the apples and added the grapes and oranges Betty handed to her. She carried the plate back to the men, while Betty followed with water glasses. They ate and chatted till after nine, when Jake said they had to get home. He had work to do tomorrow.

Mr. Brunson stopped by on Tuesday afternoon with the report that Eldon wanted another piece. He also left a check, just large enough to cover the mortgage, although he had no way of knowing that. A week later he said Eldon wanted another piece, and the week after that he stopped by to say they were to ship all the pieces Jake had built to Boston.

Two weeks later Mr. Brunson found a place in town to rent, setting Jake up as the owner of the new business. Of this Hannah was certain, because she asked. Jake said he would have worked for Mr. Brunson same as he had for Mr.

Howard. Yet Hannah could tell he was overjoyed to be his own boss.

Spring broke early that year — at least Betty said it did — coming with a warm breeze from the south. Hannah stood outside the cabin just after Jake left for work, the dawn breaking around her, the peaks of the Cabinet Mountain splashed in reds, yellows, and bright orange. The glory of it filled her soul. She suddenly remembered her old desire to move to Indiana; it had not even crossed her mind these past months.

"This is home," she said the words softly, savoring the sound, still surprised that it was true.

"Yours too," she added a moment later, the awareness having come last night while Jake was sleeping. There was life awakening inside her again.

Jerry Eicher and his wife were raised and married Amish. They live in central Virginia with their four children.